COLD
SUMMER

COLD
SUMMER

GWEN COLE

Sky Pony Press
New York

Sky Pony Press books may be purchased in bulk at special discounts for sales promotion, corporate gifts, fund-raising, or educational purposes. Special editions can also be created to specifications. For details, contact the Special Sales Department, Sky Pony Press, 307 West 36th Street, 11th Floor, New York, NY 10018 or info@skyhorsepublishing.com.

Sky Pony® is a registered trademark of Skyhorse Publishing, Inc.®, a Delaware corporation.

Visit our website at www.skyponypress.com.

10 9 8 7 6 5 4 3 2 1

Library of Congress Cataloging-in-Publication Data is available on file.

Cover design by Sammy Yuen
Interior design by Joshua Barnaby

Print ISBN: 978-1-5107-0766-5
Ebook ISBN: 978-1-5107-0770-2

Printed in the United States of America

For Corri, because without you, there would be no words.

COLD
SUMMER

O.
Kale

For me, seasons don't exist.

Only I know what it feels like when summer turns to winter in an instant. When one minute I'm in my bed and the next I'm staring up at snow-covered trees, wondering what year I'm in.

Even now I feel it coming.

I sit on the back steps, gripping the wood with one hand like it's possible to anchor myself here in the present. No matter how hard I try, it never works. The only thing I can do is delay it, sometimes not even that.

Trying to take my thoughts from it, I stare across the field behind the house where we once played baseball in the summers. Swatting at bugs and shielding our eyes with our gloves from the sun's glare. The grass was kept short then, always ready for us to spend the last hours of the day throwing ball and hoping the sun wouldn't leave. Mom would watch us from the back porch, a few feet from where I'm sitting now. Cheering us on and never taking sides.

Now the field is overgrown.

Just a memory of the family who used to live here.

I hear Bryce inside, coming down the stairs fast and hard. The jingle of car keys and his audible sigh—the only evidence

1

he's seen me. And because of that, I'm surprised when he walks across the kitchen and opens the screen door behind me.

"What are you doing out here?" he asks, lingering on the top step. The screen door bangs shut behind him.

I manage to give him a one shoulder shrug. It's all I can do—I feel like if I move again, I'll disappear.

That one sentence is probably the most he's said to me in a week. Without Libby here—with her constant sisterly comments and snide remarks—the house is submersed in silence. We dance around conversations and slip past whichever rooms the other is in.

Not brothers. Strangers.

That's what we've become, and it's my fault.

I can feel him staring. It has to be close to ninety degrees out here and yet I'm wearing a sweatshirt. I shiver like it's twenty. My body knows what's coming before it happens. I tighten my grip on the wooden stair even more.

Bryce shifts his weight, making his keys bump against his hip. I don't like him standing there, saying nothing, like I'm the one who came to find him.

"Did you want something?" I finally ask, gripping the stair tighter. My forearms flex, not strong enough to keep me here.

"I'm going to the store, so I was wondering if you wanted to come." He's lying—he only came out here because he felt like he had to.

"No, thanks." My voice is tight.

"Why not?"

I keep my eyes forward.

"Because I—" Because I won't be here in an hour? Because I don't want to disappear while we're driving to the store? I'm sure he would take that well. I start again, coming up with a normal answer. "I just don't want to," I finally tell him.

Bryce only sighs behind me.

I wrap my free arm around myself and shiver again, a place of winter invading my thoughts. If I close my eyes, I'll see nothing else. So I keep them open, hoping I'll stay here longer.

I can't give into it. Not yet.

Bryce says, "So—" He pauses a long moment "—are you . . ." He takes a quick breath and starts again, his voice lower. "Are you going to be here when I come back?"

I almost lie to him but end up saying, "I don't think so."

"Okay, well—" If I turn around, I would see him flex his jaw because that's what he does. But I don't, so the door opens and he says, "I'll see you later."

Bryce's footsteps fade away into the house, followed by the slam of the front door and the roar of his truck starting.

Then I'm alone.

After putting it off for so long, I close my eyes and picture the place my body wants to take me. I don't want to go, but I also don't want to stay.

Two worlds I don't want to be a part of.

Two worlds I don't belong in.

And the worst part is I don't have a choice.

I stand and take a step off the porch, my foot landing on snow instead of grass. Cold bites at my skin and fills my lungs. Everything changing in an instant. I don't have to open my eyes to know I'm here.

This is what my life has come to.

I don't have a superpower.

I have a curse.

1.
Harper

When I decided to move to Uncle Jasper's house permanently, I didn't think it would happen so fast, and I definitely didn't think it would actually *happen*. Boy, was I wrong.

It doesn't hit me until I'm staring at the house.

Not during the plane ride or when the pilot announced our descent. Not even when Uncle Jasper picked me up from the airport and we drove past miles and miles of familiar fields and driveways marked with old mailboxes.

But now that the truck has shut off and the only thing I have left to look at is the farmhouse, I can't ignore the truth: I'm back in the place where I spent my summers every year—a place filled with memories of a boy with secrets and a house I loved more than my own. But this time I'm not just visiting. This time I'm staying for good. Same girl, different life.

What the hell just happened?

I glance over at Uncle Jasper. He stares out across the field to the left, his hand still on the top of the steering wheel. His short graying hair is hidden beneath his Royals cap, the blue faded and the bill fraying around the edges.

My throat feels dry, but I ask him anyway, "Do you think this was a mistake?"

He blinks and looks over, giving me one of his rare smiles.

"People don't make mistakes," he says. "They make decisions."

"Ah, wise Uncle Jasper is at it again."

"I try my best. Come on, let's get your stuff upstairs."

He grabs my duffel bag and I follow him to the house with my backpack, leaving my biggest check-in bag in the back for later. I'm still wondering what I'm doing here. Inside, it smells like old wood and toast, just as I remember. The pictures in the hallway show past holidays, Dad and Uncle Jasper when they were young, and even some of me. I glance at Aunt Holly's empty chair before following him upstairs, noticing the afghan still draped over the back and the way the green is still that faded color.

Being in this house without her doesn't feel right. It probably never will.

I follow Uncle Jasper upstairs. He stops at the door at the end of the hall where my room looks untouched, as though nobody has been in here since I left. My clock glows green from the nightstand and my bed has a single pillow on it. The top of the dresser is bare, save for the mounted mirror on the wall above.

Uncle Jasper sets my bag on the floor, the old hardwood creaking under his weight. He looks around the room. "If you need anything, just let me know," he says. "All right?"

I only nod and stare at my comforter. The bed calls to me, whispers for me to hide away under the covers and sleep the days away until I wake up, realizing everything was a dream. I want this whole summer to be over with. When school starts up, there will be more distractions, things to take my mind off everything that's gone wrong.

Uncle Jasper pauses at the door.

"Harper?" I look up, trying not to show how I feel. "I'm

really glad you're here. I know it may not seem that way, but I am."

Despite everything, I smile. "I think I am, too."

"You sure?"

"No, but it's like you said. I made a decision." Then I say, "And I actually do need something. Do you still have that extra TV that used to be in the guest room?"

He raises an eyebrow and steps back into the room. "Yes? You want it in here?"

"Yeah, it's just . . . I game."

"You *game*? What do you mean, like, Nintendo 64?"

I try not to laugh. "No, like Xbox. I play with other people online. And you don't have to worry about me staying up here all day—I limit myself. You still have wifi, right?"

Now he's the one who wants to laugh, but he finally shrugs and says, "Yes, I still have wifi, and I'll move the TV later tonight."

At least something will be somewhat normal.

After he leaves, I unpack my clothes, and when I go to put my sweatshirt into the third drawer, I find a picture from my last summer here, laying exactly where I left it. I never took it with me, because I felt it belonged in this house more than anywhere else. And it does. Everything about this picture is proof of how much I loved it here.

Uncle Jasper's property line borders with our neighbor's house on the other side of the woods. A river runs halfway between our houses, and that was where I found my company every summer. If it wasn't for the Jackson kids, my summers here wouldn't have been so memorable. My aunt and uncle were fun, but a kid can only hang out with grownups for so long.

The picture was taken in the yard under the oak trees, the three of us hanging off each other's shoulders, grinning like nothing could make that day better. They labeled Uncle Jasper and Aunt Holly as their Aunt and Uncle, too, since they never saw theirs and they were around enough for them to be exactly that.

I stare at Libby, and then Kale. Bryce was always doing something with school or hanging out with his older friends, so it was always just the three of us.

Looking at Kale again, even after all these years, sparks something inside. His smiling face and single dimple. And this is a picture from six years ago—I can't help but wonder what he's like now, and how much he's changed. Because my parents couldn't have any more kids after me, I hadn't known what it felt like to have siblings until I met Libby. She was the sister I never had. But Kale—I felt something entirely different about him.

He makes me look forward to the days here.

Maybe this wasn't a mistake after all.

2.
Kale

Everything about this place is cold.

It's in the air around me. In the earth underneath my boots. Through every breath I take.

I hate it.

My numb fingers fumble with the cigarette as I try to get it out of the package. When I finally manage, I bring it to my lips and cup my hands around the match, waiting for it to catch. My hands shake too much.

I just want a smoke, and even this seems too hard.

"Here, let me try." Adams crouches in front of me, leaning his rifle against his shoulder so he can use both hands. I can only see parts of him where the moonlight catches breaks between the clouds.

I give him the matches, just wanting the damn thing lit. And when it does, my hands don't shake as much. I take a long drag and offer it to Adams, who does the same, half smiling when he hands it back.

"Where did you say you got these again? They're terrible." He settles down next to me, his leg pressing against mine.

I tell him. "I'm not saying it's true, but I might have found it lying next to a Kraut officer last week."

"Just lying there, huh? No wonder they're so bad. The Germans don't know the meaning of a good cigarette." He laughs—right not to believe me. I wanted to smoke so bad, I went as low as searching for them. Most guys do it—to find watches or other souvenirs—but it was my first time.

I never realized how cold a dead body could become.

We sit in our foxhole and pass the cigarette between us until it's gone. There's something about sharing a smoke—something I could never explain. And because I'm not alone here, next to someone who's going through the same thing, it's the warmest I've been all night. I hear the guys five yards from us, in their own hole, smoking their own cigarettes, talking about the girls they left behind back home and about better times.

When I think of home, I don't think the same way these guys do. In this world—in this time—I have no home.

And the place I call home in my own time isn't much of one anyway.

"What did you say your sister's name was again?" Adams asks.

"Libby." I stuff my hands into my armpits. A sad attempt to warm them.

"And how much younger is she than you?"

I glance over, my eyes shooting a glare. "Lay off. We might share a hole, but that won't last long if you keep asking about my sister."

He laughs and it vibrates through his chest. With his shoulder pressed against mine, I feel every chuckle. It makes the night a bit warmer.

"It's all right," he says. "When I save your ass one of these days, you'll *have* to introduce me. It's in the code of conduct."

"Really," I say.

"I kid you not," Adams says. But he can't keep his face from breaking into a grin.

After a while, I feel him drift off to sleep, his chest rising and falling slower and slower like it suddenly might stop. But it doesn't. He keeps breathing and the night wears on. The snow rains down on us, cold and silent, making the forest around us a forbidden land.

I don't know how the rest of the guys do it, but it's almost impossible for me to sleep at all in these holes. In this place.

My heart pounds too hard when I think of them out there. When they could bear down at us at any moment with their guns raised. Shooting through us like we're paper mache. In these woods, in this hole, there is nothing else I can think of.

Sometimes I try to think of home to make things more bearable. Of my sister and brother, from back before everything turned for the worse. Of my only friend—the only person who hasn't given up on me. It's hard to think about them when they don't even exist here.

Here, everything is cold.

Even my thoughts.

A few hours before dawn, I'm finally exhausted enough to sleep. It happens while thinking of past summers and a girl I can hardly remember in this place.

I wake to the sound of mortars.

They fall on us from above. Unseen before it's too late. Even before I open my eyes, my heart pounds and my hands shake—the side effect of being woken to the sounds of death.

Adrenaline courses through my veins, like an old friend ready to be embraced. I hear Lieutenant Gates yell for us to stay where we are, swearing at the men who would rather take their chances in the open than be trapped in holes.

Trees fall around us.

Dirt rains from above.

Mortars scream and pound the earth.

I grip my rifle to my chest, my fingers numb from holding it so tight. Adams and I stay huddled in our hole, only able to pray one doesn't land on us. So many times I've wondered if it would. If I travel back in time just to die. To become a part of history and disappear without anyone knowing what happened to me.

I glance over at Adams. His face is pale and his jaw is set.

The silence of the forest returns as suddenly as it left, but it's not alone. The broken trees creak where they're split, and the moans of men echo through the morning fog.

Adams gets to his feet, unsteady like he can't walk right, and climbs out of the hole. He's covered in dirt, probably the same as me, his clothes the color of dark ash. I watch as he looks around himself, surveying the damage before fully standing.

"Come on, Jackson." He motions me up, and after pushing my fears aside, I follow. My feet are numb in my boots, and I can't feel my legs. The forest is full of fallen trees and half buried holes. Everything around us is not what it was. Blood paints the snow where soldiers whom I once knew have died.

Parker.

Whitt.

Campbell.

My stomach turns over at the sight of their broken bodies. Knowing I could've been one of them. I'm shaking again, the cigarette long worn off.

I watch Adams look into the hole next to ours. It's bigger than it was. Misshapen. We were five yards away from death. I still can't feel my legs or anything else besides my heart, which beats unevenly.

Adams looks back at me and shakes his head. The emptiness in his eyes is something I've grown used to. The war is taking a greater toll on him than me. I don't know why; Adams has more to go back to than I ever will. Maybe it's because I only take this a couple days at a time. He doesn't get to come and go like I do. Doesn't get any reprieve. He's here for good.

I fumble for another cigarette in my pocket—needing a smoke now more than ever—when I hear a scream from the sky and someone shouting.

"Take cover!"

Those two words never fail to make my heart pound.

And there is nothing I hate more than a late mortar to catch us off guard. It's a dirty game they like to play with us.

The mortar lands close, before I can get back to our hole. It's death to those of us who aren't fast enough. The world goes black, and I'm thrown to the ground by a force nothing could compare. The air rushes from my lungs, leaving my body as fast as I want to leave this place.

I wish I could go with it.

And I will. But not yet.

Nothing but a high-pitched ringing invades my ears. The medic always tells me that's a good sign; my hearing will come back when there's ringing.

And while the darkness consumes me, thoughts enter my head without reason or order. The chaos on the outside coming in.

Ringing and blackness and the fact my heart is still pounding and maybe I'll live to see the next day and what I'll see when I open my eyes. It's so black even my thoughts are lost. My eyes are heavy. Something hard presses against my body. Everything is cold. Always cold.

I want summer again. I want warm afternoons at the river, lying under the sun with a bare chest, soaking in the heat with the cool grass under my fingers. It's easy to forget summer here. Easy to forget the things I live for.

I force myself to wake.

I open my eyes, feeling the crumbs of dirt fall from my lashes and onto my face. The ringing in my ears has lessened—I can hear someone yelling far away. The snow is frozen against my cheek, so cold it hurts. My fingers respond and twitch, curling into the dirt and snow, telling me I'm still alive.

I see Adams not far from me. For a moment, I'm glad to see he's still alive, staring at me differently than the dead do. But something's wrong. He tears his gaze away from mine and looks past the trees, toward the clouds with glossy eyes. His helmet has fallen off, left forgotten next to him.

His body convulses, dark blood dripping from his mouth. I push against the ground, somehow using the adrenaline to work my legs and arms. I can't feel myself walking toward him, but I am. I can't feel anything. Somehow I yell for a medic, hoping one is nearby and close enough to save him.

I fall to my knees beside him, curling one of my frozen hands under his neck.

He still stares at something above me.

"Adams." I can finally hear myself and my voice shakes. "Adams, look at me." I want to tell him he'll be all right, but I can't. I can't so much as look down to see what's there and what's not.

Someone kneels next to me, and I get a fleeting glimpse of a white Geneva cross. His hands are flying and cutting, covered in red as he tells me something I can't hear. The medic yells to someone else and a stretcher comes.

The only thing I can do is stare into Adams's eyes, wondering if he'll look at me one last time. They're as gray as the sky—something I never noticed before now. My mind reels through the things he'd told me, of his home and his family, of people who want him to come home alive.

"You're gonna be all right, Adams," I hear myself say.

13

Finally, after so long of getting nothing, he looks at me and tries to smile. It's hard for him, I can tell. His body still shakes and his skin is cold. He's in shock. The medic and another soldier put him on a stretcher and carry him away, leaving me kneeling in the stained snow.

I am numb.

I look down to see my hands still shaking. Covered in red.

The blood of my friend.

3.
Harper

Uncle Jasper leaves sometime after midnight.

I'm lying in bed—my sheets tangled around my legs and my eyes heavy—when the phone rings downstairs. I stare at the moonlit ceiling and hear him walk down to answer it, saying a few muffled words before hanging up.

His truck pulls away moments later.

I have no idea where he has to go in the middle of the night on such short notice, and my foggy brain doesn't care. After he leaves, the house is quiet and still, feeling so empty with only me to occupy it. The moonlight is bright coming through my window, followed by a breeze that tries to drag me back to sleep. It's like I'm nine again, waking up in the night and wondering what tomorrow will bring.

But I'm not nine anymore, and I'm not going home.

Whatever anyone says, growing up sucks.

The next morning at the kitchen table, Uncle Jasper doesn't say a word. He eats his toast and drinks his coffee across from me, looking tired but not acting like it. He says nothing about leaving in the middle of the night, and I don't ask.

My Rice Krispies make more conversation than we do.

He scribbles another word into the crossword puzzle he's bent over, silently mouthing the letters as he does. The clock ticks from down the hall. The refrigerator kicks on.

"So . . ." I start. He erases one of the words, swiping the paper with the side of his hand. "Do you see the Jacksons much? How's Libby doing?"

"I see them every now and then," he says and takes another sip of coffee from a mug that has a T-Rex on it trying to do push-ups. "Libby is actually living with her mom this summer, but she'll be back before you start school."

"Oh," is all I can say. I have my video games, but like I told Uncle Jasper, I can't stay in the house all day. I'd go stir crazy.

"I'm sorry," he says, finally looking up from his paper. "I know you were hoping to see her, but she agreed to it before she found out you were coming. Otherwise, she never would've gone."

"Yeah, that's all right. I understand," I mumble. "What about Kale?" I try to say it like I couldn't care less, but really just asking about him makes me nervous. I've been more anxious about seeing him than anyone. The boy version of Kale was always smiling, his eyes as bright as the stars. The boy who was always gone. When we were younger, his dad claimed it was a phase because all kids try to run away from home, one that would pass with time. He would get angry when Kale would go, and his mom would worry, but they never paid too much attention to it, probably hoping he would eventually stop.

I wonder if he did stop, and then grew into a Kale I probably no longer know.

"I see Kale quite a bit," Uncle Jasper finally says. He traces another word on the paper. "He comes over to help me on the cars when he's around."

16

I nod and chew my inner cheek. It can't be more obvious they were the only friends I have here—I could go see Bryce, but we were never close and that would just be awkward. Besides seeing pictures on Libby's social media accounts, I haven't seen either of them—or even spoken to them—in years. I should really text Libby, assuming her number is the same.

Before I can say anything else, Uncle Jasper sighs and gets up from the table.

"I've got to get going," he tells me. "I should be back in an hour or two. And remember, if you get hungry, don't be afraid to help yourself to anything you want." With a glance over his shoulder at the fridge he says, "I know there's not much right now, but we can go grocery shopping later. Sound good, kid?"

I nod again, studying my melting cereal as he walks out. Minutes pass after I hear his truck pull down the long driveway. The house feels like a shell that holds nothing but loss. The chairs are cold and the sink is empty. The refrigerator only has condiments and milk. This is—and isn't—the house I once knew.

I don't know what to do with myself. If nothing had changed, Aunt Holly and I would be working on the garden or going to the thrift store to find random kitchen utensils. Or Libby and Kale would be over here, forcing me to go swimming with them.

I drop my head on the table and say to nobody, "This is going to be the longest summer of my life."

Sometimes I can be melodramatic.

After I rinse my bowl in the sink, I go upstairs and start unpacking my gaming console. I make sure I have all the right cords and work on setting up the TV. The remote's batteries are dead, of course, so after searching for new ones for ten minutes, I'm back to work. When everything is plugged in and ready to go, I start up the Xbox and let out a groan when it says it has to update.

To kill time, I pull out my phone, which has no new messages or missed calls, something that begs me to think about Mom, but I will not open that box right now. That box is tucked away and locked. That box is invisible.

I go through my contacts and scroll down to look for Libby's name. I can't remember the last time I texted her. I go for the ice breaker approach.

Hey friend, I'm here in the empty house wishing you were next door so I won't go crazy with boredom. Miss you . . .

I glance up. The update is only at fifteen percent.

Aunt Holly was always adamant about having good wifi, even way out here in the country, so it must be a big update if it's taking so long. Or maybe I *think* it's taking so long but really, it's only been forty seconds.

My phone buzzes with a text.

:(I'm so sorry I'm not there to entertain you. Mom's house is just as boring, trust me. Have you seen Kale yet? I know he's not as exciting as me but . . .

I smile at that.

Haven't seen him yet, hopefully later.

Car doors slam outside and I go downstairs to see who it is. Uncle Jasper's truck is near the barn, and parked by it is another truck with a trailer hooked up to it. There's an old car on the trailer with a man behind the wheel, trying to back it off. There's smoke coming from the cracks in the hood, but neither of them seem surprised by this.

That's the Uncle Jasper I know.

I don't have shoes on, but I walk down the steps anyway, knowing the grass is soft.

"A little to the right!" Uncle Jasper calls from his place behind the car. He uses his hands to direct him off the ramp like someone would an airplane.

Then a voice says next to me, "You never stop watching,

because a small part of you is hoping something bad will happen. It's like watching Nascar."

I turn to find a girl standing against the porch with her arms crossed, watching them try to navigate the ramp. She has the same dark hair as the man behind the wheel and she's probably around my age. Brown freckles are splattered across her cheeks and nose, complimenting her olive skin.

"That's kind of true," I say, agreeing. "It's basically the only reason to watch—to hope for an accident."

"Because who actually likes watching cars go around and around in circles?"

I lean in and say, "Don't let Uncle Jasper hear you say that. He secretly watches it when I'm not around."

She laughs and gives me a wink. Her hair is on the unmanageable side of curly, pulled back into a ponytail like it's the only thing she can do with it. She wears a flannel button-up shirt, rolled up at the elbows, something that's usually too warm to wear during the summer.

"Unfortunately for us," she says, "they've done this hundreds of times and are very experienced in the ways of ramps. But one of these days . . ."

I smile. "We'll just have to keep watching."

"I'm Grace, by the way. That's my dad, behind the wheel." She nods her chin at him, her arms still crossed.

"Harper."

"I know." And when I look at her, she explains, "Your uncle talks about you a lot. He said you'll be here for your senior year in the fall?"

"That's the plan," I say, holding back a sigh.

Uncle Jasper and Grace's dad finally get the car into the barn, popping the hood barely before it's in park. Even when I was younger, Uncle Jasper always got excited when a new car came for him to fix. Aunt Holly would sit on the porch and watch him with an amused expression, a forgotten book in her lap but a small smile touching her lips. She would sit that way for hours, just watching him.

The empty porch now stares at my back.

"So look," Grace says, finally turning to me now that the entertainment is over. "There's a bunch of us going into the city tonight to watch the fireworks. There's this cool place by the river where we go every year. You wanna come?"

For a moment, I'm confused about why there would be fireworks tonight, but then I realize it's the Fourth of July. Between everything going on, I lost track of the days. And right about now, going out for a night couldn't sound better.

I just can't sound desperate. Don't sound desperate, Harper . . .

"Yeah, all right. I mean . . . if I'm not imposing or anything."

Nailed it.

"Not at all," she says, shaking her head. "There will be a bunch of kids there from school, too, so I can introduce you. I hated starting school as 'the new girl,'" she says, bringing her hands up as mock quotations marks. "It sucks not knowing anyone."

I'm about to mention Libby and Kale when her dad calls to Grace, telling her it's time to leave.

"I'll pick you up at eight?" she says, taking backward steps toward their truck.

Her dad starts the engine, drowning my voice when I say, "Sure." So I nod instead, in case she didn't hear. She gives me a quick wave before they're gone, the gravel crunching down the driveway to announce their departure.

I smile, because a month ago I would have said no, and a month ago nobody would've asked. For once I have plans with someone besides my Xbox.

4.
Kale

I wake to my name being yelled.

By the time my door opens, the doorknob banging into the wall, I'm sitting up. Half awake with my palms pressing into the mattress. I let out a breath when I realize I'm home and not in the middle of the woods in winter.

He surveys me and then my room. When I swing my legs over the bed, I'm suddenly aware of how sore I am. My whole right side aches when I move, and my head still pounds with a headache.

The clock over my desk shows it's past noon.

"Dad said he heard you come in last night," Bryce says, settling his gaze on me after eyeing my dirty shoes on the floor. "I guess I had to see for myself if it was true." His tone is anything but friendly.

Bryce used to be okay with me leaving, but I've broken too many promises so I can't blame him.

"Well, you found me, so what do you want?" When I look up, it hits me how much he looks like Dad—the same brown eyes and short dark hair, even the way he stands there.

"Dad wanted me to tell you that he'll be home around

eight." In the other words, I'd better be here when he does. "He got called in today."

"Wait, what day is it?" I know I lose track of the days, but I'm almost sure it's a Wednesday.

The way Bryce looks at me makes me wish I'd never asked.

For a moment, I see myself through his eyes: I'm wearing the same clothes I was in the last time he saw me, I'm sleeping in the middle of the day, I've been gone for at least the last three days, and now I'm asking what day it is.

No wonder he looks at me the way he does.

I would, too.

"It's the fourth," Bryce says. When he turns to leave, he adds, "You have dirt on your face."

For the longest time—after Bryce goes downstairs and the numbers on my clock silently change—I sit on the edge of my bed and try to think of reasons to venture out of my room today. Or out of the house.

I want to, but I shouldn't.

It's always worse between me and Dad after I get back. It reminds him who I am, and not who he wants me to be. It's opening an old wound that would rather be forgotten.

Before I think on it more, I walk across the hallway and lock myself in the bathroom. The floor is cold and the light filters through the glass-tiled window. I turn on the shower and peel off my T-shirt. My arms are sore and my ribs still ache with every breath.

For the first time since I've been back, I take a closer look at my hands—at the dirt under my fingernails and in the lines of my palms. I want to believe it's dirt. But wanting to believe isn't making it true.

I look at the floor while I tug off my jeans, trying not to look at them. Then I step into the shower to wash away the evidence of something that happened over sixty years ago.

But no matter how much I scrub, the memories won't ever fade.

I hear voices downstairs when I'm putting on a clean shirt. The front door shuts and Bryce's voice echoes up along with his friends, Todd and Jeremy. One of them is laughing about something. A laugh that bounces off every corner of the house.

After I pull on my sweatshirt, along with my shoes, I go downstairs to find them in the kitchen.

They don't notice me at first.

Todd—with his buzzed hair and button-up shirt—texts someone while leaning against the counter. And Bryce and Jeremy pull a few bags of ice from the freezer. They're both wearing T-shirts and swim shorts.

I glance down at myself.

I'm dressed for a different season.

"Kale!" Todd shoves his phone into his pocket and smiles like something is funny. "Long time no see."

While his friends laugh, Bryce glances at me uncomfortably, torn between wanting to keep up the act in front of his friends and defending me. It used to be different between us a couple years ago. Better. Every morning, he would come into my room to see if I was back. He would sit on the edge of my bed and ask about where I went and what I saw. Back then it wasn't the war. It was places that weren't filled with snow and gun shots. California, 1969. The cotton fields of Arkansas in 1950.

I would lie in bed and tell him all the funny stories about how I would mention something that nobody would be familiar with because it hadn't been invented yet. Or how I had to spend nights in chicken coops or barns, waking up only to scare a girl coming out to do her chores.

Bryce was the first person I ever told and the first person to ever believe me.

Now he turns back to his friends to change the subject.

"We have to be there at two, right?" he asks.

Todd pulls out his phone again, probably checking an old message. "Yeah, we're supposed to meet them at two. That way we can get to the lake on time." Then he turns to me. "You coming, Kale?" He smiles again, teasing, and warmth spreads up from my neck.

"I don't know if he should." Jeremy adds, "He might run off on us. Last year my dog ran off the moment the fireworks started. We couldn't find him for days."

I stare back at Todd, daring him to say something.

He says, smiling, "Sounds about right."

I take a step forward, but Bryce puts his hand on my chest, pushing me back. "Leave it alone, Kale."

Jeremy and Todd laugh about something again, muttering words too low for me to hear. I hate the way they look at me. I hate the way my own brother looks at me.

My gaze settles on Bryce, voicing thoughts I've held in for too long. "Why, so you can pretend our family is like *theirs*? So you can pretend nothing is ever wrong?" I ask, keeping my voice low. Looking into his eyes is hard because they're too similar to Dad's.

I turn to go, but he grabs my arm.

Todd says from behind him, "You sure you don't want him to come, Bryce? We could always use him to—"

"Leave him alone, Todd. He gets enough shit as it is."

"So that's what you see me as?" I shrug away from him. "A pity project?"

Then Bryce shrugs right back and asks, "What else am I supposed to see you as?"

His friends laugh, but this time he joins them. Jeremy and Todd grab the bags of ice and push past me and out the door.

And without saying anything, Bryce follows them.

I stand in the hallway and listen as they all pile into Bryce's truck. They shut the doors and the engine roars to life.

Then they're gone.

And I wish I was.

All over again.

5. Harper

Within six hours, I'm standing next to a river in the middle of the city, surrounded by skyscrapers except for this little forgotten park where Grace said we're meeting her friends.

There's a wide bank along the river where people lounge in the grass or sit on coolers they brought with them. A few people are wading into the water, the ones not thinking to wear shorts have their jeans rolled up to their knees. Somewhere there's a guy playing guitar, and there's laughter and accusing voices from those making jokes, and water splashing from girls trying to get out before their boyfriends realize they're wearing white T-shirts.

"Grace!"

We both turn at her name being called, but she reacts before I do—she'd been expecting it.

A guy our age walks over to us wearing a black short-sleeved button up shirt. His dark hair and angular eyes remind me of a girl back home who was Japanese American.

When he smiles at Grace, I have no doubt about their relationship with each other. Even I have to admit they make a cute couple, like the kind you always root for in those stupid

TV shows you can't help but watch. Which I would probably now be watching if I weren't here.

"What took you so long?" he asks, giving her a quick kiss on the lips. When they break apart, he adds, "Another minute longer, and that girl over there was about to drag me into the woods without my consent."

"You poor thing," she says, patting his cheek, keeping one arm around his waist. "Maybe if you didn't spend so long on your hair, you wouldn't have that problem."

"You love my hair," he says low.

It feels like I'm watching something I shouldn't be.

"Not if it's attracting other girls."

"You know it's not just my hair that—"

Grace puts a finger on his lips. "We have company."

They both turn, and I can't tell if they're messing with me. So I just smile and stand there, not knowing what to say.

"This is Miles," she says. "Don't be afraid to be bold with him."

Miles cocks his head and looks back at me. "She must like you, because she doesn't give that kind of advice to anyone."

"Thanks?"

He nods assuringly.

"And Miles," Grace smiles at me, "this is Harper."

Some sort of recognition dawns over his face. "Wait . . . Harper *Croft?*" Miles asks. "*The* Harper Croft?" He quickly looks at Grace. "Are you messing with me? Is this really her?"

"Am I missing something?" I ask.

Miles says, "We never thought you actually existed. Well, Grace did—for some reason—but your name comes up so much I really thought you were imaginary."

"Miles, he showed us a *picture*," Grace says, looking up at him. "How is that not enough proof?"

"Photoshop?"

"You have serious problems."

I finally step in. "Wait, how do you know my name?" But what I'm really asking is, how do they know *me*?

"Kale," Miles says. "Sometimes your uncle, but mostly Kale."

Grace nods in agreement.

Kale.

Miles and Grace talk again—more to each other than to me, just as before—but I can't grasp anything they're saying. Since I got here yesterday, I kept wondering if Kale would remember me, or even care that I'm around again. I know he's not the same boy he used to be—just like I'm not the same girl. Time changes so many things, and I was afraid this would be one of them.

"You guys know Kale?"

Miles says, "I've been friends with him since I moved here a few years ago. And Grace has known him since we started dating."

"A year next month," she adds.

"Will he be here tonight?" I feel stupid for asking. We live next door to each other, so why can't I just go over to see him? Or better yet, call and text him.

Miles shrugs one shoulder and glances around. "I haven't heard from him in a few days, so I'm not sure." Before I can ask him anything else, a few boys come over and talk to Miles and Grace—people from school I'll probably know better in the fall. The sun has set now, and it's almost dark enough for the fireworks to start. While Grace talks with another girl nearby, I slip away to the edge of the water, dipping my fingers in to see if it's cold. It's warmer than I thought it'd be.

"Harper?"

I look up to see a blond guy standing over me—someone I feel I should recognize. I stand and wipe my wet hand across my jeans, noticing the weird smile he's giving me. "Yes?"

"I don't know if you remember me," he says, "but you came over to my house a few times the last summer you were here."

I reel through the foggy memories, and a name finally surfaces. "Conner," I say. "You always used to push people into the pool."

Conner smiles and gives me a single nod. "I guess I'm more memorable than I thought. Your uncle was over at our house a few weeks back, and he mentioned you were coming to live with him. It's good to see you again."

"Yeah, good to see you, too. Now I'll know more than two people when school starts."

"Well, look," he says. "I'm having a few friends over next week, and I can introduce you to more people. You won't be the new kid at school. You can be the new*ish* kid. Trust me, it makes all the difference."

"A few friends, huh? If I remember correctly, the last time you had a few friends over, your kitchen caught fire."

"Technicalities," he says, grinning again. "So what do you say? There's not much to do around here anyway."

"I'll think about it."

"That's all I needed to hear," Conner says, turning to go. "See you around, Harper."

As I watch Conner go back to his group of friends, I spot someone new coming out of the woods, and the way he moves makes me pause only long enough for me to realize it's true.

It's Kale.

Even when time has changed us both, I know it's him. Even twenty years from now, I could still pick him out of the crowd. There are some things that stick with you forever, even if that something is a person. He definitely looks different—the sharp lines of his jaw, the way his shoulders curve, even the way he stands. Older.

Despite the differences, it's so familiar—how it feels like he's here but he isn't. It's the same way I felt all those years ago.

Seeing him is something special, because you don't know the next time you'll get to. Even though Kale's habit of disappearing for days at a time probably ended years ago, the presence of it is still here. It makes me wonder.

Kale stands there looking at Miles as he talks with his friends, the expression on his face unreadable. He's wearing an unzipped sweatshirt, exposing a black T-shirt underneath, his hands buried deep into the pockets of his jeans. His dark hair lays across his forehead the same way it used to—something that hasn't changed.

His eyes shift to me.

And for a split second—before Miles yells his name, dragging his attention away—the smallest of smiles touches his lips. It disappears as quick as it came—leaving only a memory in its wake.

Then when Kale talks, I feel like something is wrong, and it hits me. He's not smiling. The Kale I used to know smiled almost constantly—it came as naturally to him as breathing. Everyone smiles when they talk, even in the slightest way, at the beginning or end. But Kale stands there and listens, saying a few words in response without changing his expression, even when his friends laugh.

I start toward them, trying not to look at Kale and trying to ignore the fact I'm trying not to. *Get ahold of yourself, Harper.*

I catch his eye as I come closer, wondering what I'm going to say to someone I haven't seen in six years.

"Kale," Grace says, "can you please tell Miles that he owes me ten bucks? We had a deal."

"A deal we never shook on," Miles argues. "Doesn't count."

"You're full of shit," Grace says, but she's smiling.

Miles looks over at me when I get close, then glances down at my feet. "Your shoes are untied."

I don't look, knowing he's right. But when I open my mouth, Kale says for me, "They're always untied."

I finally look at him, silently cursing the sun for making the day turn to night so I can't see the color of his eyes. But even without them, I get this feeling in the pit of my stomach that makes me smile, even if it's small and barely noticeable. It's only the edge of what I cannot contain.

I don't know what to say to him, so I say, "Hey."

"Hey," he says back.

I want to hug him like old friends do, but he doesn't make a move toward me.

"How's Libby?" I finally ask, grateful that Miles and Grace are talking to each other again and not paying us any attention. "Uncle Jasper said she's staying at your mom's for the summer."

"She's good," he says, "but she hates that she won't see you until school starts." Still no smile, something that would normally follow that sentence and tone. "She tried to back out of going, but Mom wouldn't let her."

"It'll be good to see her again. I texted her earlier but it's not the same."

He nods.

This isn't the reunion I'd imagined. I hate the space between us and the forced talk. But it's impossible to pick up where we left off. Too much time has passed. That's becoming clearer and clearer.

Miles is talking again. I don't hear what he says, but Kale pulls his eyes from mine and says, "You said that last year, and I don't have to remind you what happened," not missing a beat.

"But this year I'm serious," he says.

Grace rolls her eyes and leans over to say, "Miles wants to get into the Demolition Derby. He tries every year, and every year—"

"—I get really close," he says, looking at me like I'm the one he needs to convince. "No matter how many crashes this car is in, it'll just keep going. I really feel like this is my year."

31

"And notice," Kale adds, "that 'crashes' is plural."

"You're just jealous because your piece of sh—"

"Careful," Kale warns. His mouth curves up in the slightest way.

Stop staring, Harper.

But Miles smiles, knowing how to push Kale in ways only a close friend would. It makes me miss what we had with each other. It makes me miss *him* and wonder if we'll ever have that again. Even when we're standing mere feet away from each other, there's still this wall between us that only time and distance could've made.

The first firework goes off over the river, and everyone moves toward the water, finding a place to sit or stand to watch the show. The boom echoes, followed by another a second later. Miles and Grace sit down in the grass together, looking up at the blackening sky that's now full of color.

Kale isn't next to Miles anymore, and I look around, trying to spot him. Every face is lifted to the sky, the fireworks lighting up the features of the strangers around me. Except one.

He's walking away toward the woods, his shoulders stiff. I step around the people on the ground and go after him. He's about to disappear into the woods when I call his name. The fireworks keep going off, but he hears me and turns around.

"You're leaving?"

"I have to get home."

I'm stupid for following him, especially since I don't have anything else to say. "I guess I'll see you later then." I want to kick myself.

Kale nods and turns to go, but then something changes his mind and he turns back to me. "I remember what you promised me," he says, flinching when another firework goes off. "But is it still true?"

That day by the river. He still remembers. But that would mean nothing has changed.

"Of course it is," I say, not hesitating.

Kale nods, glances up at the sky with hunched shoulders, and then he's gone.

I stand there and think back on that day. It suddenly doesn't seem that long ago.

We went swimming in the river and Libby had to leave early, so it was only me and Kale. We were lying in the grass, letting the sun dry us.

We'd been quiet for a long time when he looked over, his eyes stormier than an angry spring rain. "You never ask me where I go," he said. "Everyone else does, but not you. Why?"

"I don't care where you go," I said, "as long as you come back."

Kale always kept his disappearances a secret from me—from his family, too, though I wasn't sure.

A few seconds passed before he spoke again. "I'm sick of people asking about it. But when I'm around you, I feel like I don't have to deal with it. It's nice."

"I'll never ask where you go, Kale. I promise." The river flowed by, the clouds skimmed the sky, but he never once took his eyes off mine. "But you have to promise me something in return."

"What?"

"Promise me you'll always come back."

And he did.

6.
Kale

I couldn't stay.

The moment the first firework went off in the black sky, I knew I couldn't do it.

To me, they are flares in the night.

Warnings of something worse to come.

It's hard keeping both worlds separate when something like this happens. When one place reminds me of the other. So much that my skin goes cold, and I can't think, and I could be seconds away from traveling. It's been happening more and more often.

As I walk away from the river, my back toward the colors in the sky, I focus on the path in front of me.

I feel Harper behind me. Watching me leave.

Because it's what I do best.

I reach the parking lot. My old, discolored Mustang sits waiting for me and I get in. The engine roars to life, drowning the sounds that make my hands shake. I turn the radio up loud to mute them completely and just focus on leaving the parking lot.

I shouldn't have come tonight, but part of me is glad I did. I left before Dad got home—I couldn't sit in that house another minute longer, waiting for him to walk through the door. Something that would only result in stiff questions from him and single word answers from me. Making that distance between us even clearer.

But seeing Harper again made me think of what I used to be like before everything went to shit. I hadn't expected to see her tonight, even though Uncle Jasper told me she was coming back.

Sometimes time goes by faster than I think it does.

The days blur together in a never ending pattern.

But seeing her again . . . I don't know, it just put me at ease. Just for a moment, it reminded me of the days when my life was easier. So much less complicated. Days when I never had the deaths of my friends on my mind.

I can still feel his blood on my skin.

Even after taking a shower until the water ran cold, I couldn't seem to get it off. No matter what I did, there was still red.

The truth can't be scrubbed away.

I grip the steering wheel harder and slam on the brakes. It sends a cloud of dust spiraling into the wind, my brake lights shining behind me until it's gone and everything is still.

I breathe heavily.

My heart pounds against my chest.

Even though the summer is warm, my skin is cold—a constant reminder.

I found out a long time ago that it's easier to keep my life here separate from where I go. When I'm here, in *my* time, I can't allow myself to think about what happens when I leave. I can't think about the things I see, or the people who die.

It's the only way I can stay sane.

But it's never been this hard.

These days it's nearly impossible.

35

I can't stop thinking about Adams. And I can't stop thinking about the hundreds of other guys I've seen die right next to me. Hearing their voices one last time until they become forever silent.

I close my eyes and press my head to the steering wheel.

I miss the easy days when travel didn't mean war. It was just me in different times—playing with kids in the street and watching debuts of movies I considered classic, but they considered brand new. My favorite decade is the seventies, just because I never know what I'm going to find or see.

I don't want to go home.

But I have nowhere else to go.

The moment I walk in the door, I can feel it's not a good night.

Dad shouts at someone on the phone in the kitchen, and Bryce is still out with his friends. The television is on, watched by no one.

Before I can disappear upstairs, Dad ends his call and breaks something against the counter. I flinch, taking a step back toward the door. He rarely gets angry—it's a sign that my timing couldn't be worse.

Dad catches sight of me and walks down the hallway. He's trying to contain himself—he tries so hard to keep his work separate from home but it doesn't always happen. Sometimes I think he sees me as an employee who needs to be fired for showing up late every day.

"Damn it, Kale," he says. "Where have you been? I told you to stay home today. The delivery guy came and nobody was here to sign for it." He takes a deep breath and looks past me, like a better version of me will walk through the door and replace me. It's what he wants. "Where were you?" This time his voice is in check.

Staring hard at the carpet, I say, "I went to see Miles."

"You've been gone three days," he says. "And the first thing I ask of you is to be here. Is that so much to ask?"

I swallow, feeling my dry tongue against the roof of my mouth.

"I'm sorry." And I am. I don't want to tell him, but I totally forgot he told me a delivery was coming.

"Sorry isn't going to cut it this time," he says, then he holds out his hand. "Give me your keys. As of right now, you don't deserve to have a car. I should have done this months ago, because *nothing* seems to get through to you."

I pull my keys out and drop them in his hand, cursing myself then cursing him because we wouldn't be like this if he only listened to me in the first place.

The first time I time-traveled, I was seven-years-old. I was playing in the woods and suddenly I was on the sidewalk somewhere totally different. I didn't understand it at first. Everything looked a little strange and I didn't recognize where I was. A shop owner took pity on me and let me eat a candy bar until the cops came to get me. They seemed a little surprised to find a lost kid in a town where everyone knows each other. I told them I was from Central City, Iowa, but they didn't believe me. How could a seven-year-old get to Idaho by himself?

I had been there for only two days when I came back. I burst through the front door yelling about what had happened and where I'd been. Mom had called the police the day I disappeared, and she could only nod as I told her my story, probably thinking I watched too many movies and was just glad I was back. I don't think she ever believed what I said. Dad told me to stop lying and tell the truth. I tried hard to convince him, but nothing I said made a difference.

After about a year, I stopped telling him altogether.

Now he begs for a truth I've already given him years ago.

When he turns away, I finally unfreeze and say, "And you think taking my car away will help that?" Then I whisper, "Fuck you."

I know it's a mistake the moment I say it. Everything from the last few days has built up, wanting to come out and scream. Giving me the courage to say reckless things. Stupid things.

Dad turns around, his eyes hard as stones. "I'm going to pretend I didn't hear you say that."

He walks back to the kitchen without saying another word. I wish he would come back and try to talk to me. Ask me again about where I've been and really believe me when I tell him the truth. But none of this happens because he thinks I'm a liar. I've thought about disappearing in front of him, and maybe someday I will, but I would rather have him believe me first. Take my word as truth like he should.

A shiver runs down my spine and my skin goes cold.

I run upstairs, taking two steps at a time, and lock myself in the bathroom. I'm breathing heavy now, not understanding why I feel cold—I haven't even been back a day yet. It's too early to travel.

I won't for another four days, maybe three from the pattern I've been in lately.

I stare at the sink, counting numbers in my head to distract myself.

The feeling drains away, leaving me more anchored to this place. Here and now. I let my breathing become steady along with my heart, becoming surer of myself. After years of doing this, I should be able to control it. And in the past, I had even started to feel like I could.

But for the last few months, something has been different. I've been trying to ignore that I've been leaving more often—more than ever before. Trying to pretend like nothing is wrong.

But I can't anymore.

I wake the next morning with Bryce shaking my shoulder. I groan and push him away, but he plants himself on the end of my bed. It dips down with his weight.

"What time did you go to sleep last night?" he asks. I hear him rub his head, his hair too short for him to mess it up.

I crack my eyes open to see daylight fighting against my curtains.

"I don't know," I mutter. "What time is it right now?"

"Eight."

"Then two hours ago."

I can hear him thinking. He grinds his teeth when he thinks.

"What happened last night?" Bryce asks.

"What do you mean?" I sit up and put a hand over my ribs. They still hurt from the mortar two days ago.

Bryce stares at my bruised body. Sees my dog tags over my chest. His eyes tell me he wants to question me, but doesn't ask. I wish he would so things can go back to being normal again between us.

"I don't know," he says. "Dad was acting weird this morning, so I figured it was because of you."

"Do you know what time he'll be back?" I ask.

"He said after lunch." Bryce looks at me, something he doesn't do often. Usually he looks at the things around me, but never *me*. "What happened last night?" he asks again.

"It was nothing, we just got in a fight. The usual."

"Kale—"

"What?" I'm running out of patience with his questions.

Bryce shakes his head and stands. "I don't even know why I try."

"You call this trying?" I ask. "What's the real reason you came in here?"

He stares back because he knows I'm right. He wishes this was trying, because then he wouldn't feel so guilty about not talking to me anymore. Not caring. Bryce started hating me the moment Mom left.

He blames me for it, I know he does. And he has every right to.

Bryce makes to leave, but pauses at the door. Then he adds, "Oh, and Kale?"

My tongue forms a silent curse before he turns back around.

"What?"

He looks me in the eye. "Dad said the next time you leave, he's going to sell your car."

I fight to keep my face expressionless—he knows exactly where to hurt me the most. "Thanks for the message," I say tightly.

After Bryce leaves, I don't know who I'm angrier at—Dad or myself. He won't be the one taking my car away; I will do it myself the moment I leave again.

I get out of bed and pull on a T-shirt, still wearing my jeans from the day before. The steps are blurs under my feet and the front door slams behind me.

I don't go back when I realized I've forgotten my sweatshirt.

It's not worth it.

I pass my car, sitting where I had left it the night before, and head straight into the woods, following the path I used to know so well. It's nearly overgrown now, looking and feeling different from when I was younger. The quiet forest does nothing to calm my heart or keep my hands from shaking.

I'm cold again.

I want to stop thinking. About Adams. About Dad. About the place I'll be traveling to in a few days.

It's a *thing* that builds up with every passing day, and one day, when the slightest breeze can make me shiver, I just disappear. I've learned when it's going to happen, down to the second, but I can't stop it—nothing I do can make me stay here.

Sometimes I can delay it. I'll take a hot shower and gain a few hours in the present. I try to prolong it by wearing a sweatshirt, but I don't know if it does any good.

When I was younger, the summers were warm to me because I would leave once a month. My body would acclimate to the temperatures, and when that month would pass and the days grew colder for me but nobody else, I knew it was almost time.

But now, when I'm leaving every four days, I'm always cold.

Symptoms of a time-traveler. Even when I travel somewhere warm, it's always the same. My ability's way of warning me.

The path before me ends, bringing me to a small clearing with green grass and calm water. I stop at the river and let the sun attempt to warm my skin. It tries . . . and I want it to succeed.

Someone comes through the woods, and my thoughts stop spinning. I know only two other people who come here, one of them being Libby, and she's gone. So that leaves Harper, which makes me feel weird inside.

She doesn't notice me right away. She has a pair of earbuds in and her eyes are on the ground, following the path from Uncle Jasper's house. Her red Converses are tied today, something always rare to see, and she's wearing a *Overwatch* T-shirt.

My heart starts to slow with her being here—that feeling of

41

leaving far, far away. Then it speeds up for an entirely different reason.

Harper catches sight of me and stops short. "Kale." She pulls out her earbuds, her eyes on me the whole time. "I wasn't expecting to see you out here."

I feel my skin start to warm. "I wasn't expecting to find myself here, either."

She smiles at that, small and fleeting. "You look horrible, by the way," she says. "Couldn't sleep last night?"

"Something like that." It becomes a problem when your nightmares come to you even when you're awake. "How were the fireworks?" I ask, needing a change of subject.

"They were all right. Nothing special, anyway."

Harper steps closer, stopping right next to me at the edge of the river. I try not to stare, though it's hard. She's changed a lot since the last time I saw her. Her hair is close to blonde in the bright sun. Some of it curling behind her ears where it's escaped her ponytail. Her cheekbones stand out now and her ears don't seem as big. She's still Harper, though. Still the girl I saw again for the first time last night.

I look away before she catches my stare.

"How was school this last semester?" she asks, bending down to pick up a small stone on the shore.

I glance away from her hands, turning over the stone in her fingers, and say, "Tedious. I don't think my teachers liked me very much. What about you?"

"It was okay." She shrugs and looks over the river again. "It'll be weird this year, though. I've never changed schools before."

"I'm sure you'll be fine."

"What's your favorite subject?"

"History."

I feel like I should smile at that, but it doesn't come.

42

"Really?" she says, smiling again. "I never would have thought that. I didn't think anyone liked history besides the teacher." Then she adds, "Are you glad it's almost over?"

I shift my weight, wondering if I can change the subject before she realizes it, but it's no use. The truth will come out eventually. "I'm actually not going back to school," I tell her. "I took my GED test a couple months ago."

The skin between her eyebrows creases together. "Why?"

"I got expelled," I say, trying to sound like it doesn't bother me. "I guess they have a problem with kids who don't take attendance seriously."

Harper doesn't have a response for this, because she knows exactly what I mean. She probably thought I didn't do that anymore. I think everyone thought it was a "phase" I'd been going through. Like most kids with problems.

If only.

I can see her thinking about something, and I wish I knew what.

Then she says the last thing I expected: "Let's go swimming."

"What?"

"Swimming," she says again. "When was the last time you went?"

"Probably the last time you were here," I admit. Libby never wanted to go without Harper here. It was never any fun with just the two of us.

"All the more reason to do it," Harper says, shrugging.

Before I can say another word, she takes off her T-shirt, revealing a dark tank top underneath. Then she kicks off her shoes, leaving them on the bank.

"I don't think I feel like—"

"Come on, Kale." Harper backs into the water, a smile playing along her lips. Daring me. "What else do you have to do?"

I kick off my shoes in response and reach back to pull my T-shirt over my head. The water is freezing and I have to hold back a shiver. A part of me is afraid it'll trigger unwanted traveling, but I convince myself it's too soon to worry about it. I sink deep into the river. Letting it wash over my chest and then my shoulders. My bruised ribs ache every time I take a breath, but the water feels good.

Harper is already in the middle of the river, where the wide bend arches around, the water coming to a standstill before moving on. It's deep enough to come up to our necks.

The pebbles are smooth under my feet, and the pull of the river lures me downstream, but I don't let it drag me away.

One summer, Libby and I decided we wouldn't swim in the river until Harper was with us. And summer came early that year. The days would make us sweat and stare up at the sun, only to wonder if it would bake you if you stood there long enough. Going down to the river was tortuous. We would stand on the shore, our T-shirts clinging to our backs and our hair damp.

On a Saturday afternoon, Uncle Jasper called the house, telling us Harper was here. We ran out the door and down the path, not caring about the sun because we were finally going to swim.

We ran through the back door and shed our shoes. I was the first up the steps and into Harper's room, where her bag wasn't even unpacked yet.

But when I saw her, I stopped, blocking half the doorway, because I instantly knew something was wrong. She was always great at faking things like that. But not with me.

When Libby pushed past me into the room, Harper put on a smile and agreed to go swimming with us.

Libby went back downstairs to find Aunt Holly, but I stood

there until Harper finally looked at me. She knew she could fool Libby—not me.

I never had to say a word.

"It's nothing," she said, digging through her bag and avoiding my eyes.

"Harper—"

"Kale," she said in the same tone. That's what she did when she wanted to change the subject. She would make it into a joke. But this time her smile fell, like the act was too much for her to keep up. "I'm fine. Let's just go swimming, okay?"

Now so many years later, this Harper has gotten so much better at hiding things. Even with me. I don't realize it until now, when—for an instant—she gets this faraway look in her eyes, like she's thinking about something she's trying to bury. It comes and goes so fast.

"Are you okay?" I ask.

She blinks and it's gone. "Yeah, why?"

"I'm not Libby," I say. "You might be better at hiding things, but this is me you're talking to." Then I ask, "Six years isn't too long to forget that, is it?"

Harper stares, the water coming up to her chin. "Maybe. I also thought a person could change in that time. But I was wrong about that, too."

The little moment of happiness that I may, or may not, have had is gone. She might have been talking about herself, or maybe her mom, but it hits too close to home for me to ignore it.

I move away from her and say, "I need to go."

"Kale, wait," she calls after me.

I wade out of the water and pull on my shoes, not caring if I get them wet.

Harper puts her hand on my arm and I stop, my wet fin-

gers clutching my shirt. I can't remember the last time someone touched me like this.

"Kale." The way she says my name makes my heart jump.
"Just . . . please, listen." She doesn't speak again until I look
at her. She lets go of my arm and says, "I wasn't talking about
you—"

"But it still applies, doesn't it?" My voice is harsher than it
should be.

Harper wants to deny something she can't, I can see it.
Then she says, "If you haven't, then I'm okay with that."

"What do you mean, you're okay with that?"

Harper looks suddenly like she doesn't know me. Maybe
she doesn't. I barely know myself. "I'm okay with it, because
it's *you*."

"Well, I haven't."

"You say that like it's a bad thing. Maybe you haven't
changed—or haven't *seen* yourself change—but you have."

"I haven't changed, because I can't."

We both know what I'm talking about. We aren't talking
about change—we're talking about me leaving. Always leaving
because I can't stop.

I can never stop.

"Why?" Her voice is desperate for an answer.

"I *can't*."

When I don't say anything else—letting those words sink
in—I think she finally understands, even if she doesn't know
the truth. Because when most people say they can't, they don't
mean they can't. They either mean they're too afraid to or
don't want to.

I am neither.

When I say I can't, I really mean it.

Words have many meanings, but one has to figure out

46

their meaning to the person using them before they can truly understand them.

I let out a sharp breath. "I'm sorry, it's just . . . I thought this would be easier."

"What would be easier?"

The answer is simple.

"Everything," I admit.

Harper starts to look away but something catches her eye. She stares at my chest.

At any other time, it would've made me flush.

But then I remember the evidence I wear there.

"Where did you get these?" Her hand brushes against my dog tags and I back away, pulling my T-shirt over my head before she can get a better look at them.

She stares at the small lump over my chest. Unsure of what she saw.

"I'm sorry, but I have to go," I say. "See you around, Harper."

I walk away before I don't have the strength to. Being around Harper is like . . . something I forgot. Something I haven't felt in a long time.

Someone I forgot.

7.
Harper

When I come home, Uncle Jasper is sitting on the back steps with a cup of coffee next to him, his paper folded to the crossword page. He moves his mug over so I can sit down. My shorts are still wet, and I can feel water dripping from my hair.

I can't stop thinking about Kale and what he said last night, about the promise I made to never ask where he goes. And then at the river just now, when something triggered inside him when I mentioned change.

It's because he hasn't.

"He still leaves, doesn't he?" I ask, even though I already know the answer.

Uncle Jasper stares into the woods behind the house where I saw Kale moments earlier, his eyes soft. "He never stopped," he says.

"But *why?*"

"That's not for me to answer, you know that."

And it wasn't for me to ask. Because of the promise I made him, I can never ask Kale about where he goes, as long as he comes back.

"I know it isn't." A sigh escapes and I admit, "It's strange being back—I thought things would be different." Then I remember who I'm talking to and wish I hadn't said it. "That's not what I mean—"

"I know what you mean," he says. "But I think more has changed than you think. You've just got to look closer."

Three days pass, and I don't see Kale.

I can't stop thinking about what happened down at the river. I should've been more careful about what I said. Sometimes my mouth speaks before my brain thinks of the outcome.

Besides trying to keep Kale off my mind, I play my video games in the afternoon and get texts from Grace about the demolition derby Miles entered that's coming up in a week. I text Libby, wishing she would bring up Kale without me mentioning him first. It never works. Giving hints over text messaging is harder than it seems. But maybe it goes both ways because she keeps bringing up her mom and wanting to come home. I make a mental note to ask Kale about it.

Sometime after lunch, Uncle Jasper comes home and sits with me in the living room, watching the twelve o'clock news and working on another crossword. His fingers are stained with car grease, and they'll probably be that way forever. I can't remember his hands ever being clean.

We both flinch a little when the phone rings. Uncle Jasper doesn't take his eyes off the television and answers it, his hand searching blindly for a moment until he finds it. He's probably the only person I know who doesn't have a cell phone yet.

"Hello?" Someone talks on the other end, and I know something isn't right. It's a long while when the other person finally stops talking and Uncle Jasper's eyes tighten with worry. "When did he take it down there?" Another pause and

Uncle Jasper clenches his jaw. "No, I understand, don't worry about it. Thanks, Bryce."

He hangs up.

"Is something wrong?"

Uncle Jasper puts his crossword puzzle on the table near his chair. "Peter told Kale that the next time he leaves, he would sell his car."

"And he did . . . didn't he?" That's why Kale hasn't been around for the last two days. It's because he's not here. "He left again."

"He's been gone since last night," he says. "Peter just dropped his car down at the dealer."

"But can he do that?" I ask. "Isn't that *Kale's* car?"

"Technically, it's not. His dad bought it for him when he got his license, and the title is still in his name." Then he corrects himself, "*Was* in his name."

Uncle Jasper grabs his keys from the table and smirks at me. "Feel like taking a ride?"

I give him my best *you're up to something* look. "What are you going to do?"

"I'm gonna buy it back." As he pulls on his Royals cap, I catch a glimpse of a side of Uncle Jasper I haven't seen since I got here—just a quick spark in his eyes, and a quirk in his smile.

It's enough for me to smile back and slip on my shoes. "I would love to come with you," I say pleasantly. "Besides, you need someone to drive it back."

"Kale's usually picky about who drives his car," he says, smiling again. "But in this case, I don't think he would mind."

"Well, technically, it's no longer his car," I point out.

He tilts his head slightly. "Touché."

I follow him out to his old truck, watching the horizon where dark clouds are looming over the green fields. It's heading away from us, going south toward the city. Inside, the truck smells like stale Doritos, and I know if I look under the seat, I would find the evidence. It makes me smile again.

After pulling onto the main road, Uncle Jasper says something unexpected. "We haven't really spoken about your mom since you got here." I keep my gaze out the window. "I want you to know that you can tell me anything," he says. "I know that sounds really awkward saying out loud but I have to, because I need you to know that. I need you to know that I'll always be here for you."

Uncle Jasper catches my eye but keeps his attention on the road.

I look away, unable to look at him while I tell him the truth. "I guess it's because it hasn't hit me that I'm really here. For good. Even though I want to be," I add. "Mom and I haven't been close for a long time now, but it still feels weird being away from her. Does that make sense?"

Probably not. I very rarely make sense.

"She's your mom, of course you're going to miss her, and that's okay. I'm proud of you for making the decision to move out here—it couldn't have been easy. You need to do what's right for you, and if you need me, I'll be here."

Uncle Jasper shoots me a smile, reminding me of the dad I barely knew, and making me grateful I have him as an uncle.

I lean against the hood of Kale's Mustang and watch Uncle Jasper talk with the dealer inside the lobby. He looks like a wild man through the glass; he keeps tipping his hat back and scratching his head, his hands gesturing to no end. They're two fish in a glass bowl, muted things that I can only watch. If I didn't know any better, I'd say he was playing with the guy, and I smile at the thought, because that's the Uncle Jasper I know.

A few minutes later, Uncle Jasper walks out with a set of keys in his hand. The guy stares at him through the window, looking unsure about what just happened. Like waking up from a dream.

I stand up and cross my arms. "Why do I get the feeling we're stealing this?"

"You don't want me to answer that," he says. Then asks, "Is he still staring at me?"

I glance over his shoulder. "Yes."

He smiles to himself. "Peter dropped this off about two hours ago, and he hasn't had the chance to look under the hood." He grins. I haven't seen him smile so much all summer.

"And since it looks like a piece of scrap metal on the out-side," I say, catching on, "They think it must be a piece of junk."

"Exactly. Little does he know how many hours that kid put into this car. It might look like shit on the outside, but it runs better than anything I've seen come into my garage in a long time." A strange sense of pride rises up when I hear that. But it makes me realize more that this is a Kale I don't know. "Anyway," Uncle Jasper continues, "he couldn't decline instant cash for more than he paid for it."

I think about it and squint up. "Isn't that a little dishon-est? We're practically ripping these people off."

"They actually made money today," he says, probably try-ing not to feel bad. "Peter wanted to get rid of it, and he didn't care how much he got for it."

"So they're making money, and Kale gets his car back." I shrug. "Sounds fair enough to me."

Uncle Jasper tosses me the keys. "Meet you back at the house." He opens his mouth to say something else but stops himself.

"What?"

"I was going to say be careful not to scratch it," he says, "but I think that's irrelevant." He leaves me standing in the parking lot with Kale's keys in my hand, and I watch his truck disappear before getting behind the wheel.

I take the long way home.

Being in Kale's car stirs my stomach. The steering wheel is smooth where his hands grip it. The seats are worn with small rips along the edges, where white fluff peeks through the material. And it smells like him. Kale's smell is like standing in an open field with a rain storm coming. It's one thing that hasn't changed about him.

I wish I could say Kale hasn't been on my mind for the last few days, but that would be lying. I can't stop thinking about his missing smile or his tired eyes, which used to be so bright—something that has really been bothering me.

And I can't stop thinking about the dog tags I saw around his neck.

They didn't look like the cheap dog tags you can get in the store, or the kind you get engraved for someone. They aren't even the real dog tags that the Army uses. They were . . . old, and worn.

Just like Kale and everything about him, there's something I'm missing.

I pull over on the side of the road and get out, looking over a soybean field. The darkening clouds overhead let the sun shine through in bright rays, lighting up a world that was dark a moment before.

It makes me think things can be good again, even after moving here away from everything I knew. Sometimes it doesn't feel that way, like there's a chance for me to heal after being left behind by my own mother. Even if it was my decision to leave her in the end.

It's something I can't forget about and move on from in a day.

But maybe this can be my fresh start.

8.
Kale

We've been in this same chunk of woods for two days. A small time compared to how long we've been in this same area. It's got to be months by now.

Eating hard bread and sleeping in frozen holes in the ground.

They tell us we're advancing today, and I ran out of cigarettes last night. I don't like the taste of them, but I don't think I can go another day without one.

With my feet cold and my stomach empty, I find the nearest fire where a few guys try to warm up. Most of them are in high spirits usually, telling jokes and stories to keep their minds off things here. They hold their hands over the flames, their white fingers turning pink. It's easy for them to smile, because a part of them yearns to.

Stiles nods to me, keeping his hands over the fire. "Hey, Jackson. I heard about Adams this morning," he says. "It's a damn shame."

"We lost Campbell this morning, too," Bingo mutters, taking a long drag and blowing the smoke through his nose. "Heard the replacements are already on their way."

I feel my hands shaking again, hidden away deep in the

pockets of my jacket. I don't like thinking about Adams and how—if I'd done something differently—he would still be alive. But that's the funny thing about time-traveling; the past has already played out, even though I'm living it now.

It cannot be changed. A fact that haunts me every day.

Everyone mumbles about the damn replacements, all wondering if any of them will last the week. The guys around me talk more about girls and the war. And if anyone would've asked me, I couldn't have told them anything they said.

My body is here, but my mind isn't.

It's at home, wondering if Dad will take me seriously if I try to tell him the truth again. Wondering if I can somehow make things right between us. Libby and Bryce, he doesn't have a problem with. They go to school. Get good grades. Have summer jobs because they can.

I'm the one who makes things harder.

Just me.

The messed-up kid he probably wishes he never had.

Stiles nudges me in the arm, offering a cigarette. "You look like you could use one."

I take it wordlessly, trying to smile.

A few guys laugh and joke about me finally breaking down a month back while Stiles lights it. They know I tried to hold off smoking at first. And they also know it's nearly an impossible feat.

Our cigarettes stand out white in this gray and brown world.

My hands are so cold, I can barely hold it to my lips, but it's already calming me. We'll be attacking soon, probably less than thirty minutes from now. I need it more than I can admit.

Voices murmur around me:

"Lieutenant."

"Lieutenant."

"Boys," a voice greets behind me.

I turn and nod to Lieutenant Gates. "Lieutenant."

"And how are we this afternoon?"

Stiles answers, "Ready to kill some krauts, sir."

He takes a look at our small group, noticing the holes left by the men who are now gone. "I think we all are." Then he turns to me. "Jackson, Captain Price is asking for you. He's at the north end of the line."

"Yes, sir." I don't ask questions, despite my curiosity.

I grab my M1 and start back through the camp. I keep my head clear of everything except staying alive. Keeping warm and making sure I eat, and finding more cigarettes. Right now, I could use them more than food.

Then somehow, out of nowhere, I think of Harper.

Seeing her down near the river. And then in the water, when her eyes reflected the sky. Just a glimpse. But then that makes me think of home and I almost get the feeling I could leave now if I wanted to.

I don't.

A couple guys from the 82nd division stare as I stand there, waiting for that moment to pass.

I turn away from them and continue on, not stopping until I see Captain Price—his back is to me, facing the tree line. He's with another captain who joined us in the night, but I don't remember his name. I try to stand tall and keep my hands from shaking. They're fine right now. They usually are when my mind is on the present—wherever I happen to be.

It's what keeps me focused and alive.

"Private Jackson." Captain Price nods and motions to the man next to him. "This is Captain Donavan from the 82nd."

Donavan looks me up and down, seeming a little confused. "You're the one they call Ace?" he asks.

I resist the temptation to shift my weight. "Yes, sir."

56

"That's quite a name to be given," he says.

"And he lives up to it," Captain Price adds. "He's the best shot we have."

Donavan turns to me. "What's your range with an M1D?"

"Never used one, sir."

"Just an M1?"

"Yes, sir."

He looks at me funny. "Scope?"

"No, sir," I answer. "Someone offered me one a month back, but I would rather use the eyes I was born with."

Donavan laughs, unsure but still finding it funny. "What's your range then? No scope, if you'll have it that way."

"Almost three hundred yards."

He nods, and I don't know if he believes me.

I was seven-years-old when I first fired Dad's hunting rifle.

He took me into the woods behind our house, the rifle wedged into his shoulder with one hand holding it, the barrel pointed at the ground. And his other hand holding mine. I remember them being so much bigger than my own. They felt safe and strong.

I don't remember a lot about that day except that.

And something he said before I took my first shot.

His arms were around me, his hands guiding mine. Then he whispered in my ear, "Aim small, miss small."

Until recently, a year never went by without me going hunting or shooting with Dad.

Then he stopped asking.

So when I got here and they put a rifle in my hands and told me to shoot, nothing could come easier.

While Donavan and Price talk, my thoughts go numb. I don't want to think about the time Dad and I spent together, because it makes me miss it more.

If I think of nothing, the pain goes away.

Novocain for my heart.

Everything is cold, and a war ranges around me. But I feel nothing when I let myself.

Sometimes it's the best thing I can do.

9.
Kale

They're waiting for me.

Waiting for me to take the shot and start a day of bloodshed. Every time I pull the trigger, I remind myself I'm doing it to survive. If I don't kill them, I am dead. If I don't shoot, my friends are dead. It doesn't make it any easier.

My helmet sits near my elbow. The wind cuts through my hair. I look down the gun's sight at the man I have to kill. They gave me a new gun with a scope today because they're low on sharpshooters, and now I look at the man who they want me to kill. I try not to stare at his face so I won't remember him later. So he won't haunt my dreams.

It wasn't always like this.

I used to like going back in time.

Different places, different people. Reliving history like nobody has before. I could've told Mr. Williams things no teacher has ever known if they hadn't expelled me.

Things not important enough to make history books, or maybe too horrifying to.

I miss the days of unpredictability. Not months of the same war, coming back like I never left, time and time again.

I'm here for reasons I don't know, and it doesn't matter to me when I'll be finished.

The truth is, sometimes I would rather be here than home. Even though I'm in the middle of a war, watching friends die every day, and not knowing if I'll be alive to see the sunrise, it's better than being with a dad who thinks I would rather tell him lies than the truth.

I miss Dad. The one I used to know. The father who hugged me when I got home and told me he was proud. Who used to take me out into the field to play catch or into the forest to hunt.

But I'm not there anymore, so I swallow down my anger and focus on what I need to do.

Thinking of Dad does nothing to help me here. But the lessons he taught me . . .

"Aim small, miss small," I whisper.

My finger rests on the trigger.

I wait for my heart to slow. It matches the rhythm of the flakes of snow landing around me.

I aim high to account for the range.

I pull the trigger.

My life is slipping away through my fingers.

I cannot catch it.

10.
Harper

I wake in the night, and my cheeks are wet with tears. The blankets tangle around my legs, evidence of the dreams that turned into nightmares, and my heart beats frantically, trying to escape the thoughts haunting my mind.

The door creaks open. "Harper, is everything all right?" Uncle Jasper asks. "I thought I heard you yell something."

He stands in the doorway, unsure, still dressed from the day like he never went to bed. The familiar smell of engine oil drifts over.

I try to wipe away my tears before he sees them, but it's too late. Instead of meeting his gaze, I stare at my comforter, thinking how it's the same color of my one back home, the one Mom bought me. My home that is no more.

"I can't help thinking if—" I swallow, finding my mouth dry "—if I made the right decision. Leaving her, I mean."

The floor creaks under Uncle Jasper's weight as he walks over and sits down on the bed, facing me. "Do you want to talk about it?"

"I don't know what good that will do," I say, my voice coming out shaky and weak. I hate it. This isn't me. I don't cry, and yet here I am.

"It'll help more than you think," he says. His face is shadowed with night, but I'm still able to see the seriousness in his eyes. "I know you too well. Sometimes when you go through things, you bottle them up inside and try to act like everything is fine. Because you want to forget they ever happened. But you have to trust me when I say that doesn't work. In order for you to move on, you have to let them out. Or one day they're gonna come out whether you like it not."

"Better to do it on your own terms?"

"It's easier to win the battle." He smiles. "Come downstairs. I'll make you some hot chocolate."

Without arguing, I slip off the bed and follow him down the steps. The television is on low, the baseball players silent as they try to hit the ball. The bright light hurts my half sleeping eyes, and it's a relief when we get into the kitchen, where only the light above the stove is on. I sit down in my regular chair, and Uncle Jasper puts the kettle on the stove and turns on the burner.

He sits down and folds his hands on the table. "So what's on your mind?"

"Mom." My throat feels tight. I throw up my arms and say, "Of course, Mom. Even here, I can't get away from her."

He asks, "Do you regret coming here? Is that what it is?"

"I don't know . . . no. I don't think so." I pause and then start over. "I just . . . I always hoped we would get through this, because we always got through everything together," I say. "We were fine until a few years ago. Things kept getting worse and we got more distant from each other. It was like we were roommates, and not mother and daughter."

I stare at the lines in the wooden table, continuing, "She would go to work and I would go to school. A couple days would pass and we wouldn't say a word to each other. Then those days turned into weeks. She started going on business trips without even telling me. I think that's when I realized something was really wrong between us. It's just . . . I never thought it would come to this. And *why*?" Then I look at Uncle Jasper and say, "It feels like I did something wrong. Like I missed my chance to make things right between us."

"None of this was your fault, kid," he says. "You have to understand that. Your mom has been going through something for a long time, ever since your dad died. Some people fight through it, and some people choose not to by ignoring it. It's up to them to get through it, and we can only support and love them. But sometimes that isn't enough. No matter what we do."

"I wish there was something I could've done," I say. "Leaving her . . . it felt like giving up."

"It's not giving up, Harp. Sometimes two people drift apart, and there's nothing anyone can do about it. And you accepted that by coming here, even if you didn't know it." He reaches forward and puts his hand over mine. "You made a choice, and I couldn't be prouder of you for that."

Even if I did make the choice in coming here, I'm still not sure if it was the right thing. I have so much doubt brewing within me, making me second guess myself. I want to know if I did anything wrong, and if there was anything I could have done differently. I miss her, but I don't miss anything more than what I won't have with her.

Uncle Jasper speaks up again, "And believe it or not, this might be the start of something good between you."

"How do you mean?"

"Maybe this is the fresh start that you and your mom need."

"By her moving to a different country and leaving me to live at my uncle's house?"

Uncle Jasper half smiles at my tone. "Sometimes being apart can start healing before it begins."

The kettle hisses behind him. He pushes his chair back and I watch him turn the burner off, get two mugs out of the cupboard, tear open two packets of hot chocolate, open the refrigerator to find the milk—filling a quarter of each mug before putting it back—and then finally pouring hot water until each is filled.

He makes it the same way Aunt Holly did.

With a spoon in each one, he puts them on the table and pushes mine over to me. It's the mug that has the DeLorean from *Back to the Future* on it, with black text under it saying, "**I know the world doesn't end in 2012 because Marty McFly traveled to 2015**."

He's had this mug for years.

I absently stir until the chocolate is dissolved. But I don't drink yet, still thinking about what he said. When I left to come live here, I was sure I would never talk to Mom again. I never thought it was a possibility until now. It gives me a little hope I didn't have before.

"You know," I say, still stirring the hot liquid in my mug, "sometimes you're pretty good at this. And maybe you're right. Maybe this is the start of something good between us."

"I know it will be," he says. Even though I know he doesn't, I like hearing him say it.

"I miss her."

The instant I say it, emotions flood me before I can push them away, too strong for me to ignore. I can't help it—I start crying, small tears leaking from my eyes before I can stop them, unable to hold it back. There's a deep ache within me, wanting to be let out. Waiting to be let out.

Uncle Jasper leans over and wraps his arms around me, pulling me into his chest. More tears spill over my cheeks, dampening his shirt. I cry more because I can't remember the last time someone held me. Not like this. Even though I can't

64

bring myself to hug him back, it's the closest thing I've come to it. It's like after all these years, I've forgotten how.

"I love you, Harper," Uncle Jasper murmurs into my hair. "Nothing will change that. . . .Nothing," he says again.

For some reason, I feel relief when he says it. Like somewhere deep down I've been waiting to hear it.

Uncle Jasper holds me the same way he did when I was younger, comforting me when nobody else was there. He always has been . . . but then so was Mom before all this began.

11.
Kale

I stare at the sky and know I'm back.

It was so fast.

I barely remember it happening.

It was only about twenty minutes after I pulled the trigger and we started our attack. I'd been taking out as many snipers as I could find until they needed me deeper in town, targeting sharpshooters from around corners under covering fire.

We needed to take the town—that's all I knew. I can't even remember its name.

I just follow orders.

When we were nearing a corner of a building, getting ready to clear the next half of the town, an explosion came from nowhere. It could have been a mortar, or tank.

I'll probably never know for sure.

The guys in the front weren't as lucky as us near the back. I was thrown to the ground, the air leaving my lungs the moment I hit the frozen earth. Dirt and rock showered from above.

I could only lay there in the snow, trying to breathe and hoping I was still alive.

Then I was gone—

—and now I'm here.

Back to wearing my jeans and T-shirt like I never left at all. The only evidence of the past are the dog tags around my neck and the scratches and dirt left from the explosion.

Any wound I get there stays with me.

The very first time I go back to a certain year, I'm still in my clothes from the present—a little shock to anyone who happens to see me. I'm forced to find clothes from that time, but when I travel back to my time—the present—I'm back in my jeans and short sleeves. But when and if I go back to that same time in the past, I'm instantly brought back in the clothes I found there—like I never left at all.

So these past few months in 1944, I appear like I never left. Boots cold and helmet on my head. If someone happens to look close enough, it's probably like I flicker—faster than the blink of an eye. A second has passed for them, but days have passed for me. A soldier made a double take once. I had just gotten back and he was there looking at me like he wasn't sure what he saw. Probably thought he was hallucinating but I wasn't going to correct him.

So for the past six months, I've been going back to the same year. The same time.

I don't feel any pain right now, but I'm not feeling much of anything. Still shocked from the blast and trying to breathe regularly. It's not going to be pleasant when I go back. The blue sky stares down from above. Through the caved-in roof, the sun tries to warm my frozen skin, as it always does.

Still, I shiver. I lay there on my back, feeling the grass beneath me instead of the snow that had been there seconds earlier.

I push myself up, aware of any pain I could be feeling, but there is none. The blast knocked the air from my lungs and nothing more. I'm lucky this time. I may be dirty and cold, but I'm breathing. Not bleeding. That's what counts most.

I take a few minutes to get my bearings. Wait for my head to stop spinning enough to stand up, and my heart to slow down once it realizes I'm really here. This is the only place I ever come back to. Like a rubber band snapping me back into place.

I leave the house with the sun high overhead, and start down the overgrown driveway through the field. It's about a mile from here to the gas station. But it's not like I'm in a hurry to get home. I stuff my hands deep in my pockets in an attempt to get them warm and follow the empty road toward town.

The cracked asphalt and gravel shoulder are too familiar.

I pass trees I've seen hundreds of times.

Pass mailboxes I know by heart. I'm still cold when I reach the main road and cross over to the Phillips 66.

A truck passes behind me, blaring its horn even though I'm already off the road. Besides the only car in the parking lot—owned by the person behind the counter—I'm alone.

I take one last glance around before walking around the building where the phone booth is. Names are scratched into the metal, others used a Sharpie as their graffiti tool.

L.B. <3s SARA.

Skool suckz.

Kirbylicious—whatever the hell that means.

Then of course the various profanity scrawled everywhere. Things I don't even like looking at, much less reading.

But among the scrawls of past people, I look for the same initials. The two letters I can always count on to be here.

J.W.

Scrawled in black Sharpie at the top right corner behind the phone.

Two letters of someone's name who I'll never know. I take a long look at them before I dig the few coins from my pocket.

The ones I keep stocked, never knowing when I'll need them. I used to have a cellphone. But then I decided it wouldn't be a good idea for someone in the past to see it. It's not like I can afford to pay the bill anyway. Now it's cold and dead under my bed.

The dial tone sounds in my ear and I punch in the numbers, half wondering why they aren't worn off yet.

It rings so many times, I'm afraid he's not there. The walk home is long when I can't get hold of him, but I wait, still hoping.

Right before I think about hanging up, he answers. "Hello?"

"It's me."

There's a moment before he speaks. I close my eyes and lean my head against the phone booth, feeling exhausted—the past few days are now catching up to me. The metal doesn't feel any colder than I am.

"Are you all right?" he asks.

From the tone of his voice, I can tell he really wants to know. It's something I don't often hear.

"I'm fine."

"I'll be there in twenty."

I slip into the bathroom without making eye contact with the man at the counter and wash my face. I don't look in the mirror, knowing I won't like what I see. On my way out of the store, the cigarettes behind the counter catch my eye, making me pause just long enough for the guy to look up. Without giving him a chance to say anything, I duck my head and make my escape out the door. Back outside, I settle down on the curb and stare at my shoes. My dog tags weigh heavily around my neck. A constant reminder of what I've become.

After a while, the truck pulls up. The brakes don't squeak and the engine doesn't complain.

Uncle Jasper sits behind the wheel, staring ahead even as I

get in and close the door. He pulls away from the gas station without saying a word.

He's good like that—not pushing for answers and not caring if he doesn't get any. He asks questions that are easy to answer. About things I actually *want* to talk about.

I already feel calmer sitting next to him. My heart warms, slowly spreading to the rest of my body. But despite Uncle Jasper's company and the summer heat, I still shiver.

"Do you want me to turn on the heat?" he asks.

"No, I'll be all right." I stare across the passing fields, trying to keep my thoughts away from home. I can't help but ask, "It's gone . . . isn't it?"

There's a moment of silence. A moment where I dread the answer.

"He took it to the dealer the day after you left," Uncle Jasper says.

My finger taps against the seat like I need a cigarette, thinking about the ones back in the Phillips 66, ready for me to buy. But I don't smoke here. I've never had to, but I'm not sure how much longer that will last.

"What did I miss while I was gone?"

"Royals won again last night," he says.

"Oh *really?*"

Uncle Jasper nods, unable to hide his smile. "I think this will be their year. Last year was just a trial run. Going all the way this time."

I laugh and shake my head then ask, "How's Harper? Is she doing all right?"

"She will be," he says. "I think she just needs some time."

I turn away and watch the fields again, the golds and greens blending together as we pass by. The corn keeps growing as summer passes. A summer in which I wish I could spend more time with Harper.

I've lost dozens of friends in a war I wasn't meant to be in. I know what it feels like to lose people who will never come back. The deaths I've seen weigh heavier on my heart than anything I've ever felt. Adams more than anyone. Every time I think of him, my hands shake and my throat goes tight.

But I have no idea what Harper is going through. I've never lost a parent or a sibling. She lost her dad years ago, and now she's not even living with her mom. The pain I see in her eyes is so evident even when she tries to hide it. I only live with Dad, but at least both my parents are still alive.

"She's lucky to have you," I say, still staring across the fields. So many times I've wished Uncle Jasper was my real uncle. And so many times I've wished my father would see me for me, and not the kid he sees when I walk through the door after I've been gone for a while. When he sees that kid, he sees nothing.

It does no good to wish for impossible things.

Uncle Jasper feels my tension and says, "Kale—"

"I don't want to talk about it."

"And ignoring it isn't going to help."

My fists tighten. "It's my problem," I tell him. "Not yours."

He says nothing because he's good like that. Then he says something I never expected to hear. He says, "You should tell her the truth."

I stare at him, not knowing what to say.

Uncle Jasper nods in response, letting the subject drop. We ride the rest of the way in silence, watching every familiar mile pass by.

He usually drops me off at the end of my driveway, but he finishes the half mile toward his house.

"What are you doing?"

"I have something to show you," he says.

"You aren't building another plane in the barn like you did after watching that movie, are you? I think that lasted a total

71

of two hours." I shrug. "It would have been funny to watch you fly it, though."

"You're just *not* going to let that go," he says, shaking his head. "It's not like you haven't done anything that only lasted a day."

"Well, you could use your one free pass and I would never speak a word of it again."

"And as I've said before, I'm saving it for something worse."

"So now you're admitting you have something even crazier in mind?" I ask. "*More* than building a plane in your barn?"

He grips the wheel and tries not to smile.

When the driveway clears away from the woods, the house looks the same as it always does. The big trees around it and the faded paint on the siding. It's one of the unchanging things I can count on. There aren't many.

The tires fit into the dents in the gravel where Uncle Jasper parks every day. I get out of the truck and stare at the house. Even though it's so familiar to me—and now feels like more of a home to me than my own house—there's one thing that's different about it now. Harper.

I can't even *think* about this house without thinking about her. She's been creeping into my thoughts more and more. Ever since seeing her that first day, and even more after the river. I hope I didn't screw it up between us.

"Do you want to see this or not?" Uncle Jasper says behind me.

I tear my eyes off the house and follow him over to the barn. The lawn mower sits on the side, overgrown grass climbing its wheels.

I've spent countless nights in here helping Uncle Jasper fix whatever needs to be fixed. Jobs that needed extra hours of work or just small projects of his own.

They're memories of black stained fingers, empty Mountain Dew cans, and horrible radio stations.

Uncle Jasper pushes the big door open, and at first I don't know what I'm looking at. My mind is elsewhere. With the cold nights. My dad, whom I'll have to face by the end of today. Harper. My car I'll never see again.

But now I realize my car is right here in front of me. In Uncle Jasper's barn. With its dented bumper and nonexistent paint job.

I can't stop staring, afraid it'll disappear like everything else good.

It takes me a moment to put the pieces together.

"You shouldn't have done this." I can't see him, but I know he's behind me. "You know I can't pay for it."

He puts a hand on my shoulder and squeezes gently. "I'm not asking you to, Kale. You do enough work for me as it is. I owe this to you."

I turn away from the barn, shaking my head. "You don't owe me *anything*. You've already done enough as it is. I don't know how many times I've told you this."

"And what did I tell you?" he asks.

I shift my weight and look down at my shoes. "You told me you do it because you want to."

I can't meet his eyes.

"So what's the problem?"

I hesitate. "I hate owing you more than I can give." I cut him off before he can say what I know he's thinking. "And don't say, 'You don't owe me anything,' because you can't possibly believe that's true. You do more than anybody ever has."

"I think we've had this conversation before," he says.

We have.

Probably more than once.

Maybe five or six years ago, Uncle Jasper found me walking home one night, all the way from that old house in the field. I'd been walking that stretch of road since I was seven. But something about him made me tell him everything.

And for once, someone actually believed me. Now, him, Libby, Bryce, and Miles are the only people who know the truth. Aunt Holly used to, but . . .

"I can't take this," I say. "It's too much."

He takes my hand and presses something into my palm. It's my keys.

"You're going to."

I can't argue with him.

He doesn't give me that look very often, but when he does, I know it's best to keep my mouth shut.

Something catches my eye over his shoulder. It's Harper coming out of the house and down the steps. She's wearing an old pair of ripped jeans and a T-shirt with some other gaming logo on it.

Uncle Jasper is talking, but I don't hear him. I think the Royals are mentioned again, so I'm sure it isn't important.

The breeze pushes her hair over her shoulder and she smiles at seeing me. I follow her legs all the way down to her unlaced Chuck Taylors.

The cold has all but left me.

I don't know if it's because I'm in a good mood right now, but it feels like I'm just now noticing her today. The last two times I talked to her, I wasn't myself. Which happens a lot these days. Being around Harper has made that even more obvious.

I probably acted like an ass, and I can't do that again.

I have to fix things between us before they get any worse.

She's almost here.

"Kale." Uncle Jasper's voice seems far away.

I finally look away. "What?" I ask him.

Uncle Jasper stares a moment. "Never mind." He sighs. "I don't feel like repeating myself today."

I nod, too distracted. "Hey, Harper."

"Hey, Kale. It's good to have you back."

Before I can respond, Uncle Jasper asks her, "Did you figure out what you want for dinner yet?"

"I think I'll look through Aunt Holly's recipes to see if I can find something. I kind of feel like cooking."

"Sounds good," he says, then turning to me, "Do you want to stay for dinner, Kale?"

"No, I should be getting back."

Uncle Jasper's smile falters but he nods to hide it. "Maybe some other time then."

"Would it be okay if I kept my car here for tonight?"

Dad gets mad enough as it is on my first day back. I don't need more attention than I'll already have.

"Of course," he says. "I've got something coming in sometime tomorrow afternoon, so make sure you get it before then. Hey, maybe I'll even get a chance to fix that bumper of yours."

"Don't get carried away, old man."

He laughs and walks back to the house.

It's only me and Harper, standing in grass that needs to be cut. That was Aunt Holly's favorite hobby—mowing the lawn. She would do it every Saturday. Listening to seventies bands while driving back and forth across the yard.

A comforting sound that could be heard through my open window if the wind was coming from the west.

Nowadays, the grass grows until it tugs at my ankles. Uncle Jasper always puts it off as long as he can. Like he'll wake up one morning and Aunt Holly will be out there mowing the grass because he let it grow.

But now I look at Harper and my thoughts of Aunt Holly and her grass drift away. I have to remember not to say anything stupid. But thankfully, she talks before I can.

"I promise I didn't make any more dents in it driving it here," she nods toward my car.

A partial laugh escapes my lips. "Not like it would make a difference."

"That's what I told Uncle Jasper," she says.

I feel myself smiling.

Truly smiling for the first time in what seems like forever.

"I'm sorry if I've been acting weird lately," I say. "Or said something I shouldn't have."

"I've noticed," Harper says, smiling again.

"You have?"

"Of course I have. I may not have seen you in a long time, but I haven't forgotten anything." Then she says, more careful, "You haven't been yourself, Kale."

I remember the reasons I've become this way. Everything all at once—and none of it I want to think about.

A muttered "yeah" comes from my mouth. I look toward the woods and back to my car, making sure it's still there. "I should go." I turn away, but she grabs my wrist. Stopping me. It's the last thing I expect and my heart jumps from her touch.

It reminds me of the river.

"Kale, I'm sorry. I shouldn't have said that," she says, letting my hand drop. A flash of embarrassment crosses her face, like she didn't mean to touch me. "Sometimes my mouth says things I don't want it to."

I answer, "But it's the truth." I back away toward the woods, reluctant to leave her, but already knowing I'm in trouble as it is. "I'll see you later, Harper."

Every happy moment is taken away as quick as it comes.

It's like I'm not meant for this time I live in. Like my body keeps pulling me back to where I actually belong.

But I want to belong here.

I just don't know how.

12.
Harper

I walk down the road with the wind to my back. It pushes me along, farther away from the house and farther away from thoughts I would rather not have right now. Uncle Jasper isn't home today, and it's always too quiet being in the house without him. I always try to get some walking in before playing Xbox—it's my reward for exercising, so when I turn back to go home, I walk faster knowing what waits for me there.

But something else waits for me besides video games—better than video games. Uncle Jasper's truck is still gone, but Kale's car is parked in its place. He sits on the hood, one leg propped up on the bumper, staring off into the woods behind the house. He's wearing a long-sleeved thermal shirt, a little frayed along the neckline.

Hearing me, he turns, "Hey."

"Hey." I stop next to his car, trying not to get too close in case I smell. "What are you doing here?"

"Honestly . . . I wanted to see if you had any plans tonight."

I shrug apologetically, "I already have plans."

He wasn't expecting that. "You do?"

"Yeah, with you."

I give him a moment to be confused and then give him a smile.

He visibly relaxes and lets out a breath. "Don't do that. I thought I was experiencing memory loss or something."

"Sorry, I couldn't resist. But come on, let's do something. It's been too long."

Kale's hesitant but I know he wants to say yes. I would pick him over a party any day.

"I could call Miles to see what they're up to tonight?" he suggests.

"That sounds great. Pick me up at six? Uncle Jasper said your cell phone doesn't work anymore, so . . ."

He's two seconds too late with a response, hiding something again. "Yeah, just the house phone for me these days. But six sounds good. I'll give Miles a call when I get home."

I nod and he starts to get into his car, but then he stops, looking back at me. "I'm glad you're here."

It's like he knew exactly what to say and what my heart needed to hear. "Me too."

And I really mean it.

13.
Kale

When I first traveled back to 1944, I was surrounded by guys in uniforms with packs on their backs, looking like they were headed nowhere good. Then there was me, still wearing my T-shirt and jeans with a surprised expression on my face. I didn't know where the hell I was.

Then an officer spotted me and asked why I didn't have my gear.

"They were stolen," were the first words out of my mouth.

He just shook his head and muttered, "Damn replacements."

A couple guys nearby laughed, making jokes under their breath. I was just looking for a way out of there. But the officer wasn't about to let me out of his sight and reminded me along the way of how stupid I was for letting my stuff be stolen.

After that, telling lies became easier and easier. They didn't have me in the books, but all they did was blame it on some guy who was in charge of the replacements. I was obviously an American and supposed to be there, so they had me fill out the missing paperwork, not thinking twice. Just in need of more soldiers.

So I rolled with it, knowing I would be gone in a few days anyway.

But then I kept coming back, and my dog tags stayed with me through each travel, almost telling me I'd be there for a while.

Two weeks later, after missing most of the training I was supposed to have, I was shipped off to join the 104th infantry division. I didn't know what the hell I was doing, but I caught on fast and was already good with a gun. I listened hard and watched others around me. Lucky for me, the officers like to repeat themselves a lot.

And even though I came here as a replacement, the guys soon forgot I was one.

I think about the beginning a lot. Wondering if I started doing something different to make me go back to the same year, if somehow I was controlling it.

Or maybe it's just fate screwing with me.

I drive home from Uncle Jasper's wondering what we'll talk about when I pick up Harper, and if it'll be awkward between us.

Again, for the hundredth time, I wish Libby was here. She would know what to say and make the night seem easy. Too soon the road ends, and the moment I pull into our driveway, I realize this will be the first time Dad will see I have my car back.

I got it out of Uncle Jasper's barn early this morning and drove until I realized I couldn't pay for the gas it would take me to drive out of the state and back. So I sat in the parking lot of a restaurant that went out of business a few years ago. Just sitting. Not being at home. Trying to think of a different way to learn control that I haven't tried already.

Now I have a sick feeling in my stomach—worried he'll take it away again.

As I park in my place under the tree, a coldness sets in. I press my head against the steering wheel and try to be thankful he isn't home yet. I don't feel like dealing with him today.

Go upstairs.

Put cleaner clothes on.

Hope he doesn't come home between now and when I have to pick up Harper.

When did my life come to this? Trying to steer clear of Dad because every time he looks at me, I see how disappointed he is.

"*Shit*," I mutter. I get out and slam the door shut.

Bryce comes out of the house, his eyes darting between my car and the road.

"Kale, what are you doing?" he asks. "How did you get it back? If Dad sees it, he's going to freak."

I breeze past him. "Just leave me alone, Bryce. I get enough shit from him, and I *don't* need it from you, too."

"You know I'm just trying to help," he says, turning to follow me. "Do you think I like the way things are around here? Kale!"

I ignore him and walk into the house, heading straight for the kitchen. I can't remember if I ate lunch but I'm starving. Bryce follows inside, still talking like he gives a crap.

"You can't keep doing this." He stands in the doorway and watches me stare into the almost empty fridge. "You're only making it worse on yourself. You need to stop."

I slam the refrigerator shut and turn around. "*Me?*" I ask him. "*I'm* making it worse on myself? You know I've tried to tell him before—he never believed me. And it doesn't help that you've stopped, too."

He visibly deflates. "You know that's not true. But this is only something *you* can stop. I can't help you if you don't try."

"I'm not asking for your help," I tell him.

I want to scream and yell. Break something until there's nothing left to be broken.

Including myself.

Is it possible to put myself back together again? To make me normal?

I don't know if there's anything I want more.

We stare at each other and hear Dad's truck pull up to the house. Neither of us move. I know it's too late to run and hide. He's already seen my car.

The truck door slams, followed by the screen door.

Nothing is between us now.

I stare at my brother, daring him to speak up. But he won't. He's worried Dad will think he's lying, too. Bryce moves aside to let Dad into the kitchen, keeping his eyes on the floor.

"Why is that car parked out there?" Dad asks. He glances from me to Bryce. My brother shrugs, still staring at his shoes. "Kale? Maybe you'd like to inform me why a car I sold two days ago is sitting in my driveway again."

"It's . . ." My mouth is dry. I can't think straight when he stares at me like that. "I got it back."

"With what money?"

"I worked for it."

He looks between us again. Probably debating on punishing me for something.

But not today.

Today, I haven't done anything wrong.

With a look over his shoulder, Dad silently tells Bryce to leave.

And he does. His retreating footsteps don't even hesitate on the stairs.

Dad steps closer and I so badly want this wall between us to go away. He looks over my shoulder and over to the stove.

"Kale . . . I don't want it to be like this between us"—me nei- ther—"you know that. But the only way we can is if you tell me what's going on. Please. You don't talk to me anymore."

I almost tell him when I look up, but I don't because I know it'll just make things worse. He'll think I'm lying again. He will think even less of me than he already does.

So I don't say anything.

Dad sighs in defeat. "Just go upstairs."

He leaves the kitchen. The television sends muffled echoes from the living room.

I sneak out the back door and I'm in my car before I real- ize where I'm going. The long roads give me too much time to think, so I don't. Stretches of road go by I don't remember driving, and my fingers tap on the gear shift, wanting to go faster but not wanting to get pulled over.

The Phillips 66 sign comes up and I pull into the empty lot, parking in the farthest spot away from the door. Then I sit there. Fighting with myself to do this and not do this.

I open the glove compartment and dig out a few dollar bills hidden inside.

Then I gain enough courage to open my door. Once I do, I don't stop, knowing I'll lose my nerve and turn around. The sun is low in the sky now, and the evening already has a chill to it—though I'm not sure if it's just me.

Setting my shoulders, I open the door and the store clerk turns from where a television is mounted behind him. It's the same person I've seen dozens of times but have never spoken to.

Now I walk up to the counter and say with a less than shaky voice, "Can I get a pack of Newports?"

"Do you have I.D.?"

I nod and hand my wallet over, showing him my driver's license. He looks at it—my birthday, which is a few months pre- mature—and then looks at me. I wait for him to deny me them, because he has every right to. But this is why I chose to come here—he recognizes me and knows something isn't right. And maybe, just maybe, he'll let it go this once, because he sees I need them more than anything right now.

"Blue or gold?" he asks, turning his body so I can see them.

I don't know the difference or the brand. It's just the first thing I saw.

So I say, "Blue."

He rings me up and I hand him my cash, taking a penny out of the penny jar. Before I leave, I hesitate while he looks at me funny.

"Thanks," I say.

Then he understands and nods.

The parking lot is still empty, and I sit in my car, the shadows hiding me like I'm doing something illegal. My fingers fumble with the packaging, but when I finally open it and stare down at the white sticks, I pause.

This isn't me.

At least it shouldn't be.

I don't smoke. I do smoke, just not here and not like this. Not in a convenient store parking lot.

A car full of pounding bass pulls into the Phillips 66, and they take the spot right in front. Two doors open, letting the music into the night, and a pair of guys get out, leaving the rest of their friends inside. I know a few of them from school, and while I'm wondering if they'll recognize me, the kid closest gives me the finger.

I guess that answers my question.

A few minutes later, they drive away again, their trunk hiding the beer until they get to whatever party is tonight.

Tonight . . . as in the night I have "plans" with Harper.

"Shit." I climb out of the car and go to the payphone, dialing numbers and realizing the cigarettes are still in my hand.

84

I talk the moment he picks up. "It's me. What are you doing in an hour?"

"Hello to you, too." There's music in the background, and Grace asking who he's talking to. "The lady and I are on our way to the movies. You know, like all the cool kids do."

"Do you want to meet us at the diner instead?"

"Us?"

"Me and Harper."

The music turns off and he asks. "Hold on, you and Harper? Is this a thing now, are you guys a thing?"

I sigh. "No, she just wants to hang out. It was either this or go to Conner's stupid party."

"Ew," he says, "Yeah, we can meet you there. Six?"

"Yeah."

"Cool."

Once I put the phone back, I already feel better. It won't be just the two of us, and Miles doesn't believe in awkward situations. Oddly enough, I'm looking forward to it.

I stash the unsmoked cigarettes in the glove compartment, replacing the money I used to pay for them. Instead of smoking, I'm gonna go see about a girl.

14.
Harper

Kale takes us to this diner about fifteen minutes away on the corner of two roads that have barely any traffic. The sign saying they're open 24/7 flickers, warning anyone who cares enough that it's about to die. But inside, it's clean and bright. The booths are blue with silver specks, and the wooden table-tops are worn down with use. There's a couple eating at the bar, but there's nobody else but the waitress in the back talking to the cook.

"They'll probably be here soon," Kale says. "Come on."

He picks the booth in the corner and slides toward the back, his eyes glancing at the front door.

"You could've said no, you know," I say. He looks at me, questioning. "To hanging out with me. I just thought—"

"I would never say no. Why do you say that?"

I shrug and pull a menu from the middle of the table for something to do. "I don't know . . . everything just seems weird right now."

So weird.

Kale sits for a couple moments, and I wish I knew what he was thinking. Then he says, "It's been six years, Harp. Of course it's gonna feel weird, but it won't forever. I promise."

I take my eyes off the menu to look at him. "You always keep your promises."

"Yes, I do."

"Has it really been six years?"

He laughs and leans back, looking tired. "It really has. The last time I saw you, we were twelve, I think."

But then his smile goes away, thinking about that day and how we ended things with each other. Rather, how *I* ended things. The day before I left, we were sitting on Uncle Jasper's porch, none of us in a really good mood because it was the end of summer. I told them I would come over in the morning to say goodbye. But I hated goodbyes and I didn't want to think about not knowing when I would see them again—Mom barely let me go that year with Aunt Holly getting sicker.

So I never said goodbye. The last time I saw Kale was when he and Libby walked toward the woods to head home. He turned and waved, like he knew he wouldn't see me again—

"Heeeeey!" I look up to see Miles coming toward us with his arms stretched wide, a grin on his face. "Fancy seeing you guys here."

He and Grace join us in the booth, and the waitress comes over, side-eying Miles. "You aren't gonna order everything on the menu again, are you?" she asks him, pointing a pen at him. "We don't have the staff tonight."

Miles gives her a smile. "I'll spare you tonight."

"Good, what'll it be?" She looks at me and I glance down at the menu, not sure.

Grace leans over the table and says, "The waffles are really good."

I nod and tell the waitress. "I'll take a waffle, maybe one with strawberries on it?"

She nods, looking at Kale next, who says, "Oh, I'm good, thanks."

Miles tells her, "He'll have what I'm having, and it's on me." Kale tries to argue with him but it's no good.

The waitress continues like it's normal. "The usual?"

"You know it."

"The same for you, Grace?" the waitress asks, already putting her pen away.

"Yes, please."

After she leaves, Kale gives Miles a look—and Miles pretends not to notice. Instead he asks me, "So you didn't want to go to Conner's party tonight?"

I make a face. "Not particularly. Parties aren't really my thing."

Miles leans forward. "So what *is* your thing?'

"Mostly staying indoors and avoiding parties." That gets a laugh from Miles and Grace.

"Yeah, us too. We hang out with those people enough at school as it is." Miles takes hold of the conversation, telling me about the few things to do around here, and the waitress brings us all water, and then our food comes shortly after that. Grace and I have waffles while the boys have burgers and fries. I sneak peeks at Kale when he laughs at something Miles says or when he does an impression of one his old teachers. Grace starts telling me about the volleyball team at school, and she actually makes it sound like fun.

I've never really been into sports, but it's always worth a shot, right? I can't let my limbs go to waste playing video games for the rest of my life.

Soon our plates are empty and the diner is more filled with people looking for dinner.

"So me and Kale went to Adventureland over spring break last year," Miles says and Kale just starts laughing. He continues. "The lines were horrible, as always, and we weren't about to pay extra money for those express passes. Because screw that."

88

Grace interrupts, "And because your family are the cheapest people I know."

"Hey, there's nothing wrong with being frugal." Then he nods and says to me, "But they really are."

Kale says, "I don't know if frugal is the right word. They save and reuse plastic wrap."

"You don't see me complaining when we go on awesome vacations." Kale shrugs at that and Miles goes on, "So anyway, there was this really popular ride we wanted to go on, but the line was a two-hour wait."

"One hour of that being in the sun," Kale adds.

"So we decided to check out the gift shop first since it had AC, which was inside the building where the ride was and where everyone came out after. Then Kale noticed something. When the line went into the building, people had a chance to put their bags in lockers, which was also connected to the gift shop so they could pick them up after the ride. There wasn't good lighting in there and it was so crowded. Then Kale says, 'Let's do it.'"

"I'm pretty sure it was *your* idea."

Miles holds up his hand. "No, no, it was yours. And it was brilliant. So, we put our stuff in the lockers and rejoined the line through the other side. We didn't look at the people waiting behind us, we just kept walking down the hallway while the people asked, "Where did those guys come from?"

Grace shakes her head. "So you guys cut your wait time in half?"

"That's why it's called *cutting in line*." Miles puts an arm around her shoulders and says, "You'll learn one day."

I smile and say, "You guys sure live on the edge. Cutting in lines at theme parks? That's extreme."

"But it goes to show," Miles says, holding up a finger, "Kale *can* have fun."

That triggers groans from half the table and I can't hide my laugh, especially when Kale's face gets a little red.

Grace laughs and Miles gives her a look. The waitress comes and clears our plates and we take our leave.

We all file out, and Miles and Grace wave goodbye as we go back to Kale's car. He starts it up and pulls onto the empty road. It's dark now, the headlights lighting up the lines as they disappear beneath the car. Along with the smell of rain and wind, I catch a scent of winter somewhere close. Then it's gone before I can make sure I'm imagining it.

It makes me think of Kale. And then I'm thinking about how I owe him an overdue apology.

"I'm sorry," I tell him. My words slice through the silence but don't carry any farther than if I'd whispered. "I didn't say goodbye, and I'm sorry."

Kale glances at me. "What are you talking about?"

"The last summer I was here. I promised I would come say goodbye, but I didn't."

"Wait, what?" he asks. "You didn't come say goodbye?"

Now I'm totally confused. "No, I thought that's why you hadn't spoken to me since then."

Then something dawns on his face and he says, "Oh, so you never knew." He leans closer to me like he's about to tell me a secret, keeping one hand on the wheel. "Harper, I wasn't even there. I thought *you* were mad at *me*."

"So we both thought the other person was mad over nothing?" Then I start laughing and ask, "Why didn't Libby ever say anything? I called her the day after, and she let me go on thinking you were as mad as she was."

"Because it's Libby and she likes to keep a certain dramatic flair. It's my fault, though. I should've called you."

"It doesn't matter now," I say. "I'm here, aren't I?"

Kale smiles at that. "And I'm glad you are. Things have

been less than exciting around here, as Miles already hinted at. Can I ask you about something, though?"

"Of course." But then I regret it when his smile falls away, warning me of what he's about to ask.

"What happened between you and your mom?" Kale must see me slip, and he hurries to say, "Look, we don't have to talk about—"

"—No, it's fine, really." Even though it's not, but it should be. "We're friends and I should tell my friends what's going on. My mom and I—we've just been drifting apart these last few years. She became so absorbed in her job that we barely ever saw each other. Then a month ago, the company she works for offered her a job in Germany. We got in a big fight about it because she didn't even tell me until she already accepted it. When she told me, 'I'm going with or without you,' that's when I knew I had to get away. It's not supposed to be like that, you know?"

My eyes are moist, holding in the tears I won't let out. I will not be crying in front of Kale tonight. The summer we were ten, I fell out of a tree and broke my arm. It was Kale and me that day, and he rushed down because he saw the look on my face. He asked if I was hurt and I told him, "I don't know."

I wanted to cry so bad. And I did, but not until later that night after Aunt Holly took me to the ER and she helped me in bed. She said I didn't have to act so tough anymore, and then I cried on her shoulder until I was tired enough to sleep.

I try to think about anything to take my mind off Mom, but she's lurking there, making me doubt everything. Kale is still quiet, so I turn and ask, "Do you think I made the right choice coming here?"

"Like Uncle Jasper says, 'You don't make mistakes, you make decisions.'"

"Do you really believe that?"

"Yeah. I do." He flashes me real a smile, his face lit up by the dashboard.

Kale has changed in so many ways that I barely think I know him. He isn't a boy anymore. There are things that made him grow up—things I don't know and don't understand. Things I wish I knew.

He reaches up and fingers something hanging around his neck, and when the light from the dashboard shines on it, I recognize the dog tags I saw him wearing down at the river. He must keep them hidden under his T-shirt, because I haven't seen them again until now.

"I've missed that," I tell him.

"Missed what?"

"Your smile."

He keeps looking between me and the road. I laugh once and say, "Just watch the road, Jackson."

15.
Kale

Jackson.

That's what she used to call me when we were kids. I'm still thinking about it as I drive home to an empty house and climb into bed a lot earlier than I usually do. The ceiling stares down at me. My body is tired, but my mind won't shut off, thoughts flickering between Harper and a white forest at night. I settle on Harper and feel sleep coming.

It was nice hanging out with her tonight. When I could, I watched her at the diner while Miles and Grace peppered her with questions. I could've stayed there for hours. Being with friends and not worrying about tomorrow.

But now I'm back in the forest again, my feet frozen and stuck to the ground. The moon makes the shadows of the trees inch closer. I try to move but can't.

Then the shadows turn into soldiers. They shout when they see me.

There's a rifle in my hands but it's heavy. Too heavy. I bring it up to my shoulder as someone walks past, toward the waiting enemy with no weapon of his own. I shout a warning but no words come out. I yell as loud as I can, but he doesn't hear.

Why doesn't he have a gun?

I look down the rifle's sights, aiming at the closest soldier. They have their guns up now, all ready to shoot at the same time. But the trigger won't pull. It's as stuck as the ground is to my feet. I'm shouting again, trying to get my gun to shoot.

Nothing works.

I can't stop them.

Someone shouts an order in German and the night is filled with gunshots.

I bolt upright in bed, my breathing trying to catch up with my lungs. My sheets are wet with blood. No, not blood. Just sweat.

It was just a dream. I repeat it over and over in my head, but it doesn't make it any better.

There's a knock on my door and then it cracks open.

"Kale?" It's Bryce. He steps in the room, wearing only shorts. "Are you okay?"

My hands are shaking and I rub them down my face, expecting to find blood, but there's nothing. "Just a dream," I tell him.

He steps closer. "Do you want to talk about it?"

With a shake of my head I say, "No, I'm fine now."

Bryce turns away too soon and shuts the door behind him, the floorboards creaking as he walks back to his room. I wish he didn't give in so easily. I think about the cigarettes hidden in the glove compartment of my car. How much better I would feel if I smoked just one. It would be easy to get out of bed, go downstairs, and smoke on the other side of my car in case someone looks out the window.

No matter how strong the urge is, I don't move.

I am not that person—sneaking around in the night, smoking cigarettes.

I'm shaking less now, so I lay down and pull the blankets over me to ward out the cold. I manage to sleep for about two hours before I can't bear to lie there any longer.

Around seven o'clock, I hear Dad leave for work. Slamming the door behind him. His truck rumbling down the driveway.

I sit on the edge of my bed, only wearing yesterday's jeans. There's a faded mark over my ribs now. It'll be gone by tomorrow. But today it's still a reminder of what happened to Adams and the dreams I have at night.

My stomach turns wrong and I sprint down the hall to the bathroom, locking the door before kneeling down in front of the toilet to let it out. My head spins and my mouth tastes of vomit. Food from the diner doesn't taste nearly as good coming up as it does going down. I spit whatever is left in my mouth and flush. But I don't have the strength to get up. I don't think I have the strength to do anything.

I lie down and press my face against the cold tile, my bare chest already becoming numb. Not bothering to move from my place on the floor, I reach into the bottom drawer of the vanity to find Libby's dwindling supply of breath mints.

As the mint slowly disappears on my tongue, I trace the gray grout with my finger.

Bryce's footsteps echo up the stairs.

I don't move. Stare at the door. Glad it's locked. Don't want to see anyone. I could almost fall asleep here. Where I know I'm safe and anchored to the floor with exhaustion.

He knocks.

"Kale?" I don't answer. "Harper is here to see you. She's outside."

My eyes were half closed a second earlier. Now I lift my head from the tile. "What?"

"Harper," he says again. "Look, I'm already late meeting up with the guys. Do you want me to tell her to wait?"

Last night feels like a lifetime ago.

"No." I clear my throat to make sure he hears me. "Just tell her I'm asleep."

She can't see me like this. Broken and lying on the floor, torn between the two worlds I live in. And I don't have the energy to make myself presentable or pretend nothing is wrong.

"Are you sure?" His voice is closer to the door now. I can imagine him out there—keys in hand but one foot pointed toward the stairs because he's already made up his mind to leave.

"Just tell her to go," I say.

Bryce sighs before going back downstairs. After he shuts the front door and I'm sure he left, I lift myself off the floor and crawl into the bathtub. The entire bathroom wall parallel to it is made from glass blocks, lighting the bathroom in a way so the light never has to be turned on in the daytime. It makes everything quiet and still.

My heart finally slows.

Hiding in the bathtub and staring at the glass is something I do as a last resort. Only when nothing else can take my mind off leaving this place and going somewhere else. It's a safe place. The tub hides me and keeps me from leaving. Something solid to trap me here.

My eyes are closing when the stairs creak down the hall.

I don't even care enough to open them.

"Kale?"

I wake to find Harper standing over me and I flinch in surprise. I glance over the side of the tub to see the door open behind her. My heart won't stop hammering, but I can talk. "How did you get in here?"

She holds up a small screwdriver, offering a smile. "Did you forget Libby used to lock herself in here when she didn't want anything to do with us?"

"Right." I push myself up a little straighter, very conscious that I don't have a shirt on. "What are you doing here?"

"I wanted to see you." Harper sighs and puts the screwdriver on the sink. She kneels down next to the tub.

There's a thin strand of hair hanging down in her face. At any other time, I would want to fix it, but not now. Right now, I want to stare at her because I'm realizing we aren't ten anymore.

"So you broke into my house because you wanted to see me?" I ask, my voice sounding too loud in this empty room.

"Yup, true story." Then she finally asks, her eyebrows coming together, "What are you doing in the bathtub?"

"Taking a nap," I half lie.

She rests her chin on the lip of the tub. I can't remember if we've ever been this close.

And I can't pretend nothing is wrong. Even when I wish it.

"You're leaving again soon, aren't you?" Her eyes search me.

I nod.

"And you'll be back?" This time it's her turn to attempt a smile. It's like this house sucks the happiness from everything, even her. "I promised, didn't I?"

"And I promised I would never ask." She looks away and brushes some hair away from her face. "Is it bad that I'm regretting it?"

"Harper—"

"It's okay. A promise is a promise."

"I want to tell you, I do. I just—" I pause and start over, saying exactly what I mean. "It's like you think you know someone, and the moment you find out the truth about them,

97

everything is suddenly different. And no matter what you do, you can't take it back."

"But I don't know you," she says. "Not anymore."

She's right. She doesn't.

Harper's eyes travel down, staring at my chest. Where my dog tags lay over my heart.

I can do this.

I can tell her.

When she first moved back, I wasn't so sure.

I was with Miles at the baseball field, where we normally meet at least once a week.

"You need to tell her," Miles had said.

I dug my toe into the dirt, pretending I didn't hear him. Inside my glove, my hand was damp with sweat, and my arms and legs ached after throwing for so long. I looked up at Miles, crouched over home plate, his catcher's glove ready.

I lifted my leg, cocked my arm back, and followed through. The ball thunked when it hit Miles's glove and he winced. It used to be his dad's—it's old and worn, not in prime condition to be catching pitches for an hour straight.

He stood but hesitated tossing the ball back. "You're going to throw your arm out if you keep going."

"Just give me the ball."

"Kale—"

"Just a few more," I promised.

He threw and I gloved the ball to shake out my shoulder. Miles gave me a look. "What?" I asked.

"You know what," he said.

"It's just a couple more."

"I'm not talking about the pitches."

I knew he wasn't. I threw again, but again, Miles kept the ball. "I'm serious. You need to tell her."

"Why do you even care so much?"

His shoulders slumped and he gave a blank look. "That's it, I'm done." He took off his glove and walked toward the bleachers.

"Miles," I said. He didn't respond. "Miles!"

If I had the ball, I would've thrown it at him. He could be as stubborn as Libby sometimes. He climbed the bleachers and sat down at the top, taking a drink from his water bottle. Blatantly ignoring me.

I probably deserved it.

I slipped my glove off and started across the field. The late sun was bright and hot, not at all helping me cool down. I joined him on the bleachers and sat next to him, staring out across the empty field and then the school a little ways off, the football field in between.

"How long have you known me?" Miles asks.

"I don't know, three years?"

"Three years," he agreed. "And how long have you known Harper?"

"What does that have to do—"

"Just answer the damn question," he said.

"Like . . . forever. Since we were eight."

When he finally looked at me, there wasn't a trace of humor. "Then why haven't you told her yet?"

I finally admitted, "Because I'm afraid it'll ruin things between us."

"But if you don't tell her, it *will*," he said. "It's a risk you're going to have to take."

I hated it, but he was right.

But now that the moment is here, it's so much harder than I thought it would be. I planned this conversation a dozen times, and yet I don't know what to do or what to say.

Why does talking to a girl seem harder than being shot at? And how is it fair that I know from experience?

When she reaches her hand into the tub, I can't move. My chest rises and falls, and when her fingers wrap around my dog tags, I only watch her eyes. The light reflecting in from the other side of the glass makes them even bluer.

"Where did you get these?" I can see her eyes read my name and the numbers below it.

"They're mine," I reply.

I know her mind is racing to find an explanation. And I also know she'll never come up with the right answer. Because according to everything she has ever known, it's impossible.

Telling Uncle Jasper and Libby—heck, or even Miles—was never this hard. Never this important.

"But where did you get them made? They look so real." The cold metal touches my skin again and she takes her hand away, keeping it on the lip of the tub.

Then I say, "They are real."

"How can they be real?" she asks, hinting it's a joke. "You obviously aren't in the Army, and they don't even make them like that anymore."

I look down and say, "Not since World War II."

A clock ticks somewhere in the house. Counting the seconds while she stares.

It's quiet enough for me to almost believe we're the only two people for miles around. And even though Harper could be anywhere right now, she chose to come here.

After everything we've been through, she deserves to know the truth. Miles was right—I need to tell her. Some things are worth the risk.

"You know how some things seem impossible?" I ask, then swallow my nerves. "Like everything the world tells you is fake?" I draw my legs up and run a finger across the hole in my jeans, right over my knee. I say, "Some things aren't. Some things are real."

When I find the courage, I lift my eyes. Harper stares. She can't be more than a foot away. It would be easy for me to close the distance. To do something my heart is telling me to.

But before I can say another word or take another breath, a door slams outside. The air breaks around us, shattering something that was barely there, bringing me back to reality. I quickly pull myself from the tub and go back to my room to grab a T-shirt from the laundry basket. I slip it on while trying to find my shoes. Harper sees them in the corner and tosses them at me.

I mutter my thanks.

As soon as I have them on, we go downstairs, where Dad is taking off his shoes. He doesn't look too stressed today and that's a good sign. He starts to say something to me but then catches sight of Harper.

"Hey, Harper! Feels like I haven't seen you in years."

"Yeah, it's been a few."

He looks between us and his eyes settle on me, probably surprised I'm still around. "You guys going somewhere?"

"I was just gonna drive Harper home, maybe see if Uncle Jasper has any work for me."

His cell phone rings then and he gives me an encouraging smile as he picks it up and walks into the kitchen. That's the most positive reaction I've had from him in a long time.

"Come on." We go out to my car and get inside.

"You don't have to drive me home, you know."

"Where do you want to go?"

Then Harper grins like she's remembering something. "Isn't that demolition derby today? The one Miles is in?"

"That's today?" I'm so bad at keeping track of the days. "Why didn't he say something last night?" I ask, but more to myself. Then I know. "It was friend test."

"A friend test?"

"Yeah, to see if you're actually listening or not. He'll only tell me things once, so it really keeps me on my toes. Good thing you remembered."

Harper shrugs. "You wanna go?"

I answer by starting the car.

16.
Harper

When I walked into Kale's house, it was like walking into a place I'd never been. For a house that used to hold a family of five, it was so, so quiet. And then there was Kale, lying in the bathtub behind a locked door and holding tight to his secrets.

I still can't stop thinking about what he told me. About some things not being as impossible as they seem.

I take a quick glance at Kale sitting next to me on the mostly empty bleachers but thinking of something else—not entirely here. The group Miles is in comes on next so we have another ten minutes or so. It's the most run down and pathetic place I've ever seen. The arena is all dirt and the bleachers will be dusty until it rains again. It's the type of place only Miles could find.

I can't get the image of Kale in the bathtub out of my head. There's nothing comforting about it.

Not even the fact he didn't have a shirt on—

"Did you sleep well last night?" he asks. "I know that diner food can settle weird."

I flinch from being dragged from my thoughts. "What? Sleep?" I shake my head and stare at the cars in the arena trying to hit each other, trying to clear my thoughts. "Yeah, it was fine."

There's a pause. "What were you just thinking about?"

"I wasn't thinking about anything."

Definitely not your naked torso.

But it's like he doesn't have enough energy to argue the point. He answers, "Okay," and that's it.

A pink bus smashes into a beat-up limo, and the guy behind the wheel lets out a war cry that makes the crowd cheer.

But Kale doesn't laugh or appear to have seen it at all. Something is bothering him again—the same thing that creeps up on him from time to time, taking him further away from me and further away from everything around him.

Damn it, Kale, just tell me. But I won't ask.

"Kale?"

"Yeah?"

"Are you okay?"

He gives me an uncertain smile, one that barely touches his lips. "I don't know."

I swallow, finding my mouth dry. "What's up with you and your dad? We ran out of there pretty fast. I know things are different now, with your mom gone and all, but—" I leave it hanging.

Kale hesitates, trying to hide the surprise when I asked. "In what way?"

I feel like I've said something wrong, and my heart kicks the inside of my chest with the mistake, unable to take it back. "It's nothing." I shake my head. "Sorry, I shouldn't have asked."

Kale really looks at me now, taking his eyes off the derby. "Harper, I'm serious." A quick sigh escapes and he looks down briefly, as if to gather his words. "I don't want it to be like this between us. *I* don't want to be like this. I want to know what you're thinking and what's going through your mind, especially if it has something to do with me." There's a loud crash and more cheering. He continues, "I don't want to keep secrets from you. Anybody but you."

"Then tell me."

"I want to." Kale's eyes are glossy before he looks down, so I won't see what he's so desperately trying to hide. "But I don't know how."

"Start with your dad. What's going on between you guys? And what has Bryce been up to? I've barely seen him."

I get a smile for that. "Bryce is still around, but he spends more time with his friends than at home. And Dad—" he shrugs "—we're just not close anymore. He works all the time, and when he does come home, he's only reminded how much of a screw-up I am. It's been hard between us."

"I'm sure that's not what he thinks." But it reminds me of Mom, and I know how much that hurts. To not be seen, or be seen and not be wanted.

"No, it is," Kale replies, nodding. "I see it in his eyes and hear it in his voice. That defeat—like he's given up trying to fix me."

"You don't need fixing."

"But I do. I would give anything to be different. To be *normal*."

I try to smile, wanting to make him feel better, even when I really don't know what to say. "Sometimes parents only see the faults in their kids, because they blame themselves for the way they turn out. They don't give themselves a chance to see the good. At least, that's what I like to believe."

"I don't think I have anything good in me, even if he does try to see it."

"And that's the mistake he makes—not seeing you." Mom keeps flashes into my thoughts, haunting me even when I'm trying to forget her. "I wish Libby was here."

Kale nods. "Me too."

"Her and her short, simple answers are kind of annoying but refreshing."

A brief smile appears. "Libby and her everlasting wisdom."

The round is over now, with the pink bus being the winner. It takes them a while to clear the arena, and Grace joins us before it's about to start.

"You guys made it!" she says, sitting next to me. "I love your shirt."

I look down, not remembering what I put on today. It's my *Battlefield* shirt. "Oh, thanks. Do you play?"

She nods. "I love that game. It's so hard to find other people who play it."

"It totally is!" I can't help but grin. "You should come over and play sometime."

Kale says, "You don't want to play with Harper; she wins at everything."

"Then it's a good thing I'm okay with coming in last."

At last, the cars come into the arena and do a show of circling around it. Grace points out Miles to us. His car is an old Nissan Maxima painted four different colors from old body parts he's had to replace. There's a spray painted #9 on the doors and a pirate flag flying out the missing rear window. All the cars take their places around the arena, facing the middle.

Miles spots us and lifts a fist out the window. Kale stands and returns it.

It starts with a plume of dust as all the cars speed off. Within minutes, cars are already limping out of the stadium but Miles is still going. He has a weird strategy of driving backward, but it seems to be working. Another car tries to take him head on, but ends up on its side, and before we know it, Miles is the only one left driving, doing donuts for the cheering crowd.

I can't help but laugh when he stops, climbs on top of his car, and waves his pirate flag covered in dust. Kale laughs, too, and it makes me forget just for a minute that anything is wrong.

17.
Kale

I drive home slowly after dropping off Harper.

A funeral procession for the living.

It's not often that Dad gets off work early, but the days he does are the ones I dread most. When I'm home doing nothing, he tells me to do something, reminding me over and over how I don't have a job.

Who knows when Bryce will be home. I feel better when he's here, even though it makes no difference. Bryce is no replacement for Libby, but he's better than no one. If Libby were here, it would be different. It would be better. Libby makes Dad happy in ways I never could—she makes us both happier.

I pull up to the house and park under the tree, my thoughts not letting go of Harper and the way her hand brushed mine as we sat on the bleachers.

I need to tell her.

I should've done it today, but then my chance was gone.

Small bumps along my arms brush against the inside of my sweatshirt, triggering another shiver before I get out of the car.

It has to be nearly eighty-five degrees, and yet I'm freezing.

I open the screen door.

Squeaking. Slamming shut.

The shower is on upstairs. From where I stand, hesitating to walk deeper into the house, I can see the stack of dishes in the sink. An old cup of coffee on the table and yesterday's newspaper on the couch.

The phone rings on the hallway table. Again. And again.

I step away from the door and silence it.

"Hello?"

"Hey, you." It's Libby. For a moment, hearing her voice while standing in this house, I forget she isn't here. It makes me wish she was even more. I feel less cold, making me forget about everything wrong with me.

"Hey." I press my back against the wall and slowly slide down to the floor, staying there with my knees drawn up to my chest. "I've been meaning to call you."

She laughs. "That's what you say every time. I did try to call yesterday, though, but Dad said you weren't there. I thought maybe . . . well, you know. I wanted to try again just in case."

"Yeah, I'm still here." The shower continues upstairs, and I trace my fingers along the hardwood floor.

"Good," she says, "because I can't talk about this to anyone else."

"Talk about what?"

"Harper!" she yells into the phone. "Seriously, Kale, I'm dying here. How is she? Is she taller than me now? I'm going to kick her if she is."

"She's . . . Harper," I say. "And yeah, she looks different. The last time I saw her, she was twelve."

And her hair is a more golden than brown. Her eyes are bluer. And her smile is contagious, as always. I already want to see her again.

Libby is quiet on the other end. "Oh my gosh . . . you like her."

I open my mouth to argue, like every other sane person would do. But I can't. I don't have the strength to.

Then she says, reading my silence, "And you aren't denying it."

"Because I can't."

"Does she know?" she asks. Not about me liking her, but about *me*. I know by the tone of her voice.

"Not . . . exactly."

Libby sighs on the other end. "Kale, you have to tell her."

"You sound like Miles."

"That's because me and Miles are wise." Then she says, more serious, "I wish I was there."

"I wish you were, too. I miss you." I never thought I would say that to my younger sister. Siblings are supposed to hate each other, not miss each other. It feels odd saying it, and I realize I'm not sure if I've ever said it before.

"I miss you, too." I hear her smile fade. "How have you been, though? For real."

"I'm fine."

"Don't lie to me, Kale."

Footsteps come down the stairs. I never heard the water shut off, and I lift my head to see him on his way down.

"I should go," I say.

"Kale, wait—"

I reach up to the table and hang up the phone. He stands on the bottom step, staring down. The floor is cold beneath me.

"Still here then?" he asks, in a worse mood now than when I left.

I don't answer.

"Who was on the phone?"

"Libby."

Right on cue, it rings.

And rings.

And rings.

His jaw flexes and he takes the remaining steps to pick it up. "Hello?"

I can hear her voice on the other end.

"Hey, Lib." Pause. "No, he can't right now."

I stand, but he holds up his hand so I wait. I just want to crawl into bed and take a nap. Even though I wouldn't sleep, just lying there might be nice.

"No, she's right," he says, not talking to me. "I talked with her earlier." Another pause. "I think it's for the best." Pause. "Well, you don't have much of a choice at this point, Libby."

I hear my name being said from the other end.

"I'll tell him for you."

He hangs up. I stare at the stairs.

"I called over to Jasper's house, but he said you never showed up."

"We decided to see Miles instead."

"So you lied. Kale, how do you expect me to trust you when you don't even tell me the truth?"

I almost lose it then, wanting to scream at him. I try to keep my voice in check and say, "Because lying is easier than telling you the truth."

"Why would you think that?"

Then I shout before I can stop myself, "Because you don't listen to me when I *do* tell the truth!"

He takes a step back, deflating with every second. His eyes flick between me and somewhere over my shoulder, like he doesn't want to look at me. "I want to believe you, Kale, but I'm not sure if I can."

All the courage I had just moments before is gone. Like it was never there at all.

"You can," I whisper.

Dad just shakes his head, not ready to hear what I have to say. "Go wash the dishes. Since you don't have a job, you can at least do that."

He leaves me standing in the hallway.

After I load the dishwasher and scrub the pans in the sink, I stare out the window at the field behind our house. I miss playing baseball with Dad and Bryce, or catch with whoever was willing. I could go for hours. Not caring if the sun set or if the bugs were bad, or if my knees were scraped and bleeding from hitting the ground too much.

It's one of the few things I'm good at besides shooting.

I brush hair from my eyes with my forearm, and when I bring it down, Dad is next to me. He leans against the counter, looking like he doesn't want to be here.

"Your mother and I decided it was best if Libby live with her. Permanently. There are good schools out there, and—well, we think it's best." They don't want me being a bad influence on her—that's what he doesn't say.

Just in case I'm contagious.

My hands go still under the lukewarm water. The information sinking in with realization. After a shiver runs through me, I'm freezing.

I can't stay here any longer.

I can't do it.

"Did you hear me?"

I'm too numb to answer him. His words still echo in my ears, trying to make sense of them because they seem impossible. Because she's coming back. Libby is coming back at the end of summer, before school starts. She has to.

I'm glad he can't see my hands shake.

"Yeah."

I can't leave in front of him, but I don't know how much longer I can hold off. I feel like if I take a step in either direction, I'll be gone. Everything in me screams to let go. If I close my eyes, I'll see snow, so I keep them open. Try my hardest to delay it, because it's all I can do.

With a long sigh, he walks away. Giving up. Down the hallway and into the living room. The television turns on.

I pull the stopper out to let the sink drain, drying my hands and slipping out the back door before he realizes I'm leaving.

I stumble around, trying to force my numb legs into a run. I breathe easier once I'm well into the woods, slowing to stop. Where it's safe. My heart aches and tugs . . . and all I have to do is let it take me.

To make this place disappear. Make my life disappear.

My only regret is not telling Harper. But it isn't enough to make me stay.

Not with Dad.

Not with Libby gone for good.

Not with my life amounting to nothing.

So I close my eyes and let go.

My body is tugged by the strings of time.

I feel snowflakes on my face before I reopen them.

18.
Harper

About an hour after I wake up, Uncle Jasper asks me come with him to the barn. He likes to call it his garage, but there's no mistaking it for what it is. It used to have cows in it, so it's a barn.

The morning dew sticks to the blades of grass, dampening my shoes as I walk behind him. A set of unfamiliar keys hang from his fingers, ones I've seen in the drawer with all his screwdrivers, old pens, lighters that might not work, and odd bolts that don't have a home. Aunt Holly called it his "shit drawer," always saying it with disdain.

After Uncle Jasper pushes open the big sliding door, I hesitate. The house is always so clean and organized, but his barn is the polar opposite.

"Come on, it's back here." He maneuvers around milk crates full of tools and odd engine parts. There's a wide space open from where Kale's car sat last week, so I tentatively start there and attempt to follow him over to the other side, trying to remember if my tetanus shot is still up to date.

"Wouldn't it be easier if you open the other door?" I ask.

"It's locked from the inside," his voice echoes from somewhere over to my right. "Give me a minute and I'll open it to let in some light."

There's a small desk piled with papers and more tools with an oil-stained chair placed behind it. The large shape of a couch hides beneath a layer of drop sheets and old Mountain Dew cans. This place is long overdue for a cleanup.

A sliver of light grows as Uncle Jasper pushes open the other big door, brightening my narrow path. I make my way over to the other side of the barn, still not sure what he's supposed to be showing me.

"Well, here it is," he says, pulling a big box off something covered with an old sheet. When the box hits the ground, a large plume of dust rises up. I don't really know what I'm looking at, so I tilt my head to study it from a different angle. "Is it a car?"

"Of course it's a car!" He laughs once and rips off the sheet. More dust pollutes the air and the sun shines on old paint.

"Are you sure?" I ask. It looks more like a metal box on wheels. I walk over and peer into the windows. The inside is suspiciously clean.

"Well, it's fine if you don't want it," he says. "I thought you'd like to have a car of your own."

I stand and stare at him. "You said you had something to show me, not *give* me."

He shrugs.

I look between him and the car. "Does it run?"

"Who do you think you're talking to?" He throws me the keys. "You need to have your own way around, and this one won't let you down, even though it doesn't look like much."

"How long have you had it?" I open the door and the smell of old car rushes out. Another scent lingers, one that I know too well, something not even time can take away. I look up at Uncle Jasper. "Was this Aunt Holly's?"

I suddenly remember the picture hanging in the hallway, between their wedding photo and one of them in New York City. It's a picture of Aunt Holly and Uncle Jasper leaning against the hood of a maroon car, her blonde hair in braids and her smile wide. The ocean is behind them, the same color as the sky. The picture is old, taken back when they first started dating. Long before I was ever born.

If I had one day I could choose to travel back in time to, that would be it. Just to see her once more, the way Uncle Jasper remembers her most.

I look at him now, my smile long faded.

His jaw tightens and he nods. "She wanted you to have it."

"Uncle Jasper . . ."

He reaches out and traces the hood with his fingers, almost like he can see her in it. "And you should have it. I'm sorry it took me so long to give it to you. It's . . . just—" He pulls away and takes a shaking breath, his eyes narrowing as he tries to keep himself from crying. "It's hard," he says.

My limbs are frozen in place, my mouth lost for words. It's how I imagine it would be to see my dad cry for the first time, and there's nothing I can do but feel everything he does. Knowing someone to be reserved and like a rock my entire life, and then seeing them on the edge of tears, is something I can't be prepared for.

I never knew Uncle Jasper without Aunt Holly. If you mentioned one of them, you automatically mentioned the other, like a hyphenated word. If you don't say the whole thing, the word loses meaning. The living room isn't the same without Aunt Holly sitting in her chair. The kitchen is always cold and never smells like it used to. The towels in the bathroom closet aren't folded the same way. And those are just the things I've noticed.

For Uncle Jasper, it must be one hundred times worse.

He's only half of what he used to be, slowly learning how to become himself again.

"For months after she was gone," he says, "I never moved anything she left behind. Her toothbrush stayed on the sink. One of her shirts was left hanging over the chair in our bedroom." He shakes his head to himself, the littlest of movements, his eyes reflecting like glass. "I couldn't bring myself to move anything. Not even the glass of water on her nightstand. It was like I would erase a part of her if I did."

I think of her green chair in the living room, still untouched, probably the only thing left besides this car. I can't imagine what he feels when he sees it, and I wonder if he remembers the ocean that day. Or what she smelled like, or what music played on the radio.

It feels like I'm stealing something away from him.

"You don't have to do this—"

"—No, I do," he says, finally looking at me. "Remember what I told you about your dad all those years ago?"

I nod. "That there's always a piece of him in me, even though he's gone."

"It's the same way with Holly. Moving her things, or in this case giving them away, isn't going to take her away. I've had to realize that." Then he says, "But I won't say it's easy. Nothing about her being gone is. But it'll make me happy to see you enjoy something of hers."

I don't know what to say.

When Uncle Jasper pulls his gaze from the car, he clears his throat and digs his wallet out from his back pocket. "Here, you can fill up the tank in town and stop by the store to pick up some food. I know my fridge doesn't have anything but condiments and cheese, so get what you want."

Uncle Jasper hands me the money. But before he turns to go, he puts a hand on my shoulder and squeezes. "I'm glad she

116

decided to give it to you. I don't think there's anyone else who deserves it."

I feel a wet streak on my cheek when a breeze blows through the door. The last person I hugged was Aunt Holly, the summer I spent here before she was diagnosed. And I want Uncle Jasper to be the first since then, maybe hoping I'll give him a small piece of her that isn't lost.

I close the small space between us and wrap my arms around him, pressing my face against his chest. His shirt smells like oil and toast.

And when he hugs back, I begin to understand what it feels like to have a home.

19.
Kale

Harper was covered in mud the first time I saw her.

Libby and I heard that Uncle Jasper and Aunt Holly's niece was coming to visit in a few months, and we were wary of the thought of another kid around to spoil our fun. So, when the day came and Aunt Holly called us to come over and meet Harper, we dragged our feet on the narrow path through the woods.

I don't remember what we talked about on the way there. Kid stuff probably. Like how our big brother Bryce was "too old" to hang out with us, and most likely ways of escaping if this girl turned out to be someone horrible.

When we walked through the back door, Aunt Holly was at the sink. We stayed near the door, knowing not to track mud into the house.

"So," Libby said, crossing her arms, "Where is she?"

Aunt Holly smiled. "Hating her already, Lib? Well, let me ask you this . . . do you hate me?"

Libby got this confused look on her face and she shook her head. "Of course I don't hate you."

"Then you won't hate Harper either. I'm sorry, kid, but that's the way it works. You'll find out soon enough." She turned back to the sink, washing the leftovers from lunch off the dishes, saying, "She's with Uncle Jasper down near the river."

Libby rolled her eyes and left. I was about to follow her when Aunt Holly stopped me.

"Kale, just a minute." I paused a step away from the door. Waiting for her to finish drying her hands on the towel.

"Are you going to tell me I won't hate her either?" I asked.

"No, I don't think you'll have a problem with that," she said.

I remember being confused. "What is that supposed to mean?"

Aunt Holly shook her head, not answering, and led me out the door with one hand on my shoulder. We stopped on the back porch. I could hear Uncle Jasper's truck revving down the hill, out of sight. After a big rain, he would sometimes take it down to the low part of the field, right next to the river where it would come over the banks during the night.

I wanted nothing more than to run down there. I hated missing the fun I could've been having.

"What did you want to talk to me about?" I wanted her to start talking so I could go.

I could feel her smiling above me and she said, "Harper."

I sighed. "I already know I'm supposed to be nice to her."

"I know, but I also wanted to say that you two might have more in common than you think."

I made a weird face. "You aren't making any sense."

"I know. Maybe you'll find out in one year or ten, but I wanted to tell before . . .well," she paused and glanced down the field, where the sounds of his truck became louder. "I wanted to tell you, in case I forget or something."

"Okay." I always remembered Aunt Holly not making a whole lot of sense when I was younger. It was something I was used to.

And I didn't think about it anymore, because Uncle Jasper's truck came into view and pulled around to the backyard where he always washed off the mud with the hose. Libby was riding shotgun, but my eyes went to the third person in the bed of the truck.

It was a girl with her hair pulled back in a long braid, wearing overalls over a T-shirt. When the truck came to stop, she jumped down from the bed and smiled at Aunt Holly.

"I think I fell," she said, laughing.

Mud was splattered on one half of her body, including her face and hair. And she was smiling. That's what got me. Libby wouldn't stand less than five feet from her, and I knew right then she wasn't just any girl.

She walked up to the bottom step and held out her mud-covered hand. "I'm Harper."

I thought it was weird, because what eight-year-old kids shook hands when they met? I took it regardless. "Kale."

"It looks like we have something in common."

"What?" I went to glance back at Aunt Holly, but she shrugged.

"We both have weird names," Harper said, giving me another smile.

I didn't really think her name was too weird at all. But I couldn't tell her otherwise.

"Yeah, I guess we do have something in common," I said, smiling back.

To this day, I still wonder if Aunt Holly somehow knew things would turn out the way they did.

I like to think so.

I walk through the quiet town with my helmet in my hand

and my rifle strap digging into my shoulder. This gun is a bit heavier than my last one, but I already like the feel of it.

Snow falls from the dark sky. Small flakes at first that grow into something more. Not a heavy snow, just one that leaves a white dusting on everything exposed. Half the buildings in this town have turned to rubble. Piles of brick and ash, covered in white to look like snowdrifts instead of memories. All painted over to mask the look of death.

But I was here when they fell.

And I was here to witness the screams.

The town is still. Echoing a silence that has never been known in this place until now.

Smoke drifts from the houses where the others have settled in for the night. The officers are in a bigger house toward the middle of town, and the rest of us get to choose between houses with caved-in roofs or crumbling walls. The townspeople are long gone—they were gone once the Germans came last week, expecting something worse ahead. Something even they saw coming.

The sky is black overhead. My hands yearn for the warmth of a fire, and my eyes itch with sleep.

But I'm not ready yet.

I take a cigarette from my pocket, where I have a few stashed away. I'm about it bring it to my lips when someone appears beside me and I flinch, trying to salute without dropping the cigarette.

"Captain Price," I say.

"Private Jackson." I take my hand down when he touches his forehead. "You wouldn't have an extra one of those would you?" he asks.

"Sir?"

He nods down to my hand, still holding the unlit cigarette.

"Oh, right."

I dig into my pocket and hand him one. After I find my lighter, I light his before my own. The first drag is always the best. I exhale slowly, my head slightly tilted toward the sky. Snowflakes brush against my cheeks.

Captain Price asks, "Were you always a smoker?"

I shake my head. "I'm still not."

I show a smile with teeth.

Standing here under an unlit sky, with a captain who would rather spend his time out here with me instead of by a warm fire, and the fact that I don't go home until a few days from now, almost has me happy. Sometimes, even if it's for a fleeting moment, it's like I belong here. Like I have a place. A purpose.

At home, I'm nothing.

"Yeah, I get that," he says, taking off his helmet and putting it under his arm. Pulling his fingers through his hair with the cigarette still between them. "I was able to go a year without smoking."

"A *year*?" I ask. "I barely made it a month."

His chest vibrates with a laugh. "I was hit in the arm. Just a flesh wound, but it scared the shit out of me. And this guy, Williams, comes up to me while I was lying on the stretcher and holds out a cigarette and says, 'What about now, Price?'" He smiles to himself and keeps his gaze down the empty street. "I didn't even realize my hands were shaking until I took it from him."

I take another drag, and then roll it back and forth between my forefinger and thumb to keep them from becoming too frozen.

He speaks again, and for some reason it doesn't bother me. Usually I would rather be away from idle conversations and laughs that don't belong. But tonight I feel different. Better. "Where are you from, Jackson?"

"Iowa."

"Never been."

"Not missing much."

He snorts a laugh. "Is your family still there?"

I nod. "For the most part."

"I hear the guys say you never get any mail." I wince at that, not even realizing anyone noticed. Of course I don't get mail. Whatever relatives I have in this time don't even know I exist. "Even though most families don't like their sons joining up, they still care enough to write them. And if it's not their family, then it's always someone else."

I shrug and try to act like the question doesn't bother me. "I guess I don't then."

"Everyone has someone back home that they think about."

"But that doesn't mean they're thinking about *me*."

He takes one last drag and flicks the glowing butt into the snow. After putting his helmet back on, he gives me a long look. "Don't be so sure about that."

I listen as his muffled footsteps fade away, wondering how often Dad thinks of me while I'm gone.

20.
Harper

Sometime in the night, the phone rings.

It barely rouses me from sleep, but I still hear Uncle Jasper's muffled voice downstairs, his tone vibrating up through the floor. I turn over and face the window, my eyes almost too heavy to keep open. I'd been dreaming about something good, but when I try to think of it, it becomes more and more impossible.

The front door opens and only the screen shuts on its own. Uncle Jasper leaves, not even pausing to let the engine roar to life before putting it in gear. I have an odd sense of déjà vu.

I stare out my window for about three seconds before falling asleep again.

It barely feels like minutes before something wakes me.

This time it's not with the phone ringing or Uncle Jasper's voice. It's from something louder, more abrupt. I sit up in bed, trying to make sense of what I hear, rubbing sleep from my eyes. I shouldn't have stayed up so late playing video games, but it's the only time my friend from Colorado is online.

It was worth it.

A car door shuts outside, followed by another and then the front door opens and slams. My heart really starts to pound when I hear the scuffling of feet and a table chair screeching across the floor, like someone sat in it too fast. Uncle Jasper talks, low and fast, but I can't make out any words.

I swing my legs over the bed and pull on a T-shirt. The hardwood stings cold into the soles of my feet, and my vision is still a little blurry from sleep as I find my way down the stairs, but all that is forgotten when I step into the kitchen.

Kale is sitting in a chair next to the table, pressing his wadded up T-shirt to his ribs. It takes me a moment to realize it's red with blood, because it's the last thing I expected. His head lifts when he catches movement, his eyes glossy and his jaw tight. He looks away and stares at the floor, slightly trembling.

Uncle Jasper brushes past me through the doorway and lays a tackle box on the table. "Harper, will you go into the bathroom and get the peroxide?"

Kale still stares at the floor. There are blood stains on his shoes.

"Harper, did you hear me?"

I jerk my head up and nod, backing into the hallway. My heart makes uneven jumps into my throat, feeling that warm rush of adrenaline through my veins. I find the peroxide in the bathroom and hurry back to the kitchen where Uncle Jasper is pulling the T-shirt away from Kale's side. A gash shows itself dug into his skin, across his ribs and reaching for his back. At least six inches long.

Uncle Jasper looks at it closely before taking the peroxide from my hand, then he says to Kale, "It's just a graze. I'll need to stitch it, but I think it'll heal fine. How long ago did it happen?"

"Just before—" Kale hesitates and glances at me "—before I called you. Maybe an hour."

125

Uncle Jasper nods and unscrews the cap to the peroxide. Kale know what's about to come—he grips the edge of the table, clenches his jaw, and flinches when it pours over the wound. A hiss escapes through his teeth.

When I take a moment and really look at Kale sitting there, his chest bare and his dog tags hanging across one of his pecks—his face and neck stained with dirt—he doesn't look like he belongs in this kitchen, but somewhere else entirely. And that gash looks like something only a bullet could do.

My mind makes assumptions I don't want to believe. Has he been mixed up with a gang? Does he have friends I don't know about who get him into trouble? Even though I think them, I know it isn't true. It's something bigger than that.

As Uncle Jasper opens his tackle box and reveals everything you need for a first-aid kit, I feel like I can't watch any longer. It makes my stomach sick in a way I've never felt. I walk out the front door and sit on the porch, staring into the dark yard where light streams out from the living room window.

I can still hear him.

Kale takes a sharp breath when Uncle Jasper stitches, and I also hear when he whispers he's sorry.

My thoughts wander to places I have always known to be impossible, and Kale's promises prove they aren't.

I don't know how much time passes until the screen door opens and Kale sits down next to me. He smells like dirt, rubbing alcohol, and winter.

Neither of us says a word, just listening to Uncle Jasper clean up the kitchen behind us. Kale feels like a different person next to me than the one I met so many years ago. He has scars and secrets, things that have made him into the person he is now.

I'm tired of not knowing him.

"If I ask," I start, "will you give me a straight answer?"

"I think you already know the truth, Harper." He looks over, his face half shadowed with the night. "You're just afraid that it *is*."

"But I can't ask, because I made a promise."

"And you don't have to break it, because you already know."

Do I? Kale disappears without a trace for days at a time. Almost like he doesn't exist here while he's . . . somewhere else. Just gone. He comes back looking like he's been through hell, or the closest thing to hell, which would be war. The same place where he said his dog tags came from. Where he got shot.

He's given me all the answers, and I just have to believe them.

I look over to see him already staring at me, waiting to prove him wrong.

I shake my head and say, "It's not possible."

"How will you know if you don't ask?"

My heart beats fast and my mouth is dry. "When you leave . . . you really do leave, don't you? Like . . . somewhere else."

Kale nods.

"Like to the place where you got those." I nod toward the dog tags around his neck, still barely able to believe it.

He glances away, looking slightly uncomfortable. "It's a place, but it's also a time."

Kale opens his mouth again but no words come out, like he's struggling saying what he wants to.

"So you're like . . ." I don't know if I want to say it. "A time-traveler?"

"If you want to call it that." There's a small lasting smile on Kale's lips.

A time-traveler. *Kale.* It's weird that it feels so right.

"Why didn't you ever tell me?"

For once, he holds my gaze. "Honestly, because I didn't

127

want things to change between us. I didn't want you to see me as a totally different person, because I'm still me . . . even though things have changed and we're older. I didn't want to mess things up."

He brings his knees closer to his chest and tucks his arms in like he's cold. He still doesn't have a shirt on, but even though it's night, the air is warm. "I'm sorry I haven't told you before now. Libby, Bryce, and Uncle Jasper are the only people who know, and I had enough trouble telling them as it is. Well, Miles knows too, but that was sort of a mistake how it happened."

"I'm not saying you should have," I say. "It's yours to tell, not mine. And besides, if you would have told me before tonight, I probably wouldn't have believed you."

He looks over. "So that means you do? Believe me?"

"Of course I do." Then have to ask, "What about your mom and dad?"

"I've tried telling them the truth for years, but they never believed me. So I stopped trying." He shrugs once, clearly uncomfortable talking about them.

I think about Kale being able to travel through time, something he's been doing ever since he was a kid when everyone thought he was running away from home, and it just makes sense. Almost crazy and impossible, but for some reason believable.

"So that day when we were eleven, and you promised you would be at the river . . ." I trail off.

His eyes look up to the sky, thinking. "Hmmm, 1974. It was pretty weird."

Kale smiles, and I laugh.

"I know there are a lot of things you want to know," he says, "and I'll try to answer everything I can. But it's not as complicated as you might think." He stares into the woods, in the direction of his house, and says, "I'm sorry I haven't told you before now. I'm just—" He struggles for a word "—ashamed of it."

"Why would you be ashamed of it?" I ask. "You can do something nobody else can do—it's amazing."

"But it's also a burden." Kale shakes his head more than he should. "I can't control it, Harper. I got kicked off the baseball team because of it, and expelled from school. I can't even get a minimum wage job. What kind of future can I hope to have?"

I can't think of something to say. "I—I don't know."

For some reason he smiles a little. "Yeah . . . I don't know either." Then before I can say anything else, he says, "I should get home." But when he stands, his right arm moves too fast and he takes a sharp breath and goes rigid with pain.

"Kale—"

"It's fine. I just need some sleep."

We both hear Uncle Jasper before he comes outside. He glances at me and then Kale, his eyes going straight for his ribs. "You're staying here tonight," he says. "You can stay in the guest room upstairs."

"I really shouldn't," Kale says, for some reason avoiding Uncle Jasper's gaze.

"Did I sound like I was asking?" Uncle Jasper holds the door open wider and nods his head for Kale to go inside, not giving him a choice.

Kale says, "I could start running, you know."

"And I would chase you down," he answers immediately. "How far do you think you'll get before those stitches come out?"

The white bandage over his ribs stands out against the black around him. I can make out a thin line of red soaking through.

Giving in with a sigh, Kale walks past him into the house. While Uncle Jasper finds one of his old T-shirts for Kale to wear, fussing over him as much as Aunt Holly would, I go back to my room and lie down, wondering if I can fall asleep again. The house soon becomes quiet and dark, the only noise coming from Uncle Jasper's light snoring across the hall. When he actually does sleep, nothing can ever wake him.

My mind won't stop processing it all, asking myself how this is even possible. What places has he seen, what kind of events has he witnessed? How long has he been doing this?

I have a thousand questions for him, but he isn't here, and I know I won't be able to sleep without them.

I try to keep quiet as I get out of bed. I avoid the places in the floor where it squeaks—a foot from the dresser, the middle of my doorway, and the right side of the hallway. And then I stand before the guest room where Kale is sleeping, my thumping heart and breathing the only sounds I hear.

I open the door and slip inside. He's sitting on the opposite side of the bed, facing the window where the moon shines in. He's got a T-shirt on now, still wearing his jeans. I sit down next to him, leaving a healthy distance between us.

"I used to be able to sleep at night," he says in a hushed tone. "Before I had to start worrying about my dreams."

"What do you dream about?"

Kale winces with an unseen wound. "Nothing I want to talk about. Sometimes it's the war, but mostly it's other things . . . everything." He shakes his head. "The only way I can sleep is when I think about the good places I've been. Times I wish I could live in instead of here. I've seen things nobody should."

"Will you tell me about it?" I'm too curious now to be left in the dark. "The places you've been?"

The muscles beneath his shirt relax, glad of something good to talk about. "What do you want to know?"

I smile. "Everything."

21.
Kale

The next morning I'm up before the sun is.

My side throbs and a headache brews at the base of my neck. I stare at the ceiling, just thinking.

I'll have to hide the fact I was shot when I go back in a few days. I can't let them see me, because they'll know something isn't right when they see it's already stitched. There's a medic that would probably cover for me, but I don't want him to become suspicious.

I think about when I came back last night. The old house so dark and my fingers wet with what I couldn't hold in. Barely able to make it to the gas station without passing out. Staining my shoes and Uncle Jasper's floor.

And then Harper saw me.

I didn't want her to see me in that way, but I'm glad for it, because without it, I'm not sure when I would've told her.

Last night she asked about everything, and I had no problem talking about it. Having her next to me and telling her about my greatest secret plays over in my mind. Explaining about the different places I've been. What it feels like when I leave and the days building up to it. Such a strange series of words I never thought I would speak, because nobody has ever asked so much.

I get a sick feeling in my stomach, thinking of a particular question she asked. Because it makes me realize how wrong things are now.

Harper asked, "How often do you go?"

"About every three or four days."

"I don't remember you leaving that much when you were younger."

"I've been going more often since Mom left, and even more within the past six months."

"The last six months, meaning when you started going back to the same place? Where you're still going back to, even now?"

Then all I could say was, " . . . yeah."

"Why do you think that is? Why do you think you keep going back to the same time?"

I had no answer for her.

I have no idea why I keep going back to the same time, and why I'm going more often. It's like I'm meant to live a different life there. Two lives at the same time.

It worries me.

I get out of bed and grab my shoes and sweatshirt from the chair in the corner. My side still throbs, but it doesn't feel any different from anything I've dealt with before.

I make it downstairs without a sound.

But when I smell coffee coming from the kitchen, I let out a quiet sigh and continue on. Uncle Jasper glances up from his paper as I pause in the doorway to the kitchen.

"Sit down and I'll have a look at your side," he says.

I glance at the door, trying to find an excuse to leave so I'll be home before Dad goes to work. "I'm sure it's fine. I should get home."

"Kale, just sit down. This will only take a minute."

I pull out the chair and sit, lifting up my shirt so Uncle

Jasper can look. I stare at the stove over his head as he peels away the bandage and tape. Not wanting to look at something that could've killed me. Just thinking about it makes my heart pound faster.

It was too close.

"It looks good. Just make sure you keep it clean and come back if the stitches start coming out before they should." He throws the red-stained bandage in the trash, replacing it with another one. "You're lucky you heal pretty quick. It's like—I don't know." He shakes his head and sits down.

"Like I was meant for this?" I pull my shirt back down.

He shrugs and goes back to eating his toast. "I don't know. Maybe. Do you want some breakfast?"

"No, I should go." I pull on my shoes, being careful of my side.

"I was going to work in the garage if you want to join me. I've got a '68 Camaro in there that needs a lot of work. Should be fun."

I stand and head for the door. "Maybe later."

Then he says, "Why are you in such a hurry to get home?" But his tone of voice is different from before. Hinting at what he already knows.

My hand pauses on the screen door. "And why do you keep trying to stall something that's inevitable? You know things aren't good between us, and not being there more won't help anything."

Uncle Jasper's chair pushes back, and I see him in my periphery, putting his dishes in the sink. He grabs his truck keys off the counter, only pausing to say, "It only is because you make it that way."

He turns to leave, but I can't keep my mouth shut. "Because I don't have a choice."

"Everyone has choices, Kale. You have the choice to tell him again, but you *don't*."

I turn around and he stands in the doorway, turning to leave. "Because I *can't*."

"That's something for you to figure out. Not me and not anyone. And until you realize that, I can't help you."

I haven't heard his voice this hard in a long time.

"And I never asked you to," I tell him.

I regret saying it the moment the words come out.

Whatever drop of temper Uncle Jasper had is gone. Like he's given up already. "Then go home, Kale. Go home and keep lying to your father thinking it'll get better on its own."

And he leaves. Not even looking back once.

Before my thoughts have any time to process, I breeze out the door and across the lawn, walking as fast as I can without pain stabbing my side. The sun is starting to rise when I disappear into the woods. I'm blinded by rage and my heart pounds too fast.

I stop suddenly and yell, *"Fuck!"*

I don't remember ever being so angry.

But I don't know if I'm angry at Uncle Jasper or myself. Because what bothers me the most is that he's right. I need to try telling him again, consequences or not. I need him to believe me and see me for who I really am.

Why does telling the truth have to be so hard?

I start down the path again, my blood still hot from what was said in the kitchen. It's one of those moments I wish I could take back. Uncle Jasper isn't the one I should be fighting with.

I pull on my sweatshirt when the house comes into view. I feel colder already. My car is exactly where I left it, and Dad's truck is parked next to Bryce's near the garage. The insides of my stomach are tight.

I never know what to expect when I get home. Some days are good. Some days are bad.

Shoving my hands into my pockets, I start across the dew covered grass. Making a darker trail from where I came from.

I could've waited until later to come home, like Uncle Jasper was trying to get me to do. But the longer I put it off, the more nervous I get. I would rather get it done with. One less thing to worry about.

Dad is on the couch watching the morning news. I let the door swing shut behind me.

He takes a long look at me. "You look like shit."

Love you, too, Dad.

The news anchor's voice echoes from the television, pushing its way between our silence. Dad finally looks away and puts his mug on the coffee table. He's too calm. Like something worse is coming.

"Kale, do you know it's a privilege to live in this house?" He stands, towering a half foot over me. I hate looking up at him. So I don't. I can't. "I work so you can eat, sleep, take showers. It costs money to live . . . something you know nothing about, because you can't get a damn job."

Then he asks something he hasn't for a long time.

He voice is soft—changed. "*Why* do you keep doing this?"

I slowly lift my head, barely able to look him in the eye. And what I see there isn't anger. They're the eyes of a father who cares. Someone I miss.

I open my mouth, but words won't come out. I'm scared to tell him the truth—scared to say anything—thinking it'll make worse all over again.

"I'm sorry." The only words I know.

I can see his mind whirling. At first, a look of disappointment crosses his face, followed by something I'm starting to see more of—anger. Dad has never hit me before but some-

135

times I'm scared he'll start. I'm scared of that more than anything.

"I know what you want from me," I start, my heart pounding so hard it hurts. Then I seal my fate with, "But I've already told you the truth."

Dad acts confused at first, likes he's forgotten, but then shakes his head. "I'm not having this conversation with you again." He turns away from me and starts down the hallway, probably wishing there was beer in the fridge even though he quit years ago. I can't let it end like this.

"Dad, wait—"

I make a grab for his arm, but he's already turning back and I can't stop him in time. His arm crashes into me and I stumble back. My head hits the side of the hallway table and then I'm suddenly on the floor.

Something stings over my left eyebrow and my side throbs where the stitches try to hold me together.

"Kale—" Dad steps toward me with his hand outstretched, but he stops like he doesn't know what to do. "I'm sorry," he says. "I—"

Bryce comes down the stairs, cutting off some sort of apology. He spares me a glance, a question on his tongue that will never be asked. Instead he says, "Dad, can I talk to you for a minute?"

I feel eyes on me. I don't look up.

"Sure," Dad replies, sounding like himself again. "Kale, go clean yourself up." But his voice shakes.

I wait until they're gone before I head up the stairs. My tight muscles and cold fingers scream for a hot shower. I need something to calm me. What just happened wasn't intentional, but it could've been.

In the bathroom, I start the shower and peel off my clothes. When I'm about to throw my T-shirt in the laundry basket, I notice a new growth of red on it. I check my side but it still looks fine; the stitches are still in place and the bleeding has stopped.

Then I remember my head and carefully touch my fingers above my eye.

They come away red.

I turn around and face the mirror for the first time in months.

A stranger stares back. There's a stream of blood trailing down my temple, making my eyes look lifeless against the vivid shade. My skin holds no color like it used to, even in the middle of summer when I should be spending my days outside. Instead, it's gray and has a smudge of dirt on the right cheek.

A knock on the bathroom door allows me to look away.

"Kale?" It's Bryce.

"What."

"Libby is on the phone for you."

I wipe my fingers on my jeans, smearing blood across them, and shut off the shower. When I open the door a crack, I make sure he won't be able to see the stitches along my ribs. He stares from the other side, his hand outstretched, holding the phone. He takes a long glance at the blood on my face before turning away, not saying a word.

"Hello?"

I shut the door.

The first thing she says is, "I don't want to live with Mom. I'm trying to convince her that I don't want to change schools." She pauses. "I don't like not being there for you."

"It's not your job to look after me," I tell her, trying to make it sound like a joke. Why am I saying this? I *want* Libby to come home. But a part of my brain is telling me she's better off away from here. Away from me.

Her argument is coming out fast, barely giving herself time to breathe.

I'm too tired to fight with her, knowing it won't make a difference once her mind is set. I sit down with my back against the tub and wait for her to finish.

"Kale, are you even listening to me?" she asks on the other end. "We both know what it's like between you and Dad, and it's only getting worse."

"I think you're making it out to be worse than it is."

"Do you think I'm stupid?" There's a moment of silence. Then she asks, "When did you get back?"

"Early this morning."

"So where are you, hiding in your room? The bathtub? You can't keep avoiding him."

I feel blood dripping off my chin. I remind myself that head wounds bleed more than everything else. I want to keep my mind off it, knowing it'll take me places I don't want to go.

Sometimes when I close my eyes, I see the forest and red snow. I feel my numb fingers and nose. I'll hear the mortars and gun shots. The bullets peppering the ground at our feet. The flares singeing the night sky. I see every friend that has died, some screaming and others silenced before they can take their last breath.

I see it all.

Hear it all.

Relive every nightmare I've had. All in the blink of an eye.

I can hear my name being called, somewhere far and out of reach. I'm cold everywhere. Shaking.

"Kale!"

I open my eyes.

I'm still in the bathroom.

"I'm sorry, what did you say?"

138

She lets out a long breath, finally fed up. "I'm going to go. Tell Harper I said hi."

Before I can respond, she's gone. The dial tone drones in my ear and I slowly pull it away. Somewhere between hearing Libby's last word and drawing my legs up to my chest, I shut it off. Now it sits on the tile, reminding me I'm alone here.

At the sound of someone coming upstairs, my eyes go straight for the door, realizing I never locked it. I always lock it. I glance down, making sure my stitches aren't visible. I move my arm over them as the door opens.

A moment passes with me sitting against the tub and him with one hand still on the door, not sure if he wants to commit to coming in. We stare at each other, because he's never cared to find me here. When the door is shut between us, it's like I'm not here at all. Or maybe that's what he likes to believe.

But he's here now, and I can't move. Not sure if I'm happy or scared.

The unknown can sometimes be a little of both.

Dad closes the door and comes toward me. Each step careful and thought out. He kneels down and pushes my hair aside, his fingers barely touching my skin.

Without saying a word, he gets up and goes over to the sink. He takes the wash cloth from the rack and holds it under the tap for a few seconds.

Then I'm seven again, coming into the house with a cut on my arm. Dad was the only one home. He took me upstairs and sat me down on the toilet to clean it. He was so calm through the whole thing. Caring for me the way every parent should.

That's why coming home has always felt so safe. Dad would always be there to make things right.

But somewhere, somehow, things have changed.

He wipes the blood with the wash cloth, being more careful than he ever has. We sit there on the cold, tiled floor without ever saying a word to each other. We both know things are screwed up and nothing will ever be the way it used to be between us.

But right now, all I want to do is pretend it is.

And hope it's the start of something better.

22.
Harper

Two days. I haven't seen him for two days.

Grace came over yesterday and we played Halo since it's the only multiplayer game I have. She talked more about the school's volleyball team, and I surprised myself by agreeing to try out.

Who would have thought? Me, playing sports.

But now another day is coming to an end, and nobody in the Jackson house has bothered to answer the home phone—I told him I would try calling before going over next time, and I have. It's his fault he doesn't answer. Uncle Jasper hasn't said a word about it, just spending time in the barn or doing crosswords at the table. Despite his normal silence, the house has been quieter than usual.

I'm finished with Kale ignoring me and Uncle Jasper pretending nothing is wrong.

Music drifts from the barn as I make my way across the lawn. The light falls in the sky as the sun dips deeper below the horizon, making the clouds wispy and pink. Fireflies have already begun to light up the forest.

The door is cracked open and I slip through, breathing in the smell of oil and potato chips. Uncle Jasper lays on a creeper

141

under an old Camaro, his legs sticking out, oil stains on his jeans. He's softly humming to the song coming from the old radio in the corner.

I wait a few seconds to see if he'll notice me, but he doesn't. "Uncle Jasper?"

"What's up, kid?" Metal clanks from somewhere below.

"I'm going over to see Kale. He hasn't answered any of my calls."

Uncle Jasper stops working and rolls himself out, staring up. His baseball cap is turned sideways on his head, his graying hair sticking out from under it. If it wasn't for the look in his eyes, it would be hard to take him seriously.

"You're gonna go over there?"

"Yeah." Then I ask, "Is that bad?"

"It can be tough on him when he comes back," he says, shrugging, "especially after going through what he does. Some days are better than others. But maybe it's a good idea you go see him. He could probably use it right now."

He rolls back underneath the car without waiting for my response. But I ask him anyway, "When did he start being like this?"

"Like what?"

"Not Kale."

There's a long pause where the music fills in. "Probably within the last year or so. Things started to get worse after his mom left."

A knot forms in my stomach, now knowing what that feels like.

"But I do know one thing," Uncle Jasper continues. "He's been more himself since you got here. Oh hey, tell him I could use his help tomorrow if he's up for it."

I nod—even though he can't see me—and slip out the door, slightly nervous about going over there again, not wanting to find something else unexpected. I think about driving over, but walking through the woods takes just as much time, so I cut across the backyard with the fading music behind me.

When Kale's house comes into view, I almost hesitate before stepping out of the woods. Coming here when I was younger was easy. It was something I did almost every day—running through the woods and entering the house without a knock or hesitation. It was a second home.

Now, like last week when I came, it feels like I'm approaching something unknown. Light glows from behind closed shades and not even the hum from the television can be heard. I step up to the door and knock, trying to ignore the weird butterflies in my stomach. It takes a few moments for me to hear footsteps, and when the door finally cracks open, Bryce stands on the other side.

"Harper?" He opens the door wider. "What are you doing here?"

The house looks empty behind him, and I have a bad feeling that maybe Kale left early. It's been only two days, and he said he had at least three or four before then.

"Um, is Kale here?" I ask. "I tried calling earlier today but nobody answered."

"Oh, sorry. I just got home, and Kale is up in his room." Bryce gives a small shrug, almost apologetic. "He doesn't usually come out to answer the phone. But come on in. You can go up if you want. I'm sure he's awake."

"Thanks."

I move in past him and up the stairs. The higher I get, the darker it becomes. Kale's is the last room on the right. There's no light coming from the crack under the closed door, but I knock anyway.

I hear the bed creak and bare feet padding softly across the floor. When the door opens, the light coming through the window behind him makes his face shadowy against the white walls.

"Harper." He says it like I'm the last person he expected to see. "Who let you in? Is my dad home?" He looks past me, down the hall, like he expects to see someone standing there.

"I don't think so. Bryce let me in."

Kale lets out a breath and relaxes a little. "Oh. So, what are you doing here?"

"Well, I wouldn't have come if you would answer your phone. I've been trying to call you all day."

His eyes close briefly and he looks down. "I'm sorry." His jaw flexes. "It seems I can't do anything right today."

"You will if you let me in," I hint.

Kale flashes a quick smile and opens the door wider. "That, I can do."

I walk past him through the door. "Uncle Jasper said to tell you if you're free tomorrow, he could use some help with that Camaro." When he doesn't say anything I ask, "How's your side?"

"It's good. I'll probably take the stitches out tomorrow." He closes the door and sits down on his unmade bed.

"So soon?" I say, still glancing around and trying to remember what has changed. Not a lot—just little things, like the place of his bed and the absent posters on the walls. It seems so bare now. With the door closed, I feel close to him.

"Well, yeah," he says. "I tend to heal fast."

I lean against his desk and shake my head. "Even though I've had a couple of days to process it, you being . . ."

"Not normal?" He only stares at the floor between his feet, his expression voided.

"I wasn't going to say that."

"But it's true." Kale looks small sitting on the bed, and when he shrugs his shoulders, I really see how tired he is. Worn out. "I don't ever remember being normal."

"It's not all that great." I finger the books on his desk and the worn bookmarks protruding from them. Pencils stand up in the old mug with a chip, showing the white porcelain surrounded by green. Kale broke that mug when he was twelve. His mom was going to throw it out, but I had no idea he saved it from that fate. There's so much that I don't know about him, and I'm starting to realize it even more than before.

Pictures are tacked on a bulletin board above his desk. There's a lot of us and Libby. My eyes linger on the ones of Kale and me, trying to remember what I was thinking and what I felt. It certainly wasn't what I feel now, but maybe close.

A few of the pictures of Kale and Miles are only a couple years old.

"How long have you known Miles?"

"A few years now. He's the only person in school who bothered to put up with me."

"You said telling him about your time-traveling was a mistake. How come?"

He gives a small smile. "You really want to know?"

"Of course."

"Well . . . we stayed late after baseball practice one evening. It was the start of the season last year and I wanted to get more pitches in before our first game. I don't know—I think it might be because I worked up a sweat and couldn't feel the cold coming on, but when we were done, we packed up our bags and started back toward the school. Suddenly it just hit me. I dropped my bag and couldn't move, tried to stop it from happening. He knew something was up because I was starting to freak out that I was about to expose myself to him."

He pauses, thinking about it.

I ask, "So what happened?"

He clears his throat and continues. "I told him, 'Please don't tell anyone.' Then I was just gone. I ended up somewhere

145

in the nineties so it was an easy year, but the whole time I was there, I couldn't stop thinking about Miles and if he would ever talk to me again."

"I guess he did—talk to you, I mean."

Kale nods. "Oh yeah, I called him when I got back and he came right over with my baseball stuff I left behind, nonstop asking questions. Almost as much as you the other night." Then he looks at me different and asks, "But what about you?"

"What about me?"

"Did you leave any friends behind when you left?"

I run my teeth over my bottom lip and shake my head. "No. Nobody worth mentioning, anyway. I had some friends in middle school, but things changed when we grew up. Well . . . *I* changed. I guess they didn't like who I turned out to be."

"I like who you turned out to be," Kale murmurs. He stares a moment before shrugging. "I mean, I always have."

I hear Bryce downstairs in the kitchen. Even so, the house still feels too quiet. "At least I'll have a couple friends when I start the school year. It's better than where I left off. Wish you were going to be there, though."

"Wish I was, too," he says, staring at the floor again, looking like he wants to say something else but doesn't. He has that look a lot, like there are things he's thinking but will never say. Not even to me.

"We're still neighbors and we'll see each other," I tell him. The floor creaks underneath my feet when I move and sit down next to him. "Even if it means you're my only source of a social life."

"What social life?" Kale looks up, smiling wide enough so his dimple appears.

"Exactly." My hearts pounds faster, my mouth dry. "But it's different with you. I don't know how to explain it."

"I do." There are bits of blue in his gray eyes, something I haven't been close enough to see in a long time. "When I'm around you," he says, "I don't care if I ever see another person."

My smile slowly disappears, too nervous to do anything but keep his gaze. The room is deafening, and the only thing I hear is something pounding against my chest.

For the shortest moment, I think Kale might kiss me. And it's the scariest moment in my life. How can something that should be simple be so confusing and cause so much anxiety?

Downstairs, the door slams shut and Kale flinches and looks away. We hear a truck start up outside and the tires crunch down the gravel driveway. Five years ago, being alone in the house with Kale wouldn't have meant a thing to me, but not now. Not when there's nothing but air between us and my heart is telling me to do something reckless.

I can't lie to myself and say he's just my next-door neighbor. Not anymore.

"I should get home," I hear myself say. "Uncle Jasper gets cranky when he doesn't eat dinner and he won't start without me."

He nods, almost too quickly. "Okay."

Once we're out of his room and downstairs, it feels like whatever happened upstairs never did, and my heartbeat returns to normal once I get outside. The sun is just over the trees now, shining an orange-yellow light into the woods. Kale follows me out the door after slipping on his shoes.

"I thought Uncle Jasper gave you Aunt Holly's old Rabbit," he says, looking over to where his car sits alone.

"He did," I say, "but I felt like walking. Driving point-four miles seems like a waste of gas when I have legs that work just fine."

Kale groans. "You're making me sound lazy."

"And I'm making myself sound like I actually care about saving gas."

He laughs once, glancing toward the woods. "Let me walk you home then. After all, it *is* my fault you had to come over here."

"You don't have to." I look over, meeting his gaze.

"I want to. Come on."

I follow Kale into the woods and along the narrow path we know so well. The birds fly between the trees, catching bugs in the evening light. When we come to the bend in the river, where there are no trees to filter the light, the sun shines down full, reflecting off the water and turning it into a mirror. I slow down, almost able to see to the bottom from how clear it is.

I feel Kale next to me, close enough to touch. But I don't look at him, afraid I'll lose my nerve. So instead, I ask, "Feel like going for a swim?"

"You really like swimming, don't you?"

"You already know that. Come on, we'll be quick." I slip off my shoes and stuff my socks inside, acting before I change my mind. I'm not going to mess this up again. I'm not.

"Seriously, right now?"

Kale stares at me like he did last time. Like I'm joking. "Why not? Besides, we haven't played Sinking Ship without Libby before, and without her here, maybe one of us will actually win."

I take off my T-shirt, keeping my tank-top on.

"I don't even remember how she did it," he says. "I think she almost made me drown once from laughing so hard."

"I don't know either. But now we have the chance to see which of us is better." When he still doesn't make a move, I say, "Come on, Kale. I promise, this will be the last time I ask you."

Kale lets out a quick breath, a sign of him giving in. "All right, fine." He kicks off his shoes, leaving them next to mine, and slips his T-shirt off. I try not to stare at his chest and flat stomach, or the lines of his hips that disappear into his jeans. The bullet gaze is barely visible across his ribs. It's hard to get used to this Kale. The one who isn't a boy anymore.

I step into the river, feeling the slippery stones under my feet and the cold water creeping up my skin. When I reach the middle where the water comes up to my neck, Kale is right behind me. We wade out in the middle, barely able to touch the bottom. There's a large rock on the river bed, right beneath us. We don't have to look down to know it's there.

"Are you sure about this?" Kale asks, his dark hair splashing black against his face.

"I don't know, but let's do it before I change my mind."

We both take deep breaths and sink down at the same time, grabbing hold of the rock at the bottom to keep us anchored.

The world underwater is a quiet one, one unlike any other. The sunlight shines through the water, right down to where we're floating at the bottom with our hair pulled by the lazy current.

We were smiling on our way down, but now, the distractions from the top world are gone and the watchful eyes of the clouds are forgotten. Everything above us slowly fades until nothing is left. Down here, it's only us. And something neither of us can ignore it any longer.

When he comes closer, I don't feel the knot in my stomach like I did before—when we were in his room and I couldn't think of anything except how hot the air felt and the lump in the mattress I sat on.

Here, nothing feels more right.

Here, I want to kiss him.

Kale pauses halfway, his eyes bright under the sun. We're inches from each other with only the water between us, feeling thinner than the air. Even though my lungs burn, I can't think of anything else but him.

He gives me one last, longing look, and the moment our lips touch, I never want us to part. A racing jolt sprints down my spine and through my stomach. Nothing I've ever felt before. Is this seriously happening right now?

It's a small kiss, like he's afraid to break whatever we have between us. Soft and careful, but something amazing. Saying more than words can describe. I want it to last forever.

I might drown down here, but I'll drown happy.

Kale pulls away and I open my eyes again, not ever remembering closing them. My lungs burn for air with my heart pounding hard, but I don't want to rise yet, almost afraid our secret world will keep our secrets with it. That once we break the surface, this will have never had happened. Like trying to remember dreams.

But when Kale finally lets go of the rock, I follow him up.

It truly is another world. I hear the breeze and river, and I can smell grass and everything that comes with summer. And whatever disappeared between us below the water is back, creating an invisible wall we can't see around. I don't know why it's there, but I don't want it. This awkwardness. It's what I was afraid of.

Kale's chin is level with the water, his eyes still staring with uncertainty.

"I'm sorry," he says.

"You don't have to be," I say, shaking my head once.

"Why not?"

"Because it's not something you should be sorry for." I start for the shore, feeling nervous again, which is weird because it's Kale, and I'm never nervous around him. I can still feel the trace of his lips on mine. Just thinking about it makes my face hot.

When I'm almost out of the water, Kale's voice makes me pause.

"Harper?" He can't be more than a foot behind me. "I was going to say, I'm sorry for not doing that sooner." I turn around, and he gives me a cute, nervous smile. "Is that okay for me to say?"

"Yeah," I nod, my heart still racing, "It's more than okay."

Because it is.

Kale lowers his eyes and walks past me onto the shore, pulling on his T-shirt. With his hair wet and away from his face, I notice a thin red line over his right eyebrow. "You can tell Uncle Jasper I can help him with the car tomorrow," he says, not noticing me looking.

"How did you get that?" I ask, pointing above my own eye.

He hesitates and touches his forehead, like he forgot it was there. "Oh, I tripped on the rug in the hallway and nicked the table. It's not as bad as it looks." Once Kale pulls his shoes on, he takes a couple steps toward the direction of his house. "I should get back."

Any other time, I wouldn't want him to go. But with what just happened, I don't know what to say or how to act around him. I think we both feel it. What do you say to someone after kissing them for the first time? Especially someone you've known your entire life.

"See you tomorrow?" I ask, because that's all I can think of.

He nods once more. "Definitely."

When Kale is gone and I'm left standing by myself, the truth of what happened is something I'm not able to ignore.

I kissed Kale Jackson.

And I think I want to do it again.

23.
Kale

For the first time in six months, I sleep through the night. A dark, dreamless sleep.

I wake up in the morning and feel somewhat like myself again. The sun is already up, shining through the cracks in my broken blinds. But it's late enough that Dad and Bryce are already gone for the day.

I don't feel exhausted, and my muscles don't ache like they have been. Then my heart pounds when I remember what happened last night at the river. I feel like I can't breathe.

I push Harper from my mind for a moment so I can think straight.

It doesn't work.

I grab some clean clothes and walk across the hall to take a shower, and I catch a glimpse of myself in the mirror. The dark circles under my eyes are less prominent and my skin is less pale.

I forgot what rest feels like.

But I never thought I'd forget what happy feels like. Even though it's a small sensation in my stomach right now, I still feel it. Slowly growing. A new plant that forgot the sun.

I can only hope it doesn't go away too soon.

After taking a shower, I eat a real breakfast. Also something I haven't done in a long time. I make myself eggs and toast, sure to clean up once I'm done.

The phone rings as I finish loading the dishwasher. It echoes through the hallway, one ring after another. I have no doubt it's Libby again and I almost don't answer it, not wanting to get in another fight.

I walk into the hallway and my hand pauses over the phone. It rings once more and I pick it up.

"Hello?"

There's a pause and I hear a door slam. "Kale?"

I recognize the voice and my lips turning up into a smile. "Miles?"

He says, "I wasn't sure if you'd be home, but I guess it's my lucky day."

"Yeah, I'm still here." I feel like I've said that a lot lately. "What's going on?"

"Well, I know you wanted to throw some ball tonight, but I think I've got a better idea."

"A better idea, or a different idea?" I ask. "There's a difference."

"Possibly the latter," he says, and I can hear him smiling.

"Well what is it then?" I walk upstairs and grab my keys off the desk, pocketing them and grabbing my baseball cap. I take a long look at my sweatshirt hanging over my chair before deciding to leave it.

I don't feel cold today.

Miles continues, "There's a band playing in the city tonight, and Grace is friends with the lead singer, so she really wants to go. And she also wants Harper to come, too, so you have to make sure that happens, because whatever Grace wants—"

"—Grace gets," I finish, nodding.

"So what do you say?"

I do want to go.

Probably more than anything right now. But tonight will be my fourth night here, and I haven't made it that long in months. I feel fine. It's like my countdown is on pause, at least for right now. But tomorrow feels like a long way off.

"Kale? You still there?"

"Yeah . . . and yeah, I'll be there."

"Really? Are you sure?"

I glance up at the old photos of me and Harper, feeling more anchored than ever before.

"Yeah, I'm sure."

I park next to Uncle Jasper's truck and cut the engine.

The Rabbit isn't parked in the driveway, meaning Harper isn't here, which means I've put the moment off for a bit longer. It doesn't make me feel any less nervous about seeing her.

I grab my hat from the passenger seat and put it on, swiping my hair away from my eyes. As I get out, I notice the dark clouds, which have been growing and getting darker on my way over here.

I've forgotten the last time it rained.

I only remember snow.

"You finally decide to show up?"

I turn to find Uncle Jasper standing in the doorway of the barn. Seeing him reminds me how our last conversation ended. It's been haunting me for the last two days. Digging a hole deeper within me.

I should have called before now, or done *something*.

"If you'll have me," I say, staying planted where I am, wondering if he's having doubts about asking me to help him.

154

I wouldn't blame him if he did.

"You don't even have to ask, kid." He smiles shortly, then says, "I am sorry for what I said. I was out of line."

"You were just telling the truth." I walk around my car, burying my hands in my jean pockets. "You shouldn't be sorry for that."

"I'm not sorry for telling the truth," he says. "I'm sorry for the way it hurt you to hear it." He looks down and fidgets with an old starter that probably needs to be replaced.

I change the subject by pointing to the part in his hands. "Have you got a replacement for that yet?"

"Just came in yesterday." He grins and tosses the lump of metal in the corner where others have been thrown in the past. "I could use your help if you're up to it."

"Always."

Uncle Jasper gives me a weird look, his eyebrows drawn together. I feel like I've seen that look before, but I can't recall when. "What's up with you today?" he asks.

"What do you mean?"

"I don't know. You seem different."

"I got sleep last night, and actually ate breakfast this morning?" I suggest.

He nods slowly, uncertain. "Maybe that's it. You seem happy, though."

"Am I not allowed to feel happy?"

He raises an eyebrow and turns away.

Oddly, I feel the same way.

After changing the clutch fluid and replacing the air filter, I hear a car pull up the driveway and glance outside. The growing clouds are taking over the morning sky, bringing the smell of rain with them.

Harper pulls up in the old Rabbit and I turn around, still not ready to see her.

I am, but I'm not. My heart is racing too fast for me to decide.

"Is it weird seeing her in that car?" I ask, trying to act somewhat normal.

Uncle Jasper's arm is halfway in the engine, oil stains up to his elbow. "I'm getting used to it. It was strange at first, for sure." He brings his arm out and wipes his hands with a rag. It doesn't improve anything. "Why, is she back finally?"

I nod. "Where did she go?"

He gives me discreet smile. "I needed something in town."

A door slams outside, too hard. Harper comes into the barn carrying a McDonald's bag with her lips pressed thin. "You didn't tell me the nearest McDonald's is twenty minutes away," she says, throwing Uncle Jasper the bag. He smiles and digs out his food. "It's safe to say that's the last time I'll be going there."

Uncle Jasper shrugs, grinning. "Fair enough. I was lucky to get away with it once."

After taking a bite of his breakfast sandwich, he starts working on the engine again with one hand, pulling the old spark plugs out with a socket wrench with the other.

I glance at Harper and she meets my eyes. I pretend to be distracted by something on the floor.

"You look good," she says.

My head snaps around. "What?"

"I mean, you look like you finally got some sleep or something." Harper tries smiling, her eyes not meeting mine for long.

"I did actually." I don't know what else to say, so I ask, "How did you sleep last night?"

"Good."

I nod.

An odd silence passes over us.

"Looks like it's going to rain," I say.

"Yeah."

More silence.

When I look back at Uncle Jasper, he's staring at us, slowly chewing his food while his mind turns over. "Are you both coming down with something?" He glances at Harper. "Are you feeling all right?"

"Yeah, of course I am." She flips her keys over in her hands. "I'm gonna go back inside."

She starts walking away but I stop her, barely able to speak. "Harper?"

"Yeah?" She stops, half turned back.

"Um. I'm going into the city tonight, to meet up with Miles. Some band is playing, or something. But . . . do you want come?"

She's barely able to keep her gaze on me for long. I don't know if that's a good sign or bad sign. "Yeah, okay."

"I'll pick you up at six?"

Harper nods again and disappears into the house.

I force my gaze away. Only to find Uncle Jasper is still staring at me. "Seriously, what is wrong with you?" he asks.

I laugh once and grab my keys off the old couch. "Nothing is wrong. Do you need any more help? I gotta get home to do some errands before tonight."

His answer is slow coming. "No, that's fine. I'll call you if I need anything else."

After I get back into my car and head home, I can't stop smiling.

Not even when it starts to rain.

24.
Harper

The moment I walk into the house, the phone rings, but I have no reason to answer it. Uncle Jasper doesn't even bother unless he expects Kale to call. Leaving my keys on the table and kicking off my shoes, I start upstairs when the answering machine picks up. I pause for the sake of curiosity.

After the beep, a voice comes through the machine I never thought I would hear. Not now, and probably never again.

"Harper? It's me." Mom doesn't sound the same as she did when she left. Maybe leaving everything behind and starting a new life does that to someone.

I grip the wooden banister as she continues, my knees weak. "Could you call me when you get this? I tried your cell phone, but you didn't answer. I—" Mom pauses, because she doesn't want to say anything more in case Uncle Jasper hears this before me. "I just want to talk with you. Call me back."

She hangs up.

I never knew something so small could ruin my entire day before it even began. I can't let her do this to me again. I *won't* let her do this to me again. I walk back down the steps and over to the table where the phone sits, silent now that she has dug her way into my life once again. The red light flashes a number one, over and over again. I press delete and almost feel like it never happened. She's still there, though, lingering in the back of my mind, but it's easier to push her away now.

My phone sits upstairs on the bed and I know I'll find a missed call from her. But I'll delete that, too, and see if she cares to call again.

My hand still hovers over the phone when Uncle Jasper walks in. I step away from the table and head for the stairs again.

"Did someone call?"

"Yeah, but they didn't leave a message." I shrug, finding it easier and easier to push her from my mind.

"It was probably some sales person," he says. "I rarely get calls from anyone else."

I laugh and shake my head, starting back up the stairs.

"Hey, wait a minute." I look down at him from over the banister. He's got his thinking face on again, the same one I saw in the barn a few minutes ago. "Did something happen between you and Kale?"

"Why would you say that?" Admitting something like that to Uncle Jasper would be as hard as admitting to Dad if he was still alive. It's just not something that can be done easily. I can't say, "Yeah, we kissed and we're both pretending it never happened." Yeah, right.

"Because you both are acting like—" He looks away, shaking his head. "You know what, I don't want to know. It's none of my business anyway."

"You don't mind me going with him tonight, do you?" I ask. "I probably should've asked first."

"When it comes to Kale, you don't have to ask me anything."

Uncle Jasper walks into the kitchen and I hear the pattering of rain outside. I find my phone where I left it and delete the new missed call from Mom.

At this point, the kiss between me and Kale is a welcome distraction. Aunt Holly would be the only person I could talk to, but just thinking about her makes my throat close up.

I almost decide to text Libby, but what happened between us feels like it should stay there. What we have is . . . well, I don't know what we have.

But either way, six o'clock feels so far away.

25.
Kale

I don't go downstairs until it's time to leave.

It's been oddly quiet all day. Something that makes me uncomfortable.

Bryce has been in his room, and the television is on low downstairs. The rain outside darkened the day early, and I stand in front of my mirror with the desk lamp glowing dimly behind me.

I don't look any different from earlier this morning. Except now I have a clean T-shirt on. One that's void of oil stains or holes. I look for the cut over my eyebrow, but it's hidden beneath my hair.

I don't know what I'm looking for, but it's not here.

I put on my baseball cap and head downstairs. Dad sits on the couch. Not even glancing once at me. He's different tonight.

I'm halfway to the door, but unable to go any farther without saying something. "Dad?"

"What do you want, Kale?" His voice comes out tired. Worn out, like he's already giving up on me. Maybe he has. He takes a drink from his beer—something he stopped doing a long time ago.

"I'm going into the city tonight with Harper. I wanted to let you know I'll probably be back pretty late."

I don't even know why I'm telling him this. I haven't told him where I'm going for years.

He glances from the television to look at me, no expression at all. "All right," he says. "Be safe."

I can only stand there and stare.

Something isn't right. He's watching a basketball game, and Mom told me he used to have a gambling problem over sports. It started small then got too big too fast. He promised to stop after Bryce was born.

"Still standing there?" he asks. But it doesn't come out angry or annoyed, just curious.

"No. Sorry. I'll see you later."

I step out into the wet evening and close the door. Something heavy is on his mind tonight, and I should be thankful it doesn't have to do with me. Maybe it's because I'm still here, and he's waiting for me to leave.

Ignoring whatever my thoughts are whispering to me, I duck my head into the rain and get in my car. Harper is waiting for me and we have to meet up with Miles and Grace.

I start up my car and pray I'll be able to stay through the night.

I picked up Harper a half hour ago and I don't know how to start a conversation. I had to stop for gas before getting on the highway using the money Uncle Jasper slipped me when she wasn't looking—somehow he always knows when I need it. I ran inside the store to get us a few car snacks, remembering how much she used to like Twizzlers, and received a smiling thanks in return. Now she stares out the window as the dark night settles in. The lights of the city are in the distance. The white lines of road blink by beneath the headlights.

When I glance at her again, she catches my eye. "What is it?" she asks.

I shake my head and mumble, "Nothing."

More silence passes between us.

Harper messes with the radio for a little while, but finds nothing good and turns it off. "So where is this place we're going?"

"It's somewhere downtown. I wrote the address down before I left." I dig two fingers down into my pocket and pull out the piece of crumpled paper. I hand it to her and she silently reads it.

"I haven't been to a show in a long time," she says. "I hope they're good."

I shrug one shoulder. "I've never been to a show, so I don't have high expectations."

"Never?" Harper laughs and shakes her head. "That's hard to believe."

"I don't get out much," I say. "I don't know if you've noticed or not."

"But you also get out more than anyone," she points out.

"It sounds like the making of a riddle."

Harper laughs again, and I wish I could make her laugh more often. It feels like I've accomplished something when she laughs, even if it's something small and unimportant.

When we pass through the city limits, I follow the signs for downtown. I can feel her eyes on me every few minutes. It's not helping calm my heart.

She breaks the silence with, "Can I ask you something about that?"

"Yeah," I glance over. "Of course."

"You only mentioned places you've been to in the past," she

says. "So, does that mean that you don't travel to the future at all?"

Whenever I start thinking of the future, it's this uncertain blackness that scares me.

It scares me so much I try not to think of it.

I put on a smile and say, "Nope, it's just the past."

"Why do you think that is? Since you have the ability to time travel, don't you think you could go backward *and* forward?"

"Well, it's simple, really. I can't travel to the future because it hasn't happened yet." I smile again when she gives me a confused look. "It's not as complicated as you think it might be."

The exit comes up and I pull off the freeway. The rain stops. The windshield wipers shriek in protest until I turn them off.

"But what about all those theories about different paradoxes and alternate timelines?" she asks. "Aren't you afraid you'll mess up the present with something you do in the past?"

"You really need to stop thinking like this is *Doctor Who* or *Back to the Future*," I say. "Time travel is the simplest thing to understand if you take a moment and really think about it." When I pull up to a stop light, I turn to her. "What's the definition of *past*?"

"I feel like I'm in school."

"Just humor me."

She sighs. "The past is history. Time that has already happened."

"And what about *future*?"

"Time that hasn't happened yet."

"Exactly." I give her another smile as an answer.

The light turns green and I start looking for the street we need. Harper is still mulling over what I said. I haven't been downtown much, but Libby always swears I have a GPS in my head, which is usually helpful when I only glance a map before going somewhere I've never been.

"So," she starts again, "when you go to the past, you don't mess anything up? I feel like I'm missing something."

I find a parking space a block away from the address and cut the engine. I don't think I've ever explained this to anyone before.

It's oddly easy.

"Like you said, the past is history," I tell her. "So, when I go back in time, everything I do has already happened. And if I try to change something, it won't matter because it has already happened. Does that make sense? Let's say at some point in the past I—I don't know, meet one of the presidents. I haven't yet, but if I'm going to, I'm going to."

"Because you already have."

"Yes."

"So the past is actually your future," she says.

I smile a little. "Yeah, I guess it is."

She stares out the windshield, her eyes bright against the city lights. "You're right. It is almost too simple."

"I think people like to overcomplicate things."

"Or maybe they've never met a real time-traveler." Harper smiles, looking over. "I don't think I'll be able to watch another movie on the subject again. Have you ever met anyone else who could do what you do?"

"No, but I've always wondered. Maybe I have and just didn't know it. It's not like I have a sign on my back saying what I am." I glance down the street, my stomach full of excitement and nerves. I couldn't even eat dinner earlier. "We should get in there. Miles will break up with me if I don't show."

"What?"

I shake my head and open the door. "Nothing. Come on."

The weather is still on the warm side, enough to leave my sweatshirt in the car. Puddles of water dampen the sidewalks, but we walk side by side toward the old theater, which has been turned into a venue.

A guy stands outside, taking money from everyone trying to get indoors before the rain starts back up. Harper pulls out a couple ten-dollar bills before I have the chance to stop her.

"You don't have to do that."

She hands the guy some money and says, "I already have. What are you going to do now? Go back in time and stop me?"

I glance at the guy, but he's already taking money from the people behind us. "Could you say it any louder? I don't think the people behind us heard you."

I open the door and Harper walks past me. "And if they did hear me?" she asks. "Do you really think they would take it seriously?"

"Maybe." Even I'm not convincing myself. Or course they wouldn't, but that doesn't mean I go around announcing it to the world.

I follow in after her.

The smell of cigarette smoke and sweat clogs the air inside, causing my fingers to itch for one. The lighting is dim and hazy. Most of it comes from the spotlights on the stage, lighting up the tops of people's heads. The place is packed. It's noisy and loud, even though the band isn't on stage yet.

I ask, "Do you see Miles anywhere?"

"No. I'm gonna go find the bathroom. If I don't come back within five minutes—"

"Assume you're dead and go on without you?"

"It's too risky to come after me." Harper shakes her head in mock sadness and walks away. I watch her disappear through the crowd and adjust my ball cap.

I feel out of place here. Something I should be used to.

166

I wade deeper into the moving mass. Some people brush by like I don't exist. Others look then forget they ever saw me.

I skim faces, trying to find Miles or Grace. Hoping I won't see anyone else from school.

The stage slowly comes closer. After going a little ways more, I see Miles with Grace at his side, talking to a guy with dark hair and glasses.

I start toward him. When he inclines his head to the side to talk to Grace, his eyes catch sight of me. He flashes a grin. "I almost didn't think you'd show."

"I almost didn't either."

He engulfs me in a hug—even though I just saw him a couple days ago—receiving a few stares in our direction because he still hasn't let go. "I was hoping you'd come so I wouldn't have to break up with you," he says, his chin still on my shoulder.

I smile at Grace while she rolls her eyes. This is the Miles we know and love.

"Where's Harper?" she asks. "You'd better have brought her, or I'm going to punch you in the face—"

"—Please don't, I brought her." I pat Miles on the back. "All right buddy, you can let go now."

"Sorry," he says, not sounding it at all. He steps away and motions to the guy behind me. "This is Blake. He's the lead singer. Blake, this is Kale."

I shake the guy's hand. "Nice to meet you."

"Likewise. I didn't know Miles was that—ah, fond of you."

"Almost embarrassingly so," I say.

Grace says, "For the both of us."

"Hey now," Miles warns me. "If it wasn't for me, you'd still be friendless and at home."

"Where I'd probably be better off."

Whereas I can hold in my smile, Miles can't.

Blake clears his throat once and says, "I've got to get ready, but I'll see you guys after the show."

Grace wishes him luck and he leaves.

"So," Miles starts, "anything new? Since the last time I saw you, that is. Other than needing a haircut."

I rub the back of my neck, feeling a draft coming from somewhere. "Nothing, really. Libby called once and she might be staying with my mom."

"Like, permanently?" Grace asks.

"Sounds like it." I catch a glimpse of Harper coming toward us. My stomach tightens. Getting nervous all over again. She stops next to me and I hear myself say, "I think it'll turn out all right, though."

Grace and Harper delve into a conversation like they've been friends for more than a couple weeks. I shouldn't be surprised. Harper was always like that, even when we were kids. She could start up conversations with strangers at the grocery store without thinking.

Within the short time my mind drifts, Miles says something to Grace that makes her blush—something that is very, very hard to do. As he likes to prove countless times.

But then he smirks and leans in to kiss her and I feel my face heat. Harper and I glance at each other before looking away.

It's impossibly hard to pretend nothing happened between us.

We're saved when someone talks into the mic, announcing the show is about to start. People cheer and push their way to the front of the stage. Packing in more tightly than I could've imagined.

Miles leans in so I can hear him over the yelling crowd. "You guys want to get closer to the front with us?"

"Nah, you guys go ahead," I say. "We'll hang out here."

He nods and they both disappear in the sea of bodies. We're

about halfway from the stage, but still close enough to see the band. A few more people push by us, knocking Harper into me. I grab her arm to steady her, feeling her soft skin under my fingers.

She flashes a smile. "Thanks."

"Are shows always like this?"

She steps away again, our arms close to brushing. "Usually, yeah."

The music starts up, a piano riff along with some soft drums that slowly build. The lights flash over the screaming crowd, more deafening than the band.

But I don't take my eyes off Harper.

The room pulses with life. The music hits its climax. The floor shakes with bass and people jumping.

But my heart is only pounding because of her. I want to close the distance between us. To be near her. To feel her fingers twined with mine.

Just when I gain the courage to say something, a gunshot goes off somewhere behind me. I flinch and bump into someone standing next to me.

"Dude, what's your problem?" he yells.

"Kale, are you all right?" Her hand is on my arm, her eyes worried. "It was just someone setting off a firecracker or something."

My head starts to spin inside itself. Too fast.

Cigarette smoke fills my lungs, reminding me of somewhere far away.

Somewhere white and red.

Lights from the stage flash above. Flares in the night sky. A warning of something worse to come.

Someone screaming. Everyone screaming.

More gunshots go off behind me and I close my eyes. Try to make them disappear. Make myself disappear.

I don't want to go back there.

I'm cold. My hands shake, and I'm too afraid to open my eyes.

To see something I don't want to.

I don't want to be there. Not now.

Not when I'm with her.

I can't.

Everything flashes black.

Then someone whispers my name. "Kale."

Then louder. "*Kale!*"

I open my eyes. Harper is crouched next to me on the floor, trying to find me when I'm right here in front of her. My body trembles. The clash of cymbals causes me to flinch again. My hands won't cover my ears because they're still shaking.

"Kale, look at me."

Harper's hand rests against my face, willing my gaze to meet hers.

"It's okay," she says, staring into me. "Take my hand. I'll get you out of here."

Her skin feels so warm against mine. I let her pull me up and lead me through the crowd. I can't get enough air. The cymbals crash once more and the lights flash. When my head starts spinning again, I can only hear the racing beat of my heart.

I'm barely able to hang on. To this time and to this life.

A door opens ahead of me and fresh air hits my lungs. Every time I blink, something flashes that I don't want to see. The images overcome me, and soon I can't open my eyes at all.

All I see is Adams lying dead in the snow. Staring up and mouthing words I can't make out. I scream at him but my voice doesn't work. I can't move or close my eyes. I can only stand there and stare while his blood melts the snow beneath him.

"Kale, open your eyes."

I can't open my eyes because they're already open. I want to close them, not open them. I want to disappear and never come back.

"Please, Kale." Harper's voice pushes through my thoughts. "Don't leave yet."

I open my eyes to a silent world. I'm sitting in an alleyway, my back pressed against a brick wall. Harper kneels in front of me. My heartbeat starts to slow, my hands shake less. My jeans are damp because I'm sitting in a puddle left over from the rain.

I'm still here.

I'm still here.

"I'm sorry," I whisper.

She gives me the smallest smile. "It's not something you have to apologize for."

I take a deep breath, rubbing my hands over my eyes, but they keep going until my fingers are buried under my hat. "I thought I was gone for sure."

"But you're not."

The music hums from inside the building. I drop my hands and stare at my jeans. I've never felt so weak. "Only because of you," I say.

I know Harper is the only reason I'm still here. Without her, I would be gone.

Seventy years into the past.

There's no doubt.

It starts to rain again. A few drops fall from the sky, slapping softly against the pavement around us. "You don't have to be ashamed, Kale. A lot of people who've been in war go through things like this."

"But none of them probably have to fight themselves to stay in the present."

"Is that what it's usually like, when you go?"

"No, it's never happened like this before." I finally look up at Harper, wondering what she thinks of me. "It's usually just my dreams at night. That's why I can never sleep for too long."

The rain comes down in full, sprouting droplets around us.

Harper's knee is pressed to her chest, her arms folded around it. She ignores the rain soaking her hair. "But you did last night," she says.

"I did." I smile and shiver at the same time. I push myself up and Harper stands with me. Drops of water drip from the bill of my hat. "Again, only because of you."

"You keep saying that," she says.

"Because it's true."

My body trembles with cold, and for the second time tonight, Harper takes my hand. "Come on, let's go home."

After dropping off Harper, I go home and expect to find Dad already in bed. But when I walk through the door, he's asleep on the couch.

I'm still on edge from earlier tonight, but I can't make myself walk past him.

I gently shake his shoulder. "Dad?"

His eyes blink open and he sits up, taking me in. "Kale?" He glances at the clock. "You're back."

I just look at him. "I said I would be, didn't I?"

He glances away quickly and gets up. "I meant early," he says.

"Oh, well, it didn't go as long as I thought it would."

He looks over me, still trying to wake up. "You should get to bed then. I don't want to be woken up by you banging around somewhere."

But before I turn to go, I ask, "Is everything all right?"

"Yeah . . . yeah, everything's fine. Go to bed."

Dad heads for the stairs and I stand there, wondering how to make things normal between us.

26.
Harper

I spend a good part of the night staring up at my ceiling, thinking about Kale and the other world he has to live through. Even though he denies it, I know things aren't well at home for him either, and I hate feeling like I can do nothing to help him.

When morning finally comes, shining through the trees still dripping from last night's rain, I go downstairs to find Uncle Jasper sitting at the table. Toast and coffee are already in front of him while he scratches letters into today's crossword. The mug sitting on the table shows a giraffe wearing a winter hat.

After grabbing a bowl and some cereal, I get the milk from the fridge and slide into my chair. The tile is cold under my bare feet and the wooden chair isn't comfortable to sit in this early in the morning.

"Did you have a good time last night?" Uncle Jasper asks.

"Yeah, I guess." I pour some cereal and I feel like he's waiting for more of an answer, so I say, "It was good to get out of the house."

Without looking over he says, "What's a four-letter word for 'too old to be fun'?"

I look at him pointedly. "You know what I mean." I watch him pencil in more letters, trying to remember if he ever did them when I was younger. "When did you start doing crosswords?"

"A few years ago." He pauses and looks up, one hand slipping into the handle of his mug. "It helps to keep my mind distracted from the times when she would normally be here."

It's an answer I wasn't at all expecting. "Does it work?"

A small, sad smile appears. "Sometimes." He puts his pencil down and his eyes shift between me and a certain spot on the table. "You know, when I first found out about Kale and his ability, I asked him something very selfish of me. Of course, now I know he can't change the past and I would do anything to take back what I asked of him. But even though I knew there was probably nothing Kale could do to change anything, I wanted to see her again. Just once more." Uncle Jasper takes a deep breath, trying to smile.

"You shouldn't feel guilty for asking that," I say. "Anyone would have done the same thing."

"But I do, especially these days when he's going through something much worse than I ever have." He picks up his pencil again, but he doesn't write more words into the squares. He's thinking about something else. "I keep confessing things to you, and I don't know why. All you do is sit there and it just comes out."

"Maybe I should become a therapist," I joke.

"Or maybe you should study something actually worthwhile."

I laugh a little, still thinking about Kale and what happened last night. "Does Kale ever have, like . . . panic attacks, or anything?"

His hand pauses over the paper and he looks up. "Did something happen last night?"

"Yeah, but I don't know what. One minute he was fine, and the next he was really freaked out. He was shaking and his skin was cold, and I didn't know what else to do but get him out of there. For a moment I thought he would disappear before I got him outside. It was like he was seeing something that wasn't there."

Uncle Jasper taps the pencil eraser to his chin. "Did something happen right before that? Something that might have triggered it?"

I shrug once. "I think someone set off a cherry bomb or something, but it wasn't very loud."

Uncle Jasper nods, like he knows something I don't. "That was probably it then. Have you ever heard of post-traumatic stress disorder?" I nod and he continues. "It's common when a person has been through a war, or even so much as a bad car accident—it depends on the person."

"So, you think that's what happened?"

"I have no doubt." For the first time since I've lived here, there's a tinge of real anger behind his eyes. He blinks it away as fast as it came. "It's something nobody deserves to go through. All we can do is be there for him." Uncle Jasper gets up from the table and puts his dishes in the sink. His face is wiped of all emotion. "I've got to get going. I'll only be gone for a few hours, then maybe I'll take a look at those brakes for you."

I nod as he walks out.

I pour some milk over my cereal, listening to the diminishing sounds of his truck. It's hard to be here without Aunt Holly. The house doesn't smell the same. Uncle Jasper doesn't smile as much. The food doesn't even taste right. I can only imagine what it would be like if she were still alive.

There's a small knock on the backdoor, and I look up to see Kale standing on the other side of the screen. He smiles and gives a small wave. Again, I'm reminded of the kiss we shared days ago.

"You're still here," I say, trying to sound normal.

"For now, anyway. Can I come in?"

I nod and continue eating my cereal. The screen door shuts behind him and he sits in the chair opposite me. He looks more tired than he did yesterday.

"Did Uncle Jasper already leave?"

"Just a few minutes ago."

Kale glances back at the counter. "He didn't finish his toast."

"The wrong subject came up."

"Aunt Holly?"

I nod and push my bowl away, feeling slightly sick. Kale swipes the hair away from his eyes. It's getting a little too long to keep tame—no wonder he wore his hat last night.

I push my chair back from the table. "You should get your hair cut." I put the milk and cereal away, having to close the refrigerator twice before it stays shut. Stupid thing is too old— always has been.

"And who's going to do it?" he asks. "You?"

I give him a one shoulder shrug. "Sure."

"Really?"

"I'm not too bad," I admit. "I used to cut this neighbor kid's hair because he didn't want to spend the money. Besides, you don't need much off. Just a trim."

He mulls over it for a little while and then agrees. "Okay."

I find the pair of scissors upstairs—the same pair Aunt Holly used when my own hair got too long all those summers ago. When I come back downstairs, I pull a chair in the middle of the kitchen. "Do you want to take your shirt off so it won't be itchy the rest of the day?"

He flashes me a smile and pulls his T-shirt off. Once he's sitting in the chair, I wrap a towel around his shoulders and wet his hair using a spray bottle.

I hesitate before touching his hair, and when I do, it drapes like black silk over my fingers. I feel my breathing thin, and I start cutting before my mind has the chance to wander any further. While I'm trimming the bangs that hang over his forehead, his eyes flicker to meet mine. There's more blue in them today. A gray and blue storm.

Stay focused.

I try to keep my heart even and make sure I don't cut my own fingers. After I think I'm done, I set the scissors on the table and finish by running my fingers through his hair, checking the lengths of the layers I cut. As my fingers trace over his scalp, Kale closes his eyes and lets out a soft groan.

"You have no idea how good that feels," he murmurs.

My fingers freeze in place. I step back and take the towel from around his shoulders. Kale catches my wrist, gently sliding his fingers over my skin. He looks up and says, "Thank you. For more than just the haircut."

I can only nod. With Kale sitting there, wearing nothing but a pair of jeans and his hair still wet and dark, it's the only thing I can manage to do. Kale stands and slips his T-shirt over his head. Needing to put more space between us, I take a step back until my lower back presses against the counter.

Kale meets my gaze again with a strange expression. One that's a mixture of uncertainty and daringness.

"I—" He glances away, his breathing deep.

"What?"

His gray-blue eyes lock with mine. "I really want to kiss you right now. For real this time."

"And what was it last time?"

"A dream." Kale takes a step toward me. He's close now, barely inches away.

"Maybe you should, then." The words are out of my mouth before I can so much as register what I've said. And I don't regret them.

When Kale leans in and kisses me, I wonder if it will feel like this every time. So new and so horribly addicting. My fingers find the bottom of his T-shirt and slip underneath, softly trailing over his skin where it dips in along his spine. His kiss deepens, his fingers sliding through my hair. I want to pull him in closer to me, to feel every inch of his back and every muscle flexing beneath.

Kale breaks away and gives me a one-sided smile, showing his dimple. "It's dangerous for me to be alone with you."

"I could say the same thing."

The front door slams shut. Kale steps away and leans against the opposite counter. I dig my hands into my pockets as Uncle Jasper walks into the kitchen. The memory of Kale's skin is still fresh, probably making my cheeks redder than they should be.

"You back already?" I ask.

"No, I forgot my wallet." He grabs it from the table and nods to Kale. "You get your hair cut?"

"Yeah, Harper just did it for me."

My uncle eyes the clippings of hair still on the floor and looks up at me. "Huh. Maybe I'll have you do mine later." He sticks his wallet in his back pocket and walks out. "I'll be back in a few hours," he yells as the front door shuts behind him.

Kale and I glance at each other, and I have to hold back a laugh. I still can't believe what happened. When we kissed down at the river, it felt secret and something neither of us would ever talk about. But here in the kitchen, where we've spent countless hours eating, playing board games, and making fun of Uncle Jasper's bad jokes, it's more real than ever.

It really happened.

I push myself away from the counter and grab the broom to sweep up the hair on the floor. I need to do something to distract myself. "Did you call Miles about last night?" I ask.

"I called him this morning," he says. "I told him something came up and we couldn't stay the whole time."

"I'm sorry you weren't able to see him for very long." I dump the hair in the trash and push the chair back under the table.

"It's all right. I see him almost every week as it is, and hopefully it'll stay that way when school starts." Kale laughs to himself. "I'm sounding more like you every day."

"And what's that mean?"

"More optimistic."

"There's nothing wrong with hoping for the best." I don't want to admit it, but it's the only way I could get over what happened with Mom—hoping everything would turn out for the better. And so far, it has.

At least I think so.

Kale shrugs. "Sometimes there is when nothing turns out the way you want it to. There's less disappointment."

"Then what are you?" I ask, not wanting to argue with him.

"A realist," he says. "Things are the way they are, and always will be. I think I know that to be true more than anyone."

I can't argue that point because it is true. Kale knows first-hand that the past is what it is. I just wish he would look to the future as something more hopeful. But for him, it's something that's not.

"Have you ever tried to control it?" I ask. "Leaving, I mean."

Kale shifts his weight uncomfortably. "I've tried and I can't. When the time comes, it's too hard to stay."

"But you did last night," I counter.

"No, I delayed it. It's not something I can control."

"Maybe. But you stopped it this time, and maybe you can stop it again."

"Harper, it's impossible for me not to leave. It's a part of who I am. It's like telling Jayne from *Firefly* he can't ever touch

180

a gun again," he says, smiling. It's short lived, and he shakes his head. "Sometimes I wish it wasn't, but it's the way it is."

I could never imagine him being someone other than he is now. His bittersweet faults are what make him Kale. But I wish they wouldn't cause him so much trouble.

"When you were younger, you only left once or twice a month," I point out. "If it was possible then, maybe it's possible now. Think about it, Kale. If you didn't leave so often, you could go to school, and maybe even get a job. You could—"

"—be normal?" His tone is hard. "I'll never be what you call normal. I couldn't even finish school, so how am I supposed to find a job? At this point, I don't even know if I'll be able to move out when I'm old enough."

Kale takes a deep breath and stares out the far kitchen window. "Sometimes I think I don't belong here."

My heart flinches at hearing that. But the more I think about it, the more I know it isn't true. The truth behind Kale leaving so often has been right in front of me this whole time, and I haven't seen it before now, because I haven't *wanted* to see it.

I stand up a little straighter and uncross my arms. "No, you're just *afraid* to belong here."

Kale's eyes snap to mine. "What?"

"That's why you've been leaving so often. It's because you don't *want* to be here. Things aren't good between you and your dad and you feel like you don't have a purpose here. I get it, okay? I get being alone and not having a good relationship with a parent. But whether you want to believe it or not, you *do* belong here."

Kale throws up his arms half-heartedly. "Then tell me what to do. Tell me how to fix this." But he knows I don't have answers. "I want to try telling my dad again, it's just a lot harder when he doesn't believe me."

181

"So make him believe you."

"It's not so easy. I've always thought about traveling in front of him because it worked so well with Miles, but I want him to believe *me*. Not just believe what he sees. Is that so hard to ask?"

"I don't know . . . but once it happens, I think you'll find yourself staying here more often."

He just nods, and I have that urge to close the distance between us, but his mind is on other things now.

Kale takes a step toward the door. "I should get home." In other words, he wants to be alone.

Before he disappears out the door, I ask, "Do you want to come over for dinner tonight?" He hesitates. "If you're still here . . ."

Kale nods. "Sure. I'll see you later."

After his footsteps disappear off the porch, I slide down to the floor and sit there, unable to think of anything except Kale and wondering when I'll see him next.

27.
Kale

As I walk home, every step becomes harder than the last. Getting closer to having to face the truth. Maybe I've known all along and only now started to believe it, but Harper is right.

Me leaving so often is nobody's fault but my own. I leave because I don't want to be here.

Both Bryce and Dad are home since it's Saturday. I rarely know what day of the week it is because they all feel the same to me. But I know yesterday was Friday because of the show. Something I still don't want to think about.

I don't like the dreams I have. Even when I'm awake.

Making me colder and trying to take me away.

I rub my eyes with my forefinger and thumb, feeling a growing headache coming from somewhere deep. The only thing I can hope is that it's not too late to fix things. That I haven't totally screwed everything up.

The house is dark and quiet when I get inside, so I head upstairs, hoping to find Dad. But as I pass Bryce's room, my legs lock in place and I can only stare at him, and at what he's doing.

A large suitcase is open on his bed, half full with folded clothes. A couple of boxes are stacked next to his desk in an empty space where everything once was. His room no longer looks like his.

"What are you doing?" I can't stop staring because I don't want to believe what I'm seeing. To believe what it means.

Bryce turns from his closet and gives me a weird look—one that he only gives when he thinks I already know something. "I told you back in March, Kale. I got accepted into KU. You didn't think I was going to stick around here forever, did you?"

I open my mouth, but no words come out.

He did tell me.

It's one of those things you don't think of because it's so far away. But suddenly it's there, smacking you in the face before you've had the chance to look at the calendar.

"But that's not for another two months," I say, my voice becoming weaker with every word. "Why are you already packing?"

"Did Libby not tell you? She said she would." I shake my head and Bryce sighs, dropping his shirt on the bed. "I'm going early so I can find a job before classes start."

"But—"

"I thought you knew," Bryce says. He glances at me—saying he's sorry without actually saying it—putting more of a gap between us. Something that's been growing bigger and bigger over the years. He isn't supposed to leave until I've fixed things with us. Because if I don't, I'm afraid he'll never come back.

"Kale?" Bryce takes a concerned step forward. "Are you all right? You look sick."

I look up from the floor, ignoring my pounding heart and the cold chills running down my spine. "So, *now* you're concerned for me?" I ask, my tone nothing under sarcastic. "Maybe it's better that you leave. This way you won't have to worry about anyone but yourself."

His eyes narrow. "Don't do that."

"Do what? Tell the truth?"

Bryce shoots me a warning look. "Blame everything on me when it's your own fucking fault. Now tell me *that* isn't true, Kale. It's not my fault you leave. It's not my fault Dad doesn't believe you. So why do you have to make *me* feel guilty for finally getting out of here?"

I'm so cold I'm almost sure I'll disappear right before his eyes. "I'm sorry," I tell him, barely able to make the words come out. "You're right. Have a good life, Bryce."

I turn to go but he catches my arm. "Tell me what's really wrong. You used to tell me things—"

"That was before you stopped listening." He looks uncomfortable at that, so I continue, knowing I won't get another chance. "You were the first person to ever believe me and the first person to give up. You were supposed to be my brother, but you spent more time with your friends than with me. I'm not easy, I know. But don't forget who your family is, because they're the ones who will be there for you when nobody else is. I guess that's all I'm asking—don't forget about me once you're gone, okay?"

I walk down the hall toward my room.

He calls after me. "Kale!"

I lock my door, breathing so heavily my vision blurs and spins. I press my back against the wood and slide to the floor, doing everything not to cry. Seventeen-year-old boys don't cry. They don't. Not when they have a brother who would make fun of him, and a father who would call him weak.

Bryce knocks on my door.

I hear Dad coming up the stairs—asking Bryce what's going on.

"Kale, please," Bryce says. "Let me in."

"Kale?" It's Dad this time.

His voice his hard and I close my eyes. I can't will myself to stay because I don't *want* to stay.

There's more pounding on my door. I feel every one of them with my back pressed against it. Will they force their way in and find me gone? Or will they give up, not caring enough?

I don't get the chance to find out.

It's hard to believe the last time I was here, a bullet grazed my ribs. It feels like weeks have passed since then, and in reality it's only been five days.

And only one day since I've been back.

Yesterday, after I washed the blood from my jacket, I was able to hide the fact I'd been shot. The less questions, the better. A few of the guys swore they saw me go down, but after I assured them it was a near miss, nobody thought twice about it. Or me.

So again, like so many times before this one, I'm stuck in a foxhole. Waiting for my watch to come around, so I don't have to keep trying to fall asleep.

Boots crunch in the snow somewhere to my right, out of sight. They get louder until Perkins looks down at me, his satchel slung over his chest to keep his hands free. I can faintly make out the white and red band around his upper arm in the moonlight.

He jumps down into my hole and joins me. Pressing his back against the dirt with his shoulder against mine. It's always warmer on the nights he's here. Ever since Adams took a hit, the blond medic took it upon himself to fill his place.

I know Captain Price doesn't want two medics sharing the same hole—for obvious reasons—but I have no idea why he chose mine.

"Isn't it weird not carrying a gun?" I ask.

"Not really," he says, pulling out a pack of cigarettes. "I used to carry a 1911, but I decided it was extra weight I didn't need."

When he offers me one, I take it. Without hesitation. After he lights mine and stows his matches away, he takes his helmet off and puts it on his knee. His short blond hair glows dimly under the moon and the front sticks up from where his helmet pressed against it.

We smoke in silence for a few minutes.

"I heard you made PFC," he finally says.

"I don't know why," I admit. "I don't do much of anything."

"That's not true. You keep your head on straight more than anyone, and when all of us feel the same fear, you're not one to show it." He looks over. "You might not know it, but most guys here look at you and see more than *Private* Jackson. All they see is someone by the name of Ace. They see someone who'll cover their asses when a sniper's hiding somewhere they can't see. Someone who'll be there time and time again, never missing a shot."

I stare. Waiting for him to crack a smile to show he's kidding.

It never comes.

Perkins nods to himself, finally looking away and finishing his cigarette. "They see someone they can count on."

"You're full of shit," I tell him, shaking my head.

"Large words for a youngster like you." He flicks the butt of his cigarette into the dirt near his boots. "How old are you anyway?"

"Twenty."

"Like hell you are. How long ago did you sign up?"

"About four months now." I take one last drag. "It feels like a year."

"So how did you do it then?" he asks.

"Do what?"

"Enlist. Did you forge your father's signature or something?"

I laugh once and say, "Luck. Dumb luck."

He thinks I'm joking, but I'm serious.

Another pair of footsteps approaches our foxhole. Captain Price appears and smiles down at us. "Jackson, Perkins," he says. "Staying warm on this fine night?"

I smirk. "I thought you didn't make jokes, Captain."

"And I thought you never smiled, Jackson. It's good to see we're both wrong." He averts his attention from me. "Perkins, I heard you were low on supplies. Did you check around for everyone's aid kits?"

"I did this afternoon, sir. There wasn't much."

"All right, well head back into town and see if they have anything to spare before we move out tomorrow. And make sure you get enough. It may be your last chance."

"Yes, sir."

"If everything goes smoothly enough, you should be back before dawn." Captain Price turns to leave but pauses. "Actually. Jackson, why don't you go with him. I'll have Bentley take over your watch tonight."

"Yes, sir," I say.

Perkins puts on his helmet again and gives me a hand out of the hole. We silently make our way through the camp and past the line—if it can be called that. Out here in these woods, it's hard to know where the front is and where the Germans are.

I have to be more alert here, but it's good to be doing something different. It's better than keeping watch with cold feet and trying to sleep when I know I won't.

I have Perkins walk behind me since he's without a weapon, keeping my rifle pressed into my shoulder and pointed down.

We're both quiet until we reach the small town that has served as a drop point for the last week or so. A hospital was set up in the school where the wounded could be brought in from the front line and then evacuated. Perkins leads now, knowing the way better than I do.

A couple of soldiers walk by and call out to him. "Doc Dan, you back in town so soon?"

"Only to check up on that rash of yours," he says.

The soldier hesitates. "Rash?"

Perkins nods down. "Is it gone already?"

"I don't know what you're talking about." His eyes go wide, confused.

"You know, in theory, I heard it goes away faster if you stay away from any girls. Potentially, anyway. I wouldn't want to lie to you, though."

The soldier's friend laughs and he punches him in the arm. "Shut up, Kirk, it's not true."

Perkins laughs. "Take the joke as a man or don't take it at all, Johnson."

Kirk can't stop laughing.

Johnson finally lets a smile out and shakes his head. "Damn Doc, remind me never to get on your bad side." He finally notices me and nods, averting the unwanted attention off himself. "Who's this?"

"Private First Class Jackson. You might better know him as Ace."

To my surprise, recognition dawns over his face. "Yeah, I've heard of you. I also heard you're one hell of a shot."

I shrug. "I guess so."

"Well, you've got to be with a name like that." He tips his chin up at Perkins. "See ya around, Doc. Don't be going around starting any rumors."

Once they're out of earshot, Perkins laughs to himself.

"Sometimes I just can't help myself. Come on, let's get our stuff so we can get back."

A large stone building sits at the end of the street where a few more soldiers talk and smoke outside the door. They nod to us before we head down a wide pair of steps toward the basement. There are wounded men lying on every available bed and some sitting against the walls. All of them smelling of blood and sulfa powder.

I follow Perkins through the maze of beds and he's already talking with one of the other medics, listing off what he needs. Mostly morphine, bandages, sulfa powder, and plasma. Things he's constantly running out of.

There's yelling behind me and two soldiers come down the steps, carrying a man on a stretcher between them. Perkins is already there with the medic he'd been talking to, not giving a second thought about helping.

He's a different person here. When it comes down to someone's life, he doesn't take anything more seriously. His hands are already covered in blood with a pair of scissors between his fingers, cutting away the uniform. It's fascinating and frightening all at once.

I can't stay.

The scene unfolding before me reminds me too much of Adams.

I turn away and head back up the steps. The night is still cold and clear and thankfully quiet. In the far distance, mortars that can pass as thunder light the sky. I can still hear Perkins and the medic talking over the patient, trying to save him before it's too late.

He belongs here more than I ever will. And the reason I keep coming back here, over and over again, is something I have yet to find out. Do I belong here like he does?

Sometimes I'm not sure.

I almost don't want to go back home.

Bryce will be gone.

Dad will probably be even more closed off.

And I don't know what to think about Harper. She's constantly on my mind—her smile, the sound of her voice, the feel of her fingers on my back, and her lips—

I dig my last cigarette from my pocket and light up before I stop myself. As I exhale and draw it away, I stand there and stare at my shaking hands. I try to make them stop. It doesn't work.

"You ready, Jackson?"

I flinch and see Perkins standing next to me, carrying a small wooden box filled with supplies. Waiting for my response. I drop the cigarette and try to hide my shaking hands. "Sorry, yeah."

"You all right?"

I hesitate, almost wanting to tell him—anything, even if it's not the whole truth. Just something to lighten the burden. But I'm already nodding my head, so good at lying that it's become habit.

We walk back the way we came, a couple glass bottles clinking tonelessly in the box. "That guy you were helping," I start, "will he make it?"

"Looks like it. Are you sure you're all right?" he asks again. "You disappeared out of there pretty fast."

I glance behind us at the crooked building and recall its basement full of wounded. A beacon of death to those who are too far gone to make it. "Yeah, I'm fine, the smell of blood just gets to me. You're really good at that, you know." I nod behind us. "We're lucky to have a medic like you."

He doesn't reply right away. Just blinks a couple of times, processing. I've noticed that he does that a lot when he thinks before speaking. "I'm sorry I couldn't save Adams. I did everything I could, but . . ."

I shake my head and position my rifle now that we're in the woods again. "You shouldn't be sorry for something you didn't do. You weren't the one who sent that late mortar."

We're silent for a time until Perkins asks something nobody else has. "What are you going to do once the war is over? I've heard everyone else talking about it, but never you."

It's a common question among foxholes and campfires. Everyone enjoys looking to the future like they can already see themselves there. Away from this place.

"I don't know," I tell him. "I guess I haven't thought about it much. What about you? Are you going to keep doing the doctor thing?"

"No, probably not. I would be happy if I never saw another wounded person ever again. But that may be my only option."

I smile and look back at him. "Oh, come on. With a face like yours, you could become a model for one those romance novels."

"Why don't you shut your smart mouth and keep walking," he says, his mouth turning up. "But seriously, you've got to have some idea of what you're gonna to do."

I can only shake my head in response. It's hard to look into the future that far, while knowing nothing good will come from it. Because what I confessed to Harper about having nothing going for me can't be truer.

"I take one day at a time and see where it takes me," I tell him. "It's the only thing I can do right now."

"That doesn't seem like any way to live," he says behind me.

I take a long breath and say, "It's not."

28.
Harper

After dinner—which Kale never showed up to—Uncle Jasper and I retreat into the living room to watch whatever happens to be on television. Aunt Holly used to join us for the first ten minutes until she got bored, leaving the two of us laughing while she cleaned the kitchen or curled up in her chair to read her latest book.

Now, with the dishes already put away and dishwasher purring from the other room, we watch the remake of *True Grit* with bowls of ice cream in our laps, each of us in our respective chairs. It's been a quiet evening. We didn't talk much over dinner—just listened to the crickets outside and the bullfrogs in the distance. Even though it was a perfect summer night, neither of us felt like venturing outside.

And oddly enough, it was the first time we sat down for dinner since I got here. Subconsciously, we may have been avoiding it until now. Aunt Holly was the one who called us in for dinner each night, never missing a moment when we could all sit down together. She said it was against the law; there was no reason why we couldn't be together for one meal a day.

When Uncle Jasper came home and the smell of macaroni and cheese greeted him, he didn't say anything. He just stood in the doorway for a little while and then smiled. He paid some bills at the table while it cooked, and I kept looking at the clock, wondering when Kale would come over.

My eyes constantly wandered over to the point in the kitchen where we had kissed earlier that morning. I couldn't convince myself any longer that Kale was merely the boy the next door. I'm not sure if he ever was.

But when dinner was cooked and I set the plates on the table—forcing Uncle Jasper to move his papers aside—Kale had yet to appear.

"Are we expecting someone?" Uncle Jasper finally asked after I glanced at the clock again.

"Kale said if he was still here, he would come, but . . ." I glanced at the door once more before settling in my chair. "I guess he's gone." And I already missed him.

"He'll be back." Uncle Jasper dipped his head to catch my eye. "He always is. Remember that."

I watched him eat for a little while before starting on my own. And even though Kale was gone—more gone than anyone could ever be—I realized Uncle Jasper would always be there. He was someone I could count on.

The movie ends and the local news comes up next. Neither of us make a move to get up or do anything besides sit here. I keep waiting for Kale to walk through the door and make my heart jump, something I know won't happen for another few days. It's weird knowing he's in the past right now, nowhere to be found until he comes back.

"All right," Uncle Jasper says, muting the news anchor. "What is it?"

I look over. "I didn't say anything."

"No, but you've been thinking about something for the last ten minutes, and it's obviously not something good. So, come out with it, kid. What are you thinking about?"

"Kale and his dad."

Uncle Jasper leans away, nodding. "I see."

He un-mutes the news and continues watching.

"That's it?" I expected more.

"What else do you want me to say?"

I throw up my hands "I don't know. Maybe figure out a way to help him?"

After a long moment he finally turns off the television—all the way this time. "I know how hard it is not being able to do anything, but this really is between Kale and his dad. Kale needs to figure out who he is before anything can change."

"He admitted today it's his own fault for leaving so much," I tell him, thinking back to this morning in the kitchen. "I think he knew before now but never wanted to believe it."

Uncle Jasper nods while standing, going over to the window as though to watch Kale come up the driveway. "He leaves because of his father, but in doing so, he makes it worse on himself. It's been hard for him to realize that, after all this time. It's like admitting you're wrong after it's too late."

"When did it become this bad?"

"After Courtney left, I think that's when Kale started leaving more. He didn't want to be home because all it did was remind him his mom wasn't there, and he kept thinking it was his fault, like all kids usually do. Then he only had his dad to come home to, who was sick of putting up with something he didn't understand. Once Kale got expelled from school, that's when he really started to leave more often."

He gives me a weak smile before heading out the door and walking toward the barn, his shoulders tighter than usual. I finally take my leave and go upstairs to play Xbox until my eyes hurt, not wanting to think about anything else.

A couple days pass in a blur of helping Uncle Jasper, grocery shopping, and hanging out with Grace. Even now she sits on my bed playing *Battlefield* while I fold my laundry. She doesn't have the headset on, but she yells at the screen nonetheless like the other people will hear her. This one tank has killed her three times in a row, and she looks a bit crazed with her curly hair coming out of her ponytail.

After she dies for the fourth time, I suggest, "You should put C4 on the jeep and then drive it into the tank."

She turns and then says, "I *should* do that."

Once she beats her nemesis and turns off the game, she asks, "So what's going on between you and Kale?"

I pause the folding. "Do people really talk about this stuff?"

She shrugs. "*I* do."

"I don't know if there's anything to tell."

"Come ooooon," she drawls, "don't leave me hanging."

The phone rings downstairs and I smile, backing out of the room. "I should get that."

"We aren't done here."

I start downstairs even though I'm afraid it's Mom again—she hasn't called since last week, but it's something I'm having a hard time forgetting. But it also might be Kale. It's about that time now, so I decide to take the risk and go downstairs to answer it.

"Hello?"

"What's wrong with your voice?" Kale asks. "You sound like a mass murderer is trying to call you."

I smile, more than relieved it's not Mom. "You're back."

"I am." He sounds tired and my stomach feels weird when I hear his voice again. "Is Uncle Jasper home?"

I glance out the door, making sure the driveway is still empty. "No, he's been gone all day."

"Well," Kale says in a sad voice, "I guess that means you'll have to come and get me."

"That's a shame," I say, matching his tone.

"Tell me about it."

"Where do I pick you up?" I ask, trying to force my heart to stay calm. After Kale gives me directions, I leave Grace at her car with a list of questions and I'm driving away before I can tie my shoelaces.

My heart hammers as I drive with the windows down. I thought the wind would help calm my nerves, but I was wrong. I can't even focus on the music coming through the speakers. I had no idea one person could make me feel this way. So discombobulated and weird.

After twenty minutes of driving down roads lined with fields and hidden driveways, I catch sight of the Phillips 66 sign. I pull in and see Kale sitting on the curb near a pay phone covered in graffiti. He's wearing the same T-shirt from when I cut his hair, and it makes me wonder how long he lasted after I saw him. Hours or only minutes?

I pull up to the curb and Kale gets in. He looks more exhausted than he ever has. Along with his smell of rain and wind, the subtle hint of snow fills the car, something that should never happen in the middle of summer.

He glances at me and says, "Thanks for picking me up."

I nod and pull out of the small parking lot. My stomach won't settle now that he's finally sitting next to me. I don't understand how I was ever able to ride next to him and not be aware of his every move. I unsuccessfully try to focus on the road.

"So . . . how was it?" I ask, my voice unsure.

He leans back against the headrest and gives a tired shrug. "Fine. Good. I guess."

It's like I picked him up from work, and he doesn't want to explain his boring day. It's so Kale. I don't see what is good about anything where he came from. But I give him a questioning look anyway.

"It's just different," he says, his eyes glued to a point between us. "When I'm there . . . I feel needed. Wanted. I feel like I'm there for a purpose, even though I don't know what it is yet."

"And what about here?"

He raises his gaze and says, "I'm still trying to figure that out."

We ride a few miles in silence, listening to the wind and passing cars. Just when Kale seems like he's about to fall asleep, he lifts his head and looks over. "Have you named him yet?"

"Named who?"

He nods to the dashboard. "Your car. Every good car needs a name."

"I don't think that's a thing," I say, shaking my head and trying not to laugh.

"It is if I'm going to ride in an unnamed car."

"And you said 'him.' How do you know it's a boy car?"

Kale thinks about it for two whole seconds before breaking into a smile. "I don't."

I eye him doubtfully. "Besides, I'm horrible with naming things, so I probably shouldn't. I named our cat Blackie . . . because he was black." Kale laughs and I say, "It's not funny. That poor cat had to live with that horrible name for the rest of his life."

"Baby steps then," he says. "Pull over."

"Why?"

Kale grabs the handle of the door, threatening to jump out. "I swear, Croft. If you don't pull over right now, I'm going to jump out and very possibly die." Then he adds at the end, "And it'll be your fault."

I throw a glare and pull over on the dirt shoulder. Kale opens his door and gets out. "Come on."

I stare at him through the dirty windshield, unable to deny that smile. I cut the engine and get out, joining him in front of the car. He grabs my hand and pulls me a foot to the left. His skin is cold against mine, but he doesn't seem to notice.

"All right," he starts. "First thing you have to do is find out if it's a boy or girl."

"And how do I do this exactly?"

"Well, when you look at your car, what do you see?"

"Red."

"Come on, I'm serious." Kale moves behind me and whispers in my ear. "What's the first thing you think of?"

Butterflies tease the insides of my stomach, making it hard to concentrate on anything but Kale. "Well . . . it's a Rabbit, and when I think of rabbits, I always think of boy rabbits. Like the ones in *Watership Down*."

"So . . .?"

"So, I guess he's a boy car." I turn around and back away a step. "Which means he needs a boy name, which I cannot do him justice with." I sit down on the hood with a small sigh. "Why don't you just give him a name since you claim it's so easy?"

"No, no, no." He shakes his head. "Only the owner of the car can name it. But it's not something you have to do right away. Give it some time, it'll come."

Kale sits down next to me, putting his feet up on the bumper with his arms resting on his knees. The wind teases his hair and his eyes are more gray again today.

"What's the name of yours?" I ask, drawing up my knees. "If you're such an expert at this."

"His name is Dixon," he answers, matter-of-factly. "I know

he doesn't look like much now, but he'll be great once I take him to the body shop."

"Uncle Jasper said you put a lot of work into him, and if your dad knew that before he sold it, he would've gotten a lot more money."

There's a period of silence and I look over. Kale's eyes are downcast. "If only he knew me better," he says, but not like it's a good thing.

The field of grass next to the road moves with the wind, every blade rustling against its neighbor and creating the sound that puts me to sleep at night. "I really missed you these past couple of days."

"Really?" Kale's shoulders stay hunched, but he turns his head, studying me to make sure I'm not joking.

"Really. And I don't like the thought of you leaving again so soon."

He looks away. "Maybe I'll try to stay longer. Because you're right about what you said. I've thought about it a lot, since I can't sleep much at night. If I lasted as long as I did all those years ago, then maybe it *is* possible now." Kale pauses, his breathing seeming forced. "Because I can't keep doing this for much longer."

Every time Kale comes back, and with every new day I see him, there can't be anything more obvious. It's too much on him. He's being broken down, piece by piece. It hits me the hardest when I realize Kale could die at any time. War is unpredictable and deadly—one day, he could just not come back at all.

It needs to stop.

"Kale?"

"Yeah?"

I hesitate, knowing where it led last time. "You need to try telling your dad again."

He continues to stare out and over the field, his shoulders tight. "I know," he says. "I've been wanting him to see me for me. I just—I'm afraid he won't like who he sees."

"But he can't see you until you let him."

"I know." Kale finally looks over, even more tired than before. "That's what I'm afraid of."

I move over, closing the small space between us, and lean my head on his shoulder. He tenses at first, then everything within him seems to melt. We sit there on the hood of my car and watch the field sway under a fading sun that reminds me too much of past summers, dancing with every touch of breeze. I close my eyes and breathe in the smell of summer and Kale—with his hint of winter—memorizing it.

Almost like I'll never get to do it again.

29.
Kale

"Just drop me off here," I say as Harper pulls up to my drive-way.

"Are you sure?" She slows down and keeps the engine idling. It's almost dark now. The lights from the house are hazy from across the field. My heart speeds up with one look at it, knowing what I'm about to do. "Kale?"

I look over. "Yeah?"

Harper has her worried face on—one I've seen countless times over the years. Before jumping from the high dive at the public pool. When I told her I might've broken my arm when I jumped off the roof because that's just what boys do. Or when we got stuck out in the rain and it thundered.

I wonder if she's still scared of storms.

She asks, "Are you going to be all right?"

I nod, trying to find the courage to talk. "I'm going to tell him tonight. About everything. Because you're right—I think it's my only chance to stop this, even if it doesn't work out in the end. He'll either kick me out for good, or . . . I don't know." I look down at her Chuck Taylors—almost becoming untied again—ignoring the tight coils in my stomach, which are a constant reminder of what I'm about it do. I stare at the house again. "But I have to try. I don't want to be afraid to be me."

I hear Harper shift in her seat. When I turn, she's leaning across the center console, looking at me with soft eyes. She smells like fresh laundry. It gives me the urge to touch her. To feel how soft her skin is, only to make sure it wasn't a dream last time.

She reaches out and grabs my shirt, pulling me toward her. I don't even have time to breathe before she kisses me. Something I can't even think about once I feel her lips. I grip the edges of my seat, shutting down a moment of instinct. It takes everything for me not to do something more.

Harper pulls away and lets go of my shirt.

"Don't be afraid to be you," she says.

My heart pounds and my mouth feels dry, so I just nod and get out of the car. I stand by my mailbox and watch her drive away. Now that she's gone and the memory of the kiss fades, the tight coils return to my stomach.

I turn and head up the driveway.

I walk into the house, expecting him to be in the living room or maybe the kitchen, but he's nowhere. The only light on is the one by the front window, leaving the rest of the rooms dark. It's so quiet without Bryce here.

"Dad?"

Nothing but silence greets me.

Something doesn't feel right, but I don't know what. I survey the room, trying to find any hints of where he could be or what happened.

An empty beer bottle sits on the coffee table. I head toward the kitchen, flicking lights on as I go. I open the fridge.

There's nothing but an empty case of beer. I think I know where he went.

"Shit."

After I slam the fridge shut, I run upstairs and find my keys sitting on my desk. I pull on my sweatshirt, still feeling the chill of winter. Once I get outside again, I notice his truck isn't in the driveway. Something I should have noticed before but didn't, only focused on what would happen once I got inside.

I should have seen the signs before now. Subtle, they may have been, but still there for me to see. Stressed out about work and watching sports. He only watches them when he's got a bet going.

Once I'm on the road, I'm blind to any speed limit signs. I take corners too fast and pass in no-passing zones. One hand grips the steering wheel tight and the other one on the gear stick, my foot slamming the clutch without thought. The car thrives at this speed.

My family would've been better off without me—that's all I can think about. Over and over. Everything I've done wrong, and all the times I left them without telling the truth.

I want to make it right with the only person I have left. Before it's too late.

I pull into the bar's parking lot and kill the engine with the tires screeching to a halt. I don't even think. I shove my keys in my pocket and head for the door, not at all ready for what I might face. Only knowing I need to make it right.

The moment I open the door, a rush of noise fills the night. I step inside and stand there, trying to decide if I did the right thing by coming here. The bar is packed with people watching a basketball game and filling the air with cigarette smoke. In the back—near the restrooms and a couple making out—a crowd of people are cheering on someone playing an arcade game.

I tentatively step forward just as a cocktail waitress walks by me. She takes one glance and stops me with her palm up, her other hand holding a tray of empty glasses.

"Are you over twenty-one?" she asks, the tone of her voice telling me she already knows the answer.

"I'm just looking for my dad."

"Sorry, kid. Can't be in here unless you're twenty-one." She tries to get the attention of the guy standing behind the bar, probably wanting to throw me out.

I hold out my hand, attempting to stop her. "Please . . . I only want to find my dad. I'm not here to drink."

The skin on her forehead softens and she takes a look around. Debating. "All right, you have five minutes. And you don't want me to see you in here a minute past that."

"Thank you." I start to move around her but she stops me.

"What's your dad's name?" she asks.

"Peter Jackson."

She raises an eyebrow, starting to regret even talking to me. "Peter Jackson, like the director?" She points to the door. "Get out."

"No, I'm serious." I start to worry when I see one of the bartenders coming over. "Please, ask anyone who's worked here for a while. I'm not lying to you."

The bartender approaches, eyeing me like I might cause trouble. "Having a problem?"

The girl answers. "Do you know anyone named Peter Jackson? This kid says it's his father's name."

"Oh, yeah. I know Peter." He glances over the heads of people and points down the bar. "He's down there at the end."

He leaves and the cocktail waitress shakes her head. "Sorry. I really thought you were making that up."

"It's okay. It's not the first time," I tell her.

She finally moves away, holding up her hand with her fingers splayed. "Five minutes," she mouths.

Walking from one end of the room to the other is harder than it seems. With people moving to and from the bar, others playing drinking games that exceed their table's limits, people blindsiding me on their way to the bathroom—including two girls with uncanny high heels—I'm lucky to get through unscathed.

I finally catch a glimpse of Dad.

He's sitting at the end, his eyes staring at the television above the bar.

There's a half-empty pint of beer within the folds of his hands. I can tell he isn't drunk yet. It takes a lot more than a few beers to do that.

"Dad?"

His head twitches—hearing something he wasn't expecting. When he turns around and his features soften when he sees me, I don't know what to think.

His eyes trail down to my feet and back up again. Everyone cheers at something that happened on the television, but he doesn't take his eyes off me. Like he's afraid I'm going to disappear.

"You came back," he says.

He doesn't say "you're here" or "what do you want?"—things I'd been expecting. I'd never considered hearing "you came back," like I had no intention of doing so. It throws me off.

"Of course I did." My forehead creases without my doing. I glance at the beer between his hands. Just when I'm about to say we should go home, everyone yells and boos at the game. Dad turns his head, looking up.

"Shit," he mutters. He pulls a few bills from his pocket and slaps them on the bar. He stands up and takes one last drink. "Come on, we have to get out of here."

"Dad—" I look from him back to the basketball game. "Tell me you didn't." His jaw tightens as he shakes his head, more to himself than to me. It's as though the moment Bryce left, his promise to mom wasn't valid anymore. "Let's just go home, okay?" I tell him.

"The faster the better," he says, moving in the direction of the door.

Halfway there, the cocktail waitress walks up, holding two beers in one hand. "Did you find him?"

I watch him walk out the door and nod. "Yeah, I did. Thank you."

"Good. Just don't come back until you're twenty-one." She smiles and moves off.

I take a deep breath and head for the door. Once I'm outside, where the noise is cut off and the smell of smoke diminished, I see Dad isn't alone. There are two guys on either side of him, another talking close to his face—one arm completely covered in tattoos.

I stop short. "Dad?"

All faces turn to me and Dad takes a step forward. One of the men grabs his arm to stop him. "Kale, just go. I'll meet you back at the house."

"No, no, let him stay," the tattooed man says, eyeing me from under the dim street lamp. It casts a yellow tinge over his skin. "Kale, is it? Do you have the same bad habits as your old man here?"

The second man holds Dad's other arm, restraining him even more. Dad says, "Derek, please, just leave him alone."

"I don't know, Peter." The man—Derek—looks at Dad and back at me. My feet are glued in place. "Maybe this is the only way for you to understand how serious I am. Tell me, Kale. Do you also run away from things you can't handle?"

The question hits me harder than if he'd hit me in the stomach. Because even though he doesn't know anything about me—obviously referring to running away over losing some bets—he's asking about the very thing I've been trying to ignore.

The fact I've been running away my whole life.

I catch my father's eye over his shoulder. Unable to say anything.

I can't deny it.

But my father hasn't run away from me, so I'm not going to run away from him. Even if he's made mistakes like I have.

"You don't have to do this," Dad says, trying to get his attention focused on him again. "I'll get you the money."

Derek turns his head ever so slightly, not taking his eyes off me. He steps closer to me, within arm's reach. "I know you will. But maybe this will remind you not to make bets you can't pay out on. You know better."

A shiver runs up my arms despite the sweatshirt.

It's summer.

I shouldn't be cold.

I just got back.

Before I can prepare myself, Derek's fist lands hard into my jaw. I stumble back with my vision dark, catching my balance so I don't fall. Blood pounds hard in my ears, every throb digging into my head. He doesn't stop. He brings his fist down again, hitting me in the temple and then again in my jaw.

Fight back, Kale.

Gathering every spark of anger within me is easier than I ever thought. Because it's already there. Just waiting for me to take hold of it.

Before he has the chance to make another hit, I spin

upward, catching him off guard. My fist slams into his jaw and then again in his stomach. I ignore my aching knuckles and throbbing head. I can only focus on what his next move will be.

I don't care if I lose as long as I fight.

Just like being in the midst of war, I use my fear to make my head clear and my thoughts quick. It doesn't help that he outweighs me by one-hundred pounds and has more experience fighting than me. It only brings my thoughts to a better place.

After I take another hard hit, I'm on the ground. My palms pressed against the asphalt with my head hanging low. I taste blood and spit it out. The edges of Derek's boots stop next to me. I can't breathe, so I can't move.

He hooks one hand under my belt and uses the other to grab the back of my sweatshirt, throwing me farther into the parking lot, where I'm finally brought down.

Even though I lost, it felt good to fight back.

Over where Dad is, the sounds of a scuffle breaks the night air and he rushes toward me—one man trying to stop him and the other already bleeding—when he stops abruptly. He's breathing heavy with rage.

I don't know why he stopped until I look up.

Derek has a barrel of a black gun pointed at me. Only inches away from my head.

"You move, he dies," he says. "Don't think I won't."

My cheek is pressed against the uneven pavement and my body weighs down like there's lead in my veins. I'm not sure if I have the strength to get up.

Derek is talking to Dad again, words I no longer hear or care to be a part of. Everything is spinning and it won't stop.

The gun is still pointed at me. I can feel it.

There's an uncomfortable lump between my hip and the ground. It triggers something I almost wish it hadn't.

It's my car keys.

I shift my eyes and see it parked barely twenty feet away.

"Wait," I say, my voice cracking, barely loud enough to grab his attention. But he stops talking and looks down at me. Maybe he'll shoot me before I can even speak again.

"You have something to say, kid?" he asks.

Somewhere inside me, in a place I didn't know existed, I find the reserve strength to push myself up far enough to lift my head off the ground, though it's pounding with too much blood. I close my eyes briefly and breathe out slow, willing the pain to stay inside of me.

"Take my car," I say, finally opening my eyes.

He looks at me like I'm a waste of his time. "Which one is it?"

I nod in the direction, unable to move my arms.

"That little Fastback piece of shit?" he asks, grinning like it's a joke. "Nice try kid, but I'm not stupid."

He starts to turn and I say, "Just look under the hood."

Derek only hesitates for a second before motioning to one of the guys behind him. He's the one who's bleeding, blood still dripping from his nose. He crouches over me, roughly patting down my pockets until he finds my keys.

As I stare down at the asphalt, I hear the familiar squeak of the hood as he lifts it. I can't bear the thought of them driving away in it. I look up in time to see the man smile and nod to Derek, shutting the hood and spinning the keys around his finger.

"Huh, I didn't see that one coming," he says happily. He lowers the gun and backs away toward my car. He glances at Dad. "Make sure I don't see you again, Jackson."

Then they're gone. Taking two cars with them instead of one.

I feel like I might hurl.

Dad approaches me carefully—like he's not sure he should be near me—and helps me up on the curb, where I hang my head between my knees and watch the blood drip down. I feel him next to me—tense, not knowing what to do.

I don't know what to do either.

When he tries to touch my head, I brush him away. "Don't," I say. "Just leave it."

"You're hurt." Dad rubs a hand over his face, his gaze settling on me after looking everywhere else. "This will never seem like enough, but . . ." He's struggling to say the words. "I'm *so* sorry, Kale." A strangled sound comes from his throat, and his eyes are wet with tears.

I've never seen my dad cry before. Not ever.

Dads are supposed to be invincible. They're supposed to be a rock through hard times and be strong when no one else is. But life throws punches to even the strongest people.

He continues, "I've made mistakes in my life, but never one as big as not trying harder with you and then putting you in danger tonight." He turns his head, and I can see the shine in his eyes. "And I didn't realize it until I saw you standing in the bar tonight. After Bryce left a few days ago, it suddenly hit me that my entire family had left me. And I was sure that you did, too. I didn't think you were coming back, and I could only blame myself for that."

For what everything is worth, I can't be mad at him for the way things turned out between us. He's human, just like me. We've both made mistakes and have to live with them.

I'm in need of a second chance as much as he is.

"But I always come back," I remind him. I never knew until

211

now how important it was to him that I did. "And I always will. You know that."

"You're right, you do," he says, attempting to smile. "I think people make bad decisions when they're scared. And for me, I was scared you wouldn't come back. I wondered every morning if I would see you again. Why *did* you keep coming back?" His jaw flexes and his eyes roam the night, maybe looking at something I can't see. "I don't deserve you, Kale."

His eyes search me—asking.

"Because you're my dad. And this is my home." My jaw throbs in pain when I talk. I try to ignore it and the reason it came to be. "I still remember when we used to play catch in the back field—especially in the late evening when the mosquitoes were the worst. And when I helped you with the truck when it broke down, even though I didn't know a thing back then. I hold onto those things, because I want to believe we can be like that again."

I look away, unable to meet his gaze when I tell him something I never thought I would again. Something I *have* to tell him, because if I don't now, I might not ever.

"I came home tonight wanting to talk to you," I say. "About why I've been leaving so often."

He's silent next to me, and I need him to believe me so badly. But I'm not sure if I know the right words to say.

"You know what, I'm going to stop you right there," he says, and I feel like nothing is ever going to change between us and he'll never believe me. Then he says something else—"Bryce talked to me before he left." Dad looks at me hard, making sure I'm listening. "He told everything you've been trying to get me to believe for the past ten years. And I'm so, so sorry I didn't take your word for it, Kale. Trust me, I almost didn't believe him, either, but then he starting telling me these stories nobody could make up."

My thoughts take a moment to catch up and understand what he just said. Bryce told him? I can't believe he did it. Especially after how I left things between us. But maybe that's why he did—his way of apologizing.

I shake my head. "So . . . you really believe me? For real?"

He nods. "I really do. Doesn't seem possible, but that's who you are, isn't it? Someone who does the impossible."

"No, I'm just kid who can't control the one thing he *does* have."

All the stress I've had is suddenly gone. Dad knows. He knows, and he seems okay with it. Right now, even if it's for this small moment, everything else doesn't matter.

Dad says, "So these last few days, you've been—"

"In the past," I finish, unable to hold back my smile. "Sounds crazy, right?" I reach inside my shirt for my dog tags and pull them over my head. When I hand them to Dad, he tentatively takes them, rubbing his thumb over the indented letters. He stares at them for the longest time.

Then he looks up and says, "I think it's safe to say I didn't see this coming." He gives my dog tags back. "My grandfather had dog tags just like those. I used to look at them while he told his old war stories." Dad pauses. "I'm sorry you've been having to go through this alone, but you're not alone anymore. Okay? You can talk to me whenever you need to."

I've been waiting to hear those words for years, and I lean in to hug him in response, my throat choked up too much to talk. Another thing I've been waiting to do for a long time.

"Thanks, Dad."

He nods. "As you can imagine, I have more questions for you. But they can wait for later."

He helps me to my feet and we climb into his truck. I've never felt so tired in my life. Not just from the beating I took, but for the relief I have now that he knows. I might even be able to sleep tonight.

Dad puts the keys in the ignition but doesn't start the engine right away. He's looking at the empty parking space where my car no longer is. "I've really made a mess of things, haven't I? You could've been killed tonight. It's not something you ever have to forgive me for."

"I could say the same thing." I give him a small, encouraging smile even though losing my car has a bigger impact than he knows. I'm just not ready to think about it yet. I dug a hole and buried it the moment it happened.

30.
Harper

Breakfast the next morning is a quiet one. We speak a little about Kale talking with his Dad last night and wondered how it went. Uncle Jasper has to be somewhere in ten minutes and I have plans—well, to play video games with my BBFF (*Battlefield* Best Friend Forever), but neither of us has moved.

We both sit up when Kale slips through the door. My heart stumbles. The door closes and he stands there, trying to put on his best smile despite his bruises and cuts on his face.

"What the hell, Kale?" Uncle Jasper stands from the table, an expression on his face I've never seen until now. He's angry. Uncle Jasper says, his voice low and serious, "This has gone too far."

"It wasn't him."

Uncle Jasper stops but is on the cusp of walking out the door. "You better tell me who did it then."

Uncle Jasper doesn't take his eyes off Kale, waiting. Kale shoots me a quick glance and then sits down, having trouble looking at Uncle Jasper. I would, too, if the situation were reversed. Uncle Jasper is usually so relaxed and carefree; I've never seen him so determined before.

"You better start talking," he says, slowly lowering himself into his chair.

Kale takes a deep breath and tells his side of what happened last night. About how he came home and his dad wasn't there, and how he found him at the bar. Uncle Jasper's jaw tightens even more when he hears about Kale's dad betting on the basketball game. He must know he used to have problems with that before, even though I had no clue.

Kale stares at the table and tells us what happened in the parking lot. Before and after how his face got to be the way it is. When he opens his mouth to tell us what happened after that, he hesitates, and then closes it.

He lifts his steady gaze from the table and says, "Bryce told Dad before he left, so I didn't have to tell him much. The bottom line is, he believes me." He shrugs it off like it's not a big deal even though I know it is. He's been waiting for his dad to believe him his whole life.

Kale looks between us, waiting for some sort of reaction.

Uncle Jasper finally speaks up. "Why did they leave?"

"Who leave?"

"The guys your dad owed money to. You just said 'after they left.' How did he get them to leave?"

Kale struggles to answer this one, swallowing hard and looking away. "I gave them my car as payment."

"Your—" Uncle Jasper has trouble ending the sentence. He clears his throat and attempts to act calm. "They took your car?"

He nods and Uncle Jasper abruptly stands. "Where are you going?"

"I have some business to conduct." Then he says to me, "I'll be back later."

Uncle Jasper leaves and the house is quiet save the clock ticking above the sink.

"You haven't said a word since I got here," Kale says. I look up to see him already staring at me from across the table.

216

"That's because I don't know what to say. . . . How does it feel having your dad know?"

Kale smiles—dimple showing—and leans back in his chair. "Better than I ever thought it would be. It's like this weight has lifted and I can breathe again." His gaze focuses on something between us, something I can't see. "I really feel like it's going to be okay between us. For a while, I didn't think it would ever be possible."

"But now it is," I say.

"Yeah, now it is." Another smile shows.

For weeks after seeing Kale unhappy and so unlike himself, he's finally becoming more and more of the boy who I remember. Not the same, because after the things he's been through, there's no way he could be, but he's becoming something even more than that. He's becoming the person he was meant to be. "Do you think this will change things? With your time-traveling, I mean."

"I don't know, but I hope so. I guess we'll find out. It would be nice to spend more than four days here at a time." He leans forward, putting his elbows on the table. "Who knows? Maybe I'll get to know the girl next door a little better. I heard she's a lot different than she used to be."

"Does this mean you'll be able to take me on a date now?" I try not to show how hard my heart pounds when I smile back.

"Is that a yes?"

Kale and I haven't said a word about whatever it is that's going on between us.

And I have no idea what to do. The closest thing I've had to a boyfriend was in fifth grade when a kid named Jeremy pulled on my ponytail under the yellow slide. I'm crossing into unknown territory with a reckless heart, ready to take a step toward something new.

"Yes," I start, wincing a little, "but I don't know how good I'll be at this."

"Like I'll be any better? The girls at my school wouldn't even look at me."

"I don't know, you seemed like you knew what you were doing last week." I bite the inside of my lip to keep myself from smiling any wider. I have to force myself from looking down at his lips—even when there's a cut running across the bottom one, I still want to kiss them.

Something flickers across Kale's face, too fast for me catch. "Are you sure this is okay? Me and you?"

Every second of silence that passes between us feels like forever, and the table separating us is a mile too wide. I can't bear it anymore. My feet touch the tiled floor and I walk around to the other side of the table. I bend down, softly touching the side of his face, and kiss him. His jaw moves under my fingers and he leans into me, his lips matching with mine. I slowly pull away, going against every fiber within me.

Kale looks up with eyes I know too well, his lips still wet from mine.

"Is that enough of an answer for you?" I ask.

"I'd say it's more than enough." Then he smiles—a real one this time that I can't help but return.

I sit down in Uncle Jasper's empty chair, still wishing the cuts and bruises on his face would disappear. "At least you'll be okay in a few days, right?"

"Should be." Kale's smile fades and he absently picks at his sleeve. "It feels weird that the only thing I have to worry about now is trying to control my traveling. It feels good, though. Like I'm finally moving on." He steals a quick glance from downcast eyes, not able to hold my gaze. He used to do that all the time when we were kids when he didn't want to admit something. "Sometimes I wake up thinking maybe I'm not the only one like this, and it makes me feel more normal. That there are others out there who struggled with the same thing or still are."

I lean in with my elbows on the table. "Kale, you don't have to feel normal, because you're better than normal. I know you hate the fact that you aren't, but without it, you wouldn't be you. *This* makes you, you."

He finally lifts his eyes—committing this time. "And that's a good thing?"

I can't imagine him being anyone different. "A very good thing. Plus, it'll probably make dates more interesting once you can control it."

"What do you mean?" His question sounds too serious.

"I mean your time-traveling. Dates in this time will be fun, too, but—" When his eyes become hard, I know I've said something wrong. "What?"

"Harper, you can't—" Kale takes a deep breath and stands up too fast. He walks over to the sink and grips the edge of the counter. A blue vein laces the swell of his bicep. After taking a deep breath, he says, "I'm sorry, it's just . . . even if I can control it someday, I'm not sure if I'll ever be okay with taking someone with me." He stares down at the sink, his shoulders drawn tight. "If you ever went with me to the past, and something happened and we got separated . . ." Kale turns around and his chest raises and falls with forced breaths. "You could be stuck there forever. Okay?"

I stand up, keeping close to the table. I can't imagine a worse outcome than being stranded in some past time, not ever able to go home again. The possibility never crossed my mind, but now that he's said it, it's so obvious. "Can you even take anyone with you?"

"I'm not sure, but I don't want to find out." Kale reaches out for my wrist and draws me closer. "But I won't ever let that happen. I'm always careful so nobody is around when I think I'm going to leave. It's a mistake I'll never make."

I nod, still imagining myself gone from here forever. I wonder if this is how Kale feels when he leaves. Does he ever worry he won't come back at all? He already told me he did once, but I never knew what that would feel like until now. It's a frightening thought.

There's nothing more I want than for Kale to learn to control his time-traveling, for him to have a chance at a normal life. But even if he can't, my feelings for him won't ever change. He's Kale, and he always will be. Flaws and all.

31.
Kale

Three days pass and I don't feel any different.

I feel anchored here more than I have in years.

I've gone to Harper's house every day, but every day I've been stuck working with Uncle Jasper in his garage. I don't complain, and I don't try to get out of it when he asks me to help him. Harper and I haven't done anything in front of him that might've tipped him off about what's going on between us, but I think he already knows.

And I think he's doing it on purpose.

Just to see how long we can last before we slip up in front of him.

So between working with Uncle Jasper during the day, and spending time with Dad in the evenings when he gets home from work—since he's been persistent about having dinners together now—I've barely talked to Harper at all.

I've seen her sitting on the porch. I've seen her come and go from her car at least once a day. Hanging out with Grace.

Once in a while, she'll come visit us in the barn. Harper will sit on the old couch and flash me smiles when Uncle Jasper isn't looking. I make more mistakes when she's here.

It's hard acting normal with her because it *isn't* normal with her.

We're passed normal.

Now it's my fourth day stuck in Uncle Jasper's garage, and I'm determined to escape when he's not looking. Unfortunately, he seems set on keeping an eye on me.

"How 'bout those Royals last night, eh?" he says from under his latest project.

It's a 1975 Mustang. And it looks too much like my own car for me to look at it long without creating an ache in my heart. Dad promised me he'd make it up to me. Something I don't see possible.

"Yeah . . . sure," I finally mumble, leaning against the car.

I flip a wrench over in my hand absently.

Top to bottom. Top to bottom.

Uncle Jasper keeps talking about the game last night and how the Royals are looking like they'll make it into the post-season. Something he's very proud of. Enough to keep him talking for so long.

The faint sound of the front door closing echoes across the lawn. I look up in time to see Harper stepping off the porch. I stand up a little straighter and watch her as she heads for her car.

Uncle Jasper's voice is background noise.

I say "uh huh" when he pauses, and he keeps going, unfazed.

I silently take a couple steps forward and catch Harper's eye. The corners of her mouth turn up when she sees me. She's about to yell something from across the yard so I hold my finger up to my mouth, motioning for her not to talk.

Then I mouth "Save me" and point back to Uncle Jasper, whose legs still stick out from under the car. Harper catches on quick. She holds up one finger and points to her car. I nod and glance back at Uncle Jasper.

"—really think they could make it this year. And I'm not just saying that."

Harper gets into her car and gently pulls her door shut.

"That's what you said last year," I say over my shoulder, ready to make my escape.

Just when Harper gives me the signal, Uncle Jasper starts rolling himself out. I make a break for it. Harper starts the car as I'm running across the lawn. Uncle Jasper shouts my name from behind.

My heart races, but I'm grinning as I open the passenger side door and jump in. Harper gives Uncle Jasper a friendly wave as she swings around the driveway. He stands in the large doorway with his arms crossed, shaking his head.

I'm not blind enough to miss the smallest smile touching his lips.

We finally won his game.

Once we're on the main road, my heart starts to calm to its normal rhythm. Or whatever that rhythm could be called when I'm around Harper.

I look over and say, "Hi."

The breeze from the window blows loose hair across her face as she looks over. "Hi."

"So where are we going?" I buckle my seat belt and hang my arm out the window. I'm not cold today. I haven't been since I got back.

Harper slips on her sunglasses and shifts gears. "We're going to the grocery store. We ran out of bread, which is some-thing of a tragedy in the house, as you know. Sorry it couldn't be more of an exciting trip for you."

"I don't care as long as I'm out of that garage. Plus . . ." I steal the chance to look at her while her eyes are on the road. Even now, I can't believe things turned out the way they did. Harper—the girl who lived next door every summer when we were younger, and the girl I've never been able to forget—is sitting next to me now, making the summer warmer and my blood run fast. "Plus," I start again, "as long as you're there, it doesn't matter where we go."

Harper grins. "That was really corny." She pauses and looks over. "But I like it."

Even when I look away, I can feel myself smile. The familiar fields and houses pass by. The gas stations and empty lots. Even though I've driven down these roads countless times in my life, it feels different today. Newer. I haven't felt this happy in months.

I keep waiting for something to take it away.

"I'm sorry about your car," Harper says when she stops at a stoplight.

I stare ahead at the traffic waiting in front of us, trying not to think too deeply about the fact I'll never see it again. The bruises and cuts on my face have healed over the last few days.

I wish I could say the same about what I lost.

I turn the subject around in a way she doesn't notice. "Have you named yours yet?"

The light turns green. "No, but I will. I promise," Harper says after she sees my unconvinced look. "Naming things is hard."

I give a skeptical look. "I think it's just you."

She pulls into the parking lot of the grocery store and finds an empty space. We've never been here by ourselves before. It was always with Aunt Holly, or Bryce when my parents would send him to get something. Libby would rarely tag along, but we would.

So, like it was all those years ago, Harper and I are here again.

Just the two of us this time.

We pass through the sliding doors where the dry air of the

air conditioning battles against the hot air from outside. The beeps from the checkout lines echo through the store. There are only two cashiers on duty—proof of the small town.

Harper has already grabbed a cart and is making her way over to the meat department. I'm about to follow her before a couple of book titles catch my eye, claiming to have time-traveling in them. I haven't read a book in years, but I miss it. Leaving the books without seeing what they're about, I catch up to Harper and do my best to walk up quietly behind her. Her hair is in a ponytail, pulled over one shoulder and leaving the back of her neck exposed. I can't stop looking.

"Does Uncle Jasper like pork or sausage more?" she asks, tilting her head back toward me.

"How did you know I was here?"

Harper places a package of pork chops in the cart, already knowing the answer. "Maybe you aren't the only one with a superpower."

My smile fades. "Don't call it that. Please."

"If it's not that, then what is it?" She waits for my answer with her eyebrows raised.

I can't count how many times I've wished I was normal, though I know some people would do anything to have what I have. But all I want is for it to go away.

"An inconvenience," I answer.

I push the cart for her down the mostly empty aisles. Harper doesn't say anything else, but I know she's thinking—she's biting one corner of her lip and her eyes roam the shelves, not really seeing anything.

An old country song plays over the store radio and people pass by, pushing their carts with squeaky wheels. The lights overhead need replacing. This place hasn't changed since I was born.

"If you could go to school for something, what would it

225

be?" Harper asks, stopping in front of the shelf of canned soups.

"I don't know—I haven't thought about it." Why would I? I'll never be able to go to school unless I learn to control my *inconvenience*. With it as it is, the future has never been my top priority.

"You've got to have some sort of idea." She glances from over her shoulder. "What were you best at in school?"

I smile jokingly. "History."

"What about being a history teacher?" There isn't an ounce of sarcasm in her voice.

"You're serious."

She's still staring at the canned soup. "Why wouldn't I be? Give me one reason why you wouldn't be a great history teacher."

I open my mouth.

And no words come out.

I've never thought of myself in any other place except where I am now—it's never been possible. I don't like dwelling on things that might never happen. There's less disappointment later on. For years, I wanted to graduate with a baseball scholarship, because that's what I loved. When that was taken away, I never felt more lost. So now when she's asking me about my future, I don't have an answer.

"What soup are you looking for?" I step forward, grateful for a store full of distractions.

"Cream of mushroom," she says. "I swear, looking for the right kind of soup is almost as bad as looking for a certain spice."

I grab the can off the shelf and place it in her hand. "Come on, Sherlock."

We roam the rest of the aisles slowly. Harper doesn't need many things; we're mostly killing time before we have to go

226

back. I want to reach for her hand, but I'm afraid to. I want to kiss her again, but I don't know how.

I follow Harper down the frozen food aisle. Most of the glass doors are fogged up from people opening them, and a few of the lights are burned out. We stop somewhere in the middle while Harper tries to decide which frozen vegetables to get.

My mind keeps going back to what she said near the soup. About the possibilities of having a life I never thought I would. About becoming something more. If I can control my ability, I'll actually have a chance at a life.

It's something to think about. I've tried to control it so many times before that I've grown used to the idea of never being able to.

Harper opens the freezer door and a rush of cold air trails up my arms. Raising the hair along my neck and causing a shiver to trace my spine.

I flinch from something unseen, my muscles already stiff.

It's happening. I can feel it.

The white, shining floor turns to snow. A growing patch of red surrounds my feet, soaking me with Adams's blood. Urging my heart to beat faster.

It's not real.

It's not.

It's not.

When I close my eyes, all I can see are the woods. All I can hear are the gun shots and mortars. The screams.

I don't want to be there.

Not now when everything is going so well.

I force my eyes open, hanging on to the reality around me. I'm afraid to look down and see red, and my heart won't stop pounding.

There's no blood on the floor.

It's not real.

Harper turns around, her mouth moving with words I can't understand. She hasn't noticed anything wrong yet. I don't want her to.

But it's so cold.

So cold.

Her eyes catch mine and her sentence is cut short. My chest heaves too fast. My eyes fill with of a fear only I can feel.

"Kale." Her hand is on my face, her skin warm against mine. "Stay with me."

I'm afraid if I relax my jaw, it'll shake.

So I only nod.

Harper looks down the aisle. It's empty. "Maybe you should sit in the car while I check out. You'll warm up faster."

I nod again and force my legs to move.

"Just don't leave," she says behind me. "Promise?"

I turn back to her, pushing my mind to better places so my skin will unfreeze.

"I'll try," I tell her.

I don't make promises I can't keep.

I sit in the passenger seat of Harper's unnamed car, soaking in the heat coming through the windshield. I watch people load their groceries and fight their children into their car seats.

My arm hangs outside, feeling the hot waves roll off the black pavement.

I'm still cold.

It's set deep in my bones, slowly leaving with every passing minute.

I don't understand why I was so eager to leave all those

times before this. When I couldn't stand being in the house with Dad. Couldn't stand being *anywhere* but here.

Only a week ago, I couldn't decide where I belonged.

I have little doubt now—with me and Dad making it better between us, and Harper . . . I do belong here. But I know I have to keep going back in time. Because somehow—in ways I don't understand and probably never will—I belong in those places, too.

I try to think about the reasons I went to certain times before but none of them seem as significant as a war. Did I go back to those other years for a reason or is everything just random?

Harper opens her door, dropping the grocery bags in the backseat. She doesn't move to start the car. "Are you all right?"

"Getting there. I'm sorry . . . about what happened in there." I shake my head, daring the lump in my throat to grow. I haven't shed a tear months, and I'm not going to start now even though this is frustrating as hell. "I don't know what's wrong with me."

"Nothing is *wrong* with you, Kale. A lot of people have gone through what you're going through now. Not many from the same war as you anymore—" I smile a little at that "—but I'm sure it's no different. It is what it is—nothing to be sorry for."

I lean back against the headrest and stare out the windshield. "It makes me feel like a different person, like I can do nothing at all to stop it from happening. The smallest of things can remind me of that place and it triggers something bigger." Then I say, "I hate it. I didn't think I did before, because when I'm there, I really do feel like I belong, but I hate knowing it's inevitable. I *am* going to go back. It's just a matter of when."

"You really don't think you can control it?"

I give her a look. "Trust me, I've tried. I've tried so many times, I lost count. Remember Libby's tenth birthday party and how I wasn't there? I knew she wanted me there—I knew it was important. But a couple hours before the party, I felt it coming. I took a hot shower, and I tried to keep myself busy to keep my mind off it, maybe hoping it was all in my head. Nothing worked."

"I had no idea," she says. "But we can figure this out, I promise. You might've given up, but I'm just getting started."

I smile at that, seeing her stubborn side come out. "Maybe I'll be able to once my time in the war is over. Right now, it feels hopeless."

"When do you think that'll be?"

I pause, coming up with no explanation. "Only the past can answer that. But I hope it's soon. The war can't last forever, right?"

Harper leans back in her seat, a small sigh escaping her lips. "I hope it ends soon, too. This last time you left . . . I couldn't stand it. Every day I wanted you to come through that door."

"And every day I wanted to," I confess. I wanted nothing more than that while sitting in my frozen fox hole, counting the minutes until sunrise so time would go by faster. Nights are the worst. "I don't want to go back. More now than ever."

Harper doesn't say anything, which I'm glad for. There is nothing to say. It feels fake when people try to make something seem better than it is.

"What's it like? The war?" she asks quietly. I turn my head, but she's staring at her steering wheel. "I'm sorry, I shouldn't even ask. You're probably—"

"Harper. It's all right." She's still avoiding my eyes. "It's . . . the scariest and worst thing I've ever been through." And when I say those words, it really hits me how true they are. Every moment I'm there, I note an underlying fear is always present. Every time I fire my gun, a drop of remorse fills my heart. I dread every moment we enter a battle. I stare at my hands, remembering them covered with blood. "There's no worse feeling than watching your friends die . . . *knowing* you can't do anything to save them. I've killed people, and all I can ever think is that someone on the other side is going through the same thing I am. But I can't hesitate to pull the trigger, because if I do, I'm dead."

I try not to think of Adams more than I already am.

I finally say, looking over at her, "I just want it to be over."

When Harper finally lifts her eyes, they're glazed. "I know it doesn't mean much that I hate the thought of you there more than anything else, but I need you to know I'll always be here when you come back. I wish I could do something more."

"It's more than you think," I say. "Really. Before I heard you were coming back here, there were times I didn't want to come back at all. Not while knowing what waited for me."

"And now?"

"And now, I don't even want to leave."

Harper wipes the corners of her eyes and wipes her fingers on her jeans, leaving wet streaks across them. "I wish you didn't have to. At least not back to where you've been."

"I'm hoping it won't be much longer now."

Harper starts up the car and heads back, glancing at me like I'm going to disappear at any minute. I might have felt the pull back in the store, but it's gone now, replaced with the warm summer air.

A reminder of where I am and where I belong.

She slows down at the bottom of my driveway, engine idling.

I open my door, not yet stepping out. "See you tomorrow?"

"You promise?" she asks.

I can't promise, even though I want to. It could change in

an instant. Without warning. "You know I can't. But I'm really going to try this time. I've made it this far, haven't I?"

Harper nods. Something more is clearly on her mind.

"Hey." I lean toward her and she looks up. "It's going to be all right."

"I know," she says, nodding like she's trying to convince herself. "But I don't care what you say. I'll see you tomorrow." She gives me a heart-pounding smile. "And you know what else you're going to do tomorrow?"

I remember to breathe. "What?"

"You're going to kiss me."

"Really."

"Really," she says.

I finally step out and shut the door. I lean down, looking at her though the window. "Tomorrow then."

Harper nods. "Tomorrow."

32.
Harper

I don't remember driving home. I don't remember bringing the groceries into the house. All I can think about is something Kale said to me in the car, and I'm trying to figure out why it's bothering me so much.

I snap awake when Uncle Jasper comes through the back door, shedding his shoes on the mat. I have a can of soup in one hand and a bottle of orange juice in the other, not at all remembering how they got there.

"Are you okay?" Uncle Jasper eyes me, grabbing a pencil from the mug on the counter.

"Um . . . yeah." I nod and put the orange juice away. "Just thinking about something."

"Would this *something* be Kale?"

I put down the can of soup and turn around. "Is this the part where we have that weird and awkward talk about the two of us . . ."

"Dating?" he finishes for me.

He can't hold back his all-knowing grin. I fight not to roll my eyes, because Grace says I do it too much. She's probably right.

"I don't know what we are," I admit. "And I have no idea why I'm having this conversation with you."

I turn back and finish putting the groceries away. For some reason, I put the orange juice in the cupboard, and I quickly take it out before Uncle Jasper notices. Seriously, what is wrong with me?

"Look, Harper. It's been no secret to me that you both have had—" he debates "—something between you for a while now—"

I turn around. "What? How long have you known? *I* didn't even know."

"I wasn't me, it was Holly," he says. "She saw something since you guys were eleven. Or so she claimed."

"She really said that?"

He nods. "She did. And I never believed it until this summer. I've got to say, it's been amusing watching you two pretend like nothing is going on whenever I'm around."

I think of Kale kissing me right here in the kitchen before Uncle Jasper almost walked in on us, and my cheeks warm. He saw right through us. Of course he did. He always does.

Uncle Jasper clears his throat and returns his attention to the paper. "I'm sorry, I won't say anything else. That's something between the two of you and it should stay that way."

"I think you're the only parent to ever say that." I realize what I just said, and Mom pops into mind because Uncle Jasper isn't my real parent. But he pretends not to notice for my sake and I love him for it.

"But it's true, isn't it?" He smiles just as the phone rings.

I flinch, unable to stop myself from thinking it might be Mom. Speak of the devil and she shall come. She's the last person I want to think about right now. Uncle Jasper stands and starts for the hallway.

"It's just the phone," he says, looking at me with his eyebrows raised. He's still looking as he picks it up. "Hello?" I wait, hoping it isn't her. "Oh, how's it going, Jacob?" There's a short pause and he laughs. "I hear ya. I had an old Camaro in my garage last week. How's that Mustang working out for you?"

Now that I know it isn't Mom, I stop listening altogether. Uncle Jasper can talk to his old friends about cars all day.

I slip past him in the hallway and head up to my room. Once the door is shut, all I can hear is the shifting grass outside, growing tall in the field next to the house. I can just make out the small creek at the bottom of the hill, where in a few weeks I won't be able to see it until fall.

Then it hits me again—what I was thinking of before Uncle Jasper came inside. The very thought drops into my stomach, hard and unwelcome because I'm scared to find something I'm not even sure exists.

But I have to know.

When Kale and I were sitting in my car in the parking lot, he said something that got me thinking: "Only the past can answer that." *That* meaning Kale's future. I knew the truth before now, but am only now grasping what it truly means.

The past is Kale's future. There's no way to tell the future, but the past is something I can find out.

I pull out my laptop from under my bed. It starts up slow since I haven't turned it on in a while. My phone buzzes with a text, and I glance at the screen. It's from Libby.

So have you guys kissed yet?

It's like she knows even when she's hundreds of miles away. I send back a winking face just to screw with her. I turn back to the computer and try to ignore the growing fear in my stomach. I don't know what I'll find, and I don't know what to expect, but I need to know. I can't go another minute being in the dark.

I open Google and search Kale's name tagged with World

War II, something that looks out of place in the same sentence. There's one match at the very top of the screen. It's too easy. Why does the Internet have to be this easy? I click the link, hoping it's not him and the heading is wrong.

It's a long article about The Battle of Hürtgen Forest, and there's a small section where Kale's name pops up. My eyes are the only things moving, scanning the words faster and faster until I've read it all. I read them again, just to make sure I'm reading it right. Because this is the very thing I've been dreading. I'd hoped it wasn't going to be this way.

Because it's Kale.

And if history proves to be true, he's going to die.

33.
Kale

I head upstairs, trying to ignore the growing ache in my stomach. Trying to steer my thoughts away from leaving.

I need to stay.

I want to stay.

I pause at the bathroom door. The light filtering in from the glass tiles invites me in. The bathtub sits quiet, a constant reminder of the comfort it gave me during the past year. The only thing that makes me feel safe.

I move into the bathroom and run my fingertips across the cold porcelain.

Without thinking—like a hard-to-break habit—I step inside and slowly lower myself down. The cold seeps through my jeans and T-shirt, freezing the back of my neck. This is a different type of cold. Not the cold I feel deep in my bones that calls me away from here. It's a cold I can touch. Something my body warms. Something to hold onto when there is nothing else. Anchoring me.

I sink deeper, pretending there's water to slip into, remembering the baths I once took when I was young. Memories I can barely hold onto. It's been too long since I've seen Mom's smile, or heard Libby's voice when she's happy.

I stare at my shoes pressed against the other end of the tub.

The faded blood stains are still visible, now looking more like dirt than blood.

Sometimes I can't help thinking, what the hell am I doing here? In the middle of nowhere, Iowa. Living in a mostly empty house. Hiding in a bathtub from something I can't escape. Haunting me with a past I have to return to.

I feel lost.

While everyone has their whole lives planned out in front of them—even if they're vague and not set in stone—I have nothing except trying to focus on not leaving this place. I don't understand why some people have it *so* easy when, for others . . . nothing seems to go right.

It's like trying to figure out my map when I don't understand the directions.

I instinctively put my hand over my heart when a different kind of cold sets in. It pounds harder. Knowing what's to come.

The phone rings downstairs.

I sink deeper into the tub and close my eyes.

I'm not sure if I have the strength to fight it this time.

On days like this, it's easier to just let go.

34.
Harper

Kale's phone is ringing and nobody is answering. It rings and rings, and my heart pounds too quickly between each one. I hang up. I'm lightheaded because I'm breathing too fast. I close my eyes and focus only on calming myself down. It won't do Kale any good if I pass out before I can tell him.

And I *need* to tell him because there's no way I can't, right? I make myself believe it.

Uncle Jasper's truck isn't in the driveway, and I don't remember hearing him leave. It doesn't matter now. Instead of trying to find my car keys, I head out the back door and run the moment my feet touch the yard. Kale didn't answer the phone, but it doesn't mean he's not there. He could be in the shower. Or outside.

I think of all the possibilities as I run through the woods, down the path made so many years ago by kids who never could've imagined things would turn out this way. Because this can't be possible. It just can't. There has to be some sort of mistake.

I tear through the woods, my feet pounding in my ears louder than my heart. Once I'm out of the trees, I run straight toward his house, the long grass grabbing at my ankles. The driveway sits empty, neither Kale's car nor his Dad's truck are here. Then I remember Kale doesn't have his car anymore. So he could be inside, not bothering to answer the phone because he never does.

I can hardly breathe when I step on the small porch and knock on the door. I let a few seconds pass, and after not hearing anything, I knock harder. "Kale!"

I can't stand waiting out here. I grip the doorknob and twist. It's unlocked—I don't know why I thought it wouldn't have been—it has always been unlocked. Like Kale's parents were afraid if they ever locked the door, he wouldn't be able to come back home. That's what Libby always liked to think and what Kale liked to believe.

It's dark and quiet inside, reminding me of the day I came over to find Kale in the bathroom. Nothing would make me happier than finding him there now. I move toward the stairs, not trying to be quiet. At any other time, I would have been. It never feels right entering someone else's house in the middle of the day when nobody is home.

But Kale is home. I just have to find him.

Natural light pours out the open bathroom door and I slowly walk toward it. "Kale?" I step in the doorway. The bathtub sits empty and cold, hiding no boy for me to find like last time. I glance toward his bedroom—the door is shut, giving me no indication whether he's here or already gone.

Within the brief moment that I close my eyes, I can see the article I read on the Internet. That horrible moment I wish would've never happened. I take those last few steps and knock on his door, hard and impatient. "Kale?" I don't wait for a response and let myself in.

"Harper?" Kale slowly sits up on his bed, one hand rubbing his head. "What the hell is going on?"

One of the windows has its blinds drawn down, making it

darker than it normally is. Then I understand; he was taking a nap. That's why he didn't answer the phone or hear me knocking on the front door.

I lean against the doorframe, weak with relief that he's still here.

"You're here," I breathe out. "You're still here."

But what difference does that make? It doesn't change what I saw. That short moment of relief is taken away too soon.

Kale swings his legs over the bed, looking at me through tired eyes. He's still wearing his jeans and T-shirt. I don't want to take my eyes off him, afraid he'll disappear.

"What's going on?" Then his eyes really take me in and something must give me away. "Harper, what's wrong? Is it Uncle Jasper?"

"No," I shake my head, pushing off from the doorframe. He moves a blanket aside, making room for me to sit next to him. It's not uncommon for him to sleep on top of his comforter, just using an old blanket if he gets cold during the night. I've always loved the smell of his room—the smell of him. I don't want it to ever leave.

"Then tell me what's so important to—Did you run over here?"

I nod, still catching my breath. "I had to. I—" Why am I suddenly at loss for words? Kale's eyes aren't straying, wanting to know what I came here to say. He has no idea. "I was thinking about something you told me, about the past being your future. I just . . . I'm sorry."

I finally pull my gaze away and stare at the floor, afraid to admit what I found. Maybe if I don't tell anyone, it won't come true.

"Harper . . . what did you do?" Kale asks, his voice careful.

"I had to know what happens to you." I try to keep my voice from wavering.

He tilts his head down, forcing me to look at him. "Are you saying you looked me up . . . in the past?"

The corners of my eyes burn. "Yes," I whisper.

Kale gets up and runs a hand through his tousled hair. I stare at his back, his hand resting on the back of his neck. He slowly turns around.

"Don't you think I've been tempted to do that?" he asks, burying his hands deep into his pockets. His jaw is tight. "That I didn't know it was as simple as looking up myself on the Internet? I avoid computers at all costs because once I go down that rabbit hole, I'll never come out. Years ago, I made Libby and Bryce promise to never look me up."

"So you don't know?"

He flinches like my words slapped him. "No, I don't know! Harper, don't you get it? I don't *want* to know. Not now and not ever." The floor creaks under his weight when he paces to the other side of his room, to the window, and back toward the door like the walls are a prison he can't escape. He finally turns away from me, pressing his forehead against the wall. I want to do something for him, but I'm afraid to move. Like he'll suddenly remember I'm here and tell me to leave. "I've never wanted to know anything, because then I would have to live with it," he says.

Kale turns around and leans against the wall, keeping an invisible barrier between us. "Sometimes it's better not knowing."

"But if you knew, you could—"

"—I could what?" he says, cutting me off. "Stop it from happening? Don't you remember what I told you, about the past being the past? It can't be undone, Harper." His chest rises and falls a few times before he says, "Whatever it is, it's going to happen."

I'm trying so hard to hold back everything inside that

wants to spill out, but I can't. A tear runs down my cheek, followed by another. "You don't want to know, then?"

"No."

"I'm sorry I looked, but I couldn't *not*. Not while knowing where you've been and where you'll be going back to." I swipe at my cheek, willing them to stay dry. "I hate the thought of you in that place. I'm sorry," I say again.

"Don't—" Kale shakes his head and closes his eyes, fighting back something more. "I've had to do everything to hold myself back from doing what you did." He pushes away from the wall and sits next to me. I feel better when he's here, within reach. Like it's possible to keep him here forever. "It's like knowing a storm is coming, but not knowing when or how bad it'll be. But I know it's coming one way or the other—I always have. I just don't think about it, because I can't bear it."

"How long have you known?" I ask.

He gives me a pained look. "It's war, Harp. I've been thinking about it a long time now, and there's no way I'm coming out of it the same way I went in. I'm not that lucky."

I can't say anything, because I can't lie.

Kale might not want to know the whole truth, but he already knows something is going to happen. I can't imagine how hard it is—knowing something is coming without the power to prevent it.

"But why don't you want to know?" I whisper.

Today, even when the sun lights up his room through his broken blinds, nothing can make his eyes bright. "It's easier to pretend than be afraid of the truth."

Kale looks at me for the longest moment, enough for me to see everything; the pain he's been though, the lingering fears, the self-doubt. Maybe it is easier to pretend, because I can't bear the thought of him not coming back.

I don't know what compels me to do it, but I kiss him. His skin is cold and smells of snow, lips made of melting ice. This is the Kale I can't let go of. Not now and not ever.

I pull myself away from him and stand up.

"Wait—" Kale slips his hand around mine, his thumbs gently touching my wrist. "Can you stay for a little while? I just . . . I don't want to be alone right now."

Kale lets go of my hand and lays down on his back. With my heart kicking a little more than usual, I give him my answer by slipping off my shoes. I've never been in Kale's bed before, at least not like this. Not with him already in it.

"Harper, you're overthinking things," he says, knowing me too well. "Just come here."

He takes my hand again and draws me in, leaving no space between us. I rest my head on the side of his chest, my hand over his heart. It pounds a steady rhythm under my fingers, and his arm wraps around me, keeping me close.

Kale has never held me like this, and it's something I wished we could have done sooner. Not now when our time suddenly has an end. Life is playing a cruel joke on us, one I wish never has to become reality.

"Kale?" I'm not sure if he's even awake; he's been quiet for so long.

"Hmm?"

"What will the date be, when you go back?" I try to sound curious, not at all like I need to know. Kale is in a state right before falling asleep, and I'll be lucky if he doesn't remember me asking.

"Um . . . I don't know." I don't pry; just wait, hoping he'll answer. "It's about to be the new year."

"1945?"

"Yeah."

Kale takes one last real breath before falling asleep. I don't want to think about the past right now, or what will happen when this perfect moment is over. All I want to do is sleep next to the boy who has always kept his promise.

But if the past is true, he dies on January 8.

35.
Kale

I'm cold when I wake.

Harper is no longer lying next to me, and the light coming through the window is dull. I sit up and blink my eyes awake, ridding myself of the dreams I had. Even with her sleeping next to me, they still came, but . . . they weren't as bad.

Harper sits on the edge of my bed, pulling on her shoes.

"Trying to sneak out without waking me?" I ask, trying to make it sound like a joke.

Harper doesn't smile. "I should go home. Uncle Jasper will be wondering where I am and your dad will be home from work soon. I don't know about you, but I'm not ready to be caught—"

"Doing what? Taking a nap?" Still, she doesn't smile. I lean in closer and tuck a strand of hair behind her ear. "Harper, look at me."

She does. Barely. This is a side of Harper I've never seen— not even when she thinks about her mom or Aunt Holly. At least then she tries to smile and only focuses on the good. Being the optimist she is.

Something is wrong.

More wrong than I first thought.

I almost ask her to tell me what she knows. The temptation is so strong.

"This is where you tell me everything will be okay," she says.

"Will you believe me if I do?"

"I don't know if I can. But I want to." Harper presses her lips together, willing herself to stay calm. She used to do it all the time when we were kids. She's always been so easy for me to read. "I don't know what I expected when I came over here," she says. "Maybe I was thinking that once I told you, it wouldn't be true. Like I could prevent it from happening. It's stupid, I know." She sniffs once and looks away. "Like you said, there's nothing to be done."

I can't take this another minute. It's like watching a movie and knowing exactly where the end is heading, but then you have to stop watching and you never get the chance to see it for yourself.

I know what's coming, and I've been trying to ignore it.

But I can't anymore.

"I die . . . don't I." I don't bother phrasing it as a question. There's no doubt with her acting this way. "Is that what you read?"

Harper nods silently, still turned away.

I can't pretend anymore. This is why I didn't want to know.

There's a hole burning through my heart. The things I've done to make things right—with Dad and Harper, talking about me having a *future*—all of it was for nothing. All of it. It was all shit to fill in the place of false hope.

What was the point of anything if I am to die?

"You should go," I hear myself say.

"What?"

I don't look up.

I need Harper to leave, and I can't do that if I look at her again. "Please just go. I'll see you tomorrow."

"Kale—"

"*Please.* I need to be alone."

I close my eyes, hearing and feeling nothing but the growing rage within me. I'm drowning without water, under the pressure of something larger. It hangs over my head, waiting for me to break.

When I have enough strength to open my eyes again, she's gone.

My door is open, and a cool breeze comes from somewhere down the hall. I follow it with my feet on the cold floor and my hands in fists so they won't shake. I think of nothing, because if I do, I'm sure I'll explode.

I'm teetering on the edge of sanity.

The house is darker now, the day coming to an end. A day that started so well.

I go down the stairs, one at a time, counting each step to keep myself in control.

I can't do it anymore.

I can't act like nothing is wrong. Because everything is wrong. Just this morning, with Harper in the car next to me and wind breezing through my fingers, things were finally starting to look up. I was *happy.*

Now death presses in around me. Shattering the smallest hope of the future I might have had. Gone. Not even there to begin with.

I hear something crash to the floor and I look down. A broken lamp lays at my feet. I don't know if it was an accident or if I did it on purpose. But it feels good breaking something. I've always been this controlled and relatively calm person, never losing my temper or acting out, even when I was young. I always keep it together.

I've been a shaken bottle, and now I'm ready to burst.

The sounds of crashing and breaking echo off the walls, shared with a raging yell that I don't realize is coming from me until my throat is sore. Ripping at things the moment I see them. I can't see straight, my vision dotted with red and black spots.

I'm in the kitchen now, and I don't know how I got here. The table is tipped over, the chairs thrown across the room. I whip my arms across the counters, everything tumbling to the floor. I grab dishes and throw them into the wall. Hearing every break and wanting more.

It's not enough.

When everything around me is broken and silent, I finally stop. My chest is heaving and I've ruined the entire house.

But I'm still shaking. My hand stings. I look down to see I've cut it on one of the plates. There's a long gash across my palm.

I sink down to the floor. The cabinets press into my back. The refrigerator chooses this moment to kick on, as though telling me it had witnessed nothing previously. My hands hang over my knees, and I watch the blood drip from my fingertips.

I'm going to die.

And there's nothing I can do to prevent it. The only thing I can hope is that recorded history is wrong. It's been wrong plenty of times before, so it could be wrong about me, too.

It's the only thing that will save me.

When I was in the bathtub earlier, I was so close to leaving. I could have if I wanted to. I could have let go without trying. But I didn't because I promised Harper I wouldn't. For once in my life, I had an ounce of control—just enough to delay my leaving.

Now, I'll do anything to stay longer, even just one more day. One more hour. I don't want to go back where it's winter. Where there's blood on the snow and screams in the night. My nightmares have been full of empty foxholes and shadows that come through the trees when I'm not ready. Death from the ground and death from the sky. It will kill me all the same.

I'm still shaking. From what, I don't know.

The front door opens and shuts, followed by Dad's voice. "Kale? Kale!"

There's movement in the doorway, and I look up to see Dad taking in the scene around me. His eyes move from me, to the mess around me, and back.

I can't stop trembling. At some point, I started to cry.

My hands and shoulders shake as if they aren't connected to me at all. I am someone I don't know. I don't want to think about tomorrow or the day after that. I don't want to think about leaving again. And I don't want to think about what will happen to me when I do.

Dad doesn't say a word. I don't have to say anything for him to know something is wrong. Something very wrong.

He steps over a broken chair and some shattered dishes and sits down next to me without hesitation.

And then he's holding me—his arms wrapped around me with my head pressed against his chest.

I'll never be too old to be held by him.

His shirt becomes wet with tears I've held in for months. His warm hands are on my back and behind my head, making the world safe again. Even just for a little while. I don't ever want him to let go. And I'm scared he will.

"It's all right, Kale," he murmurs. "It's all right."

And for that small moment, it really is.

36.
Harper

I walk home after Kale told me to leave. I hesitated at first. He wasn't acting himself, and something in his voice sounded off. Still, I couldn't stay, either—I felt like he needed to be alone. I'm on autopilot, feeling numb and thinking of things too fast to make sense of them. I want to wake up and have all this be a dream—a horrible, horrible dream.

The house comes into view, and I go in through the back door, slipping off my shoes on the mat. The kitchen is dim in the fading light with the lingering smell of frozen pizza. I follow the low sounds of the television down the hall and into the living room where Uncle Jasper sits in his usual seat, staring but not really watching.

He looks up when I enter. "Hey, Harp, I was wondering where you've been. Were you over at Kale's?"

I nod numbly.

"I know I said I don't mind you being out of the house," he says, "but could you leave a note next time so I know where you are? I don't like worrying." I nod again and Uncle Jasper's carefree smile drops away. "Did something happen?"

I let my eyes drift to the television, not wanting to relive what I told Kale. "Yeah."

Uncle Jasper stands up, not taking his eyes off me. "What's wrong?" he says. "Tell me. Are you hurt? Did something happen to Kale? Harper—" He steps in front of me, forcing me to look at him and think of things I don't want to. "What is it?"

"It's Kale," I say, barely audible.

Uncle Jasper's eye flash. "Did something happen?"

I close my eyes, feeling light-headed. I back up and sit down on the bottom step of the stairs, not knowing how to tell him.

"I looked something up on the Internet earlier," I say. Uncle Jasper pauses, trying to make sense of what I'm telling him. He sits down next to me. "Let me rephrase that. I looked up *Kale*."

"Kale." I look up at him in time to see realization settle in. "You mean, you looked up the Kale in the past."

"Technically, Kale in the future." I don't smile and neither does he. What might have been funny this morning no longer is. "I needed to know if he was going to be all right. You know better than me how hard it is when he's gone. I had to know. And now I'm wishing I didn't."

"What did you find?"

I don't have to say it. I look at him and give a small shake of my head, and he knows. The tension between us is like a brick wall. The voices from the television are the only indication time is still moving. My throat tightens when I try to swallow.

Sometimes life really, really sucks, and I just want to play my video games to drown out the noise in my head. This time, I don't think there's any way to ignore this.

Uncle Jasper finally pulls his gaze away and focuses on the floor. "Can you tell me exactly what you read?"

"It was only a mention of him. How he—" I lick my lips and start again, finding this more difficult with every passed minute. "It said he was killed in action, on January eighth."

"Not missing in action?"

"No. I reread it a dozen times to make sure."

Uncle Jasper's jaw clenches and unclenches. Missing in action would make sense. Kale would go missing because he would come home. Why does it have to say the former?

"What's the date there—did you ask him?"

I regret leaving Kale when he asked me to. I could still be over there, feeling his heartbeat under my fingers and his breathing matching mine. It was safe with him. The possibilities of him leaving were far out of reach, along with every worry that clouded my thoughts.

"He said it's about to be the new year," I say, closing my eyes to fight back the rush of unwanted emotions. All I can think about is Kale. The way he looked down at the river, dripping wet and giving me a dimpled smile. The dashboard lights outlining his face as he drove me back from the diner. Every moment his eyes caught mine, my heart beat a little faster.

I want Uncle Jasper to say it'll be all right or figure out a way to prevent it. To say anything that will make this all go away. The same way I wanted Kale to. I keep yearning for something that will never come.

A few minutes pass until Uncle Jasper releases the tension in his shoulders, exhaling a defeated and tired breath. He flicks off his hat and it drops between his feet.

"I wish there was something we could do," I say, my voice barely above a whisper.

He looks over. "Me, too, kid."

I lean over to rest my head on his shoulder and his arm wraps around my back. He reminds me so much of Dad that it hurts. Even his smell and the sound of his voice. Nothing could erase that from my memory.

"The only thing we can do is hope history is wrong," he says.

Whatever happens, I just want Kale to come home to us. I'll give anything for him to walk through that door again; today, tomorrow, and even weeks from now.

We sit on the bottom step of the stairs, ignoring the constant hum of the baseball game and watching the night settle through the screen door.

There's nothing we can do.

It's impossible for me to sleep. The moon shines bright through the windows, and I toss and turn under the pale light, the sheets clinging to my legs. I give up and sit against the headboard, staring out at a night filled with crickets and grass and the faint sound of the river.

The house is empty and quiet. Uncle Jasper left an hour ago, saying nothing when he did. Aunt Holly told me he used to do it all the time. He just leaves and drives wherever the roads take him when he needed to think or let off some steam. It's his way of dealing.

Now more than ever I wish she was here. Even at night, when I would wake up after having a nightmare, just knowing she was in the next room was enough for me to fall back asleep. Missing Aunt Holly makes me miss Mom even though it feels wrong to do so.

The stairs creak, followed by the hallway floor. I never heard Uncle Jasper come home, so it could only be one other person. My bedroom door cracks open and Kale slips inside, wearing his gray zip-up sweatshirt and a ripped piece of cloth tied around his right hand. I untangle myself from the bed and move into his waiting arms.

I press my face into his shoulder, inhaling his smell and trying to memorize it. "I was afraid you were already gone."

The muscles along his back stiffen. "I didn't come to talk about that."

"Then what did you—"

Kale cuts me off with a kiss. It's soft and cold at first, deepening into something more when he draws me closer. My fingers twine into his hair, feeling like this could never be enough. I finally realize the difference between needing and wanting.

The back of my legs hit the bed, and I slowly lower myself down, Kale following me without an inch of space between us, his knees coming up on either side of me. One of his hands wraps around my waist, his thumb tracing along my hip. A shiver runs up my back and I break away, still feeling his chest move every time he takes a breath.

Something isn't right and I want to ignore it. Still— "Kale . . ."

"What?" His eyes search mine.

Screw it.

I tug at the zipper on his sweatshirt and pull it free from his arms. It falls to the floor somewhere behind him, and I can swear my heart is pounding loud enough for him to hear. My fingers trace the hem of his jeans before slipping under his T-shirt, slowly drawing it up, over his stomach and the curves of his chest. He leans away and lifts his arms, allowing me to pull the shirt over his head.

The smell of winter is everywhere.

I thread my fingers through his hair, remembering how it felt when I cut it and my stomach fluttered the same way. Wrapping my hand around the back of his neck, I draw him closer. His lips brush my chin and then my jaw, finding my mouth in the stream of moonlight.

Nobody is here to stop us this time. Uncle Jasper won't be walking in on us, and there's nothing but the night outside, keeping our secret away from the sun and everything that

255

reminds us of reality. Because being with Kale is like a dream—too good for me to have and disappearing when things become too real.

Being with him lets me forget about everything wrong. I've already forgotten why he's here and why I couldn't sleep.

But when his dog tags brush against my neck, I remember.

Kale doesn't have much time left. I feel it with every movement in his lips—like he knows his days are numbered.

I break away and put a hand on his chest. "Kale, stop."

"What's wrong?"

He looks down at me with a face I can't say no to. We both need each other, but not like this.

"This doesn't feel right," I say, "and I think you know why. You can't make it go away by trying to forget."

"Why is it so horrible for wanting to forget that I know I'm going to die? All I want right now is you."

I almost give in. My hand is still on his chest, feeling his cold skin against my palm. He's using this to forget about his problems, and I could be the solution. But it wouldn't change anything.

"And I don't want this to happen under that reasoning," I say. "I don't want it to be like *this*. And I know you don't want it to either."

"How do you know that?" he asks, suggesting otherwise.

"Because it's not you. Or else you wouldn't have waited so long to kiss me, and you wouldn't be so nervous every time we're close. This isn't you, Kale. You're only doing it because you think you're going to die."

Kale's eyes harden. "I *am* going to die, don't you get that? And not being with you would be my greatest mistake."

"You are with me. You always have been." Because it's true, even if I never knew it. Then I say, "Tell me the truth, Kale. Do you want to do this tonight? Right now?"

His jaw clenches and he looks down. "I didn't want to be alone."

Before I can stop him, he moves away and gets off the bed, searching the floor for his T-shirt. After he pulls it back on, I catch his wrist. He stops and looks down at me, his chest moving steadily.

"You don't have to be," I tell him.

"I'm sorry."

"You don't have to apologize."

"Yes, I do." Kale sits down next to me, weaving his fingers through mine. "I shouldn't be using you to ignore my own problems. It's wrong, I know. I just . . . I wanted to forget. I'm sorry." He gives me a smile; one of his rare, dimple-showing amenities. "No matter how much I liked it."

He leans in to give me a soft kiss. The short-lived smile is gone when he pulls away, replaced with an expression I've grown used to. A little of the person he was when I got here is showing again, and it pains me to know there's nothing I can do.

He pulls me into him, and there's so much of a difference between Kale holding me and anyone else. So much.

"It won't be the last time," I murmur into his shoulder.

Kale shivers against me and I lean away to look at him.

"Why are you always so cold?" I ask. "Does it have to do with something with you leaving soon?"

He nods. "The sooner I am to leaving, the colder I get. It's like a warning. And the more I think about it, the worse it gets."

"Then don't think about it."

"It's hard not to when I can't sleep."

"So sleep here tonight." Kale looks over, unsure. "Because you aren't the only one having trouble."

"Are you sure?"

"It's just sleeping, Kale." He laughs a little, probably remembering his own similar words earlier. I realize he doesn't laugh enough. "I don't want you to leave yet."

His eyes are a little sad. "Afraid I'll disappear?"

"Should I be?"

Kale shakes his head and smiles again. "Not tonight."

But maybe tomorrow or the day after. That's what he doesn't say and what I don't want to think about.

37.
Kale

During the night, I can almost believe there is no such thing as day.

Night is for the sleepless.

For the ones who don't want dawn to edge over the horizon.

Because each new day brings the reality that time is still in motion. It doesn't stop for anyone. Or change, for that matter.

Not even for someone like me.

I sit on the edge of Harper's bed and watch for the first signs of daybreak. The fields stretching away from the house are unmoving. Waiting, just as I am, for something I don't want to come. Because once it does, it means everything must move forward.

Time must move on.

Me along with it.

I glance at Harper behind me. She hasn't moved since she fell asleep hours ago. Her light brown—almost blonde—hair is webbed over her pillow, proof of her deep sleep. I envy her for that. I was able to sleep only a few hours before the dreams came and woke me.

I was wrong for coming here last night.

My mind wasn't in the right place.

I wanted nothing more than to forget about what I had ahead of me—even if it was for only a moment. And I knew Harper was the only one who could do that. It's one of those mistakes I wish I could take back.

I slowly stand, careful not to wake her. The sun peeks through the windows and I can't sit here any longer. I walk around the bed and pick up my shoes and sweatshirt.

After the door clicks shut behind me, I make my way down the dark hallway. And the moment I smell toast coming from downstairs, my shoulders relax and I give a small sigh. I didn't hear Uncle Jasper at all during the night, and I wonder if he ever went to bed.

He's sitting in his usual place at the kitchen table, staring down at the wood with an expressionless face. He doesn't even look up when I take my seat.

I'm having a moment of déjà vu.

It was four years ago, exactly two months after Aunt Holly died, and I had come over to visit. I did almost every day. But for those first two months, he tried to act like he was doing okay. He tried smiling and keeping a conversation. But there was a chunk of him missing that was too obvious to mistake.

Then one day I found him sitting at the table like this, finally realizing the reality of what had happened. That was when he started doing crossword puzzles, slowly trying to build his life back up, day by day.

There's no paper in front of him today.

No smile and no hello.

Suddenly I'm afraid of what will happen to him when I don't come back. And what about Dad? And Libby and Bryce. Miles and Grace. Harper. On the outside, I might be calm and controlled, but on the inside, I'm panicking like last night in the kitchen except not nearly as bad. Enough to stay in control, but barely.

I don't want to die.

I want to come over here every day and walk into the kitchen, which constantly smells like toast.

I want to work on cars with Uncle Jasper.

I want to kiss Harper every minute and every hour.

I want to go to school and become a history teacher because I would be better at that than anyone.

I don't want my dad to see his youngest son die and think it was his fault.

I want a future.

All the while I'm thinking this, I'm becoming colder and colder, and I don't know how to make it stop.

I close my eyes and think of Harper upstairs—the curving shape of her lips, her long lashes touching her cheeks while she sleeps, and the memory of her fingers on my skin. Pulling me closer. Wanting me as much as I wanted her.

It's enough of a distraction for now to keep me rooted here. I just can't let my thoughts stray like that again.

Not when I'm this close to leaving.

I still haven't asked her about the date she saw, and I wonder how many more travels I have left until it comes.

Neither Uncle Jasper nor I talk. There's nothing to say. I'm sure Harper told him everything last night, so there's no point confirming it or trying to come up with a way to stop it from happening.

Because it is going to happen. It's the fact that haunts me.

Uncle Jasper becomes unfrozen and glances at me, his eyes not at all bright like they usually are. "Are you hungry?" he asks.

I shake my head—my stomach is too tight to be hungry.

"Well, I'm going to make you something, and you're going to eat it." He gets up from the table and moves in front of the stove, turning on the front burner. While the pan is heating up, he glances at me from over his shoulder. "How did you sleep?"

His mouth curves upward.

My mouth becomes dry, suddenly remembering where I spent the night. "It was—" But no words want to come out.

Uncle Jasper throws me the smallest smile, letting me know he's messing with me. "You're lucky I trust you enough."

I wish he didn't say that.

Last night, *I* couldn't even trust myself.

"I think you should trust Harper more than me," I admit.

He looks at me before cracking an egg into the pan. "You underestimate yourself."

"How can I trust myself, when it feels like I don't know myself?"

I look away and listen as he fries an egg and butters a piece of toast. He sets the plate of food before me and sits down, catching my eye. "I know it feels like that sometimes. But it's within those times when you find out who you really are. We all go through them."

I stare down at the food on my plate, thinking about the mistake I made last night. Harper deserves better than me. "And what if I'm not someone good?"

"Kale, I've known you since you were four years old, ever since you wandered over here claiming you weren't lost but exploring—"

"—I wasn't lost—"

He chooses to ignore this. "—and during your whole life, I've never once seen you be anything but good. You make mistakes just like the rest of us, but you learn from them." Then he asks, "When you do something you shouldn't, do you regret it?"

I finally look up and say, "Yes."

"Then why do you keep trying to believe otherwise?"

I don't have an answer to that. Because it makes me feel less guilty? Less of a screw-up?

I pick up my fork and poke at the eggs. There's no point trying to argue my way out of eating—I've tried it too many times to bother.

This feels like too normal of a morning—other than Uncle Jasper's lack of smiles and sad attempts at joking—and it shouldn't. There's something major on both on our minds, and yet we try to have a regular breakfast like any other day.

I'm almost glad for it.

Having something normal makes it as though nothing not-normal is going to happen.

I'm halfway through my eggs when Harper walks into the kitchen. I try not to make it obvious that I'm watching her. My eyes follow her every move, forgetting about the food on my plate.

She pours herself a bowl of cereal and tries to find a spoon in the drawer—Uncle Jasper is horrible about putting them back in the right place. When she finally sits down across from me, I try to keep eating.

"Don't forget to eat your toast," Uncle Jasper comments.

I take a bite and shoot him a fake smile. Harper tries not to laugh from across the table.

Uncle Jasper starts talking about a car that will drop by today. I'm not sure which one of us he's talking to, but it doesn't seem to matter. We listen to him ramble, catching each other's eye from across the table at odd moments.

I could sit here all day and be happy. But life likes to plays games with me.

Uncle Jasper suddenly stops talking and looks down the hallway toward the door. "I think someone's here," he says, standing up and finishing off his coffee in one swallow. He glances at us, still seated at the table. "Don't worry, I've got it," he deadpans.

"We thought you liked answering the door," I tell him, smiling pleasantly.

"Don't be a smartass."

Once he's out the front door, I push my plate away. I can smell her from here—fresh, clean laundry and the deodorant she uses. "I'm sorry about last night," I say. "Really. I wish I could take it back."

"You wish you could take back kissing me?" she asks, smiling a little. "Am I really that bad?"

I resist rolling my eyes. "You know what I mean."

"I know, and it's okay." Her eyes are sad again, the same way they looked last night. "I probably would have done the same thing. Did you tell your dad about—"

"No. I don't want him to worry." I'm thinking about it again. It waits there, in the back of my mind. My thoughts. Something that cannot be ignored. I hear myself say, "I don't think I can do this much longer."

"Do what?"

I stare at the table, trying to keep my hands from shaking. The countdown within me is flashing double zeros. Flashing and flashing. Telling me it's time. Telling me I can't stall any longer.

"I can't hold it back," I say.

"Kale—" But the phone rings, cutting her off.

It rings and rings but she stares at me. I can see it again—the look she gets when she's afraid I'm going to disappear.

"Are you going to get that?" I ask.

She hesitates and says, "Just don't go anywhere, okay?"

Harper walks away without waiting for an answer.

For which I'm glad, because I can't make promises.

38.
Harper

The moment I answer the phone, I wish I hadn't, because the moment I hear Mom's voice, I realize how much I miss her. Then I hate that I miss her.

"Harper," she says.

I can't seem to get enough air. It's all around me, so why is it so hard to breathe? I almost hang up, but then my heart betrays me.

"Mom."

She lets out a breath of relief. "It's so good to hear your voice again," she says. "Listen, Harper . . . I've been thinking a lot over the last few weeks and I realize I made a huge, huge mistake. I should have never left without you. I miss you too much."

Her words hang in the air.

After so long of wishing she would change—be the person, and the mom, she was supposed to be and never was—I don't feel happy like I imagined I would be. I don't feel relieved or at all hopeful or even like we have another chance making ourselves a family again. That point has come and gone.

"*Now?*" I ask. "After all this time, you're *now* realizing this?"

I can tell she's taken back by this but recovers quickly. "I'm sorry. I just needed time to—"

"—time?" I shake my head, even though she can't see me. Every night I cried myself to sleep, brewing anger toward her I've never fully felt. Now it's all coming up at once. "You've had years . . . so why now? Why am I so important all of the sudden?"

"I've made a mistake," she says. "I didn't get to realize that until after you were gone. I miss you. Please, Harper. Please try to understand that. I should've never let you go. I know I haven't been the best mom in the past," she says, her voice cracking, "but I'm asking you to give me another try. I promise it'll be different this time. I can move back and we can find a new home. Whatever it takes."

No matter how angry I am at her, hearing the sincerity in her voice—imagining her sitting in some room by herself with a messy ponytail and dark bags under her eyes—I can't hold onto it. It only makes me sad.

"How can you promise that?" I ask, because deep down I really want her to.

Then she says, "It's all I have."

I feel myself splitting apart. It took me months to realize I had to let her go to get on with my life. I did because I had no choice. I couldn't hold onto the past and continue on with the future at the same time. I couldn't have both, and I never would've done that without Uncle Jasper and Kale.

In the end, after everything I've gone through to get to this point, I know my answer.

"I can't, Mom." A lump in my throat threatens to keep down my words. "It's too late for that."

"What do you mean?" she asks.

If Mom had told me this months ago, maybe my answer would've been different. It's easy to forgive when it still hurts.

266

We forgive in hopes it'll take the pain away. But my pain healed over time and I got over it.

"Don't you understand?" I ask. "It's too late for that. If you would have told me this a couple months ago, it would have been different. But there are times to give second chances and times to move on." I say that last part thinking of Kale and his dad. It saddens me thinking Mom and I won't get that chance. "And it's too late for us. I'm not saying this is good-bye, but I can't go back to the life I had. You have to understand that."

"So you aren't even going to think about this?"

"I've been thinking about this since I got here."

There's a long moment of silence, and I would do anything to know what she's thinking.

"Look," I start, "I'm just saying I think I'll be better off here right now." I pause, needing to say more but scared to. "You hurt me when you left. We can't make things right between us, but we can start over. This isn't forever."

"And that's more than I deserve. Will you consider visiting for Christmas?" she asks, hopeful.

"Of course I will."

I can see Uncle Jasper though the screen door, talking to another man near his truck. Now that I'm here, I couldn't imagine leaving. This is more of a home than I've ever known.

"I've got to go, Mom, but I'll keep my phone on me if you want to give me a call sometime."

"I would like that."

We say good-bye and hang up, and I don't know what to make of the conversation. Half of me wishes she never called, and the other half is glad she finally admitted fault.

I go back into the kitchen—about to tell Kale we should go out for lunch—but he isn't there. The words stick in my mouth, and I'm left staring at his empty chair.

"Kale?"

There's no answer, and I spin around and am out the door before I can catch my breath. Uncle Jasper stops mid-sentence, turning around.

"Have you seen Kale?" I ask.

"I thought he was inside," he says.

I can only shake my head and back away into the house, not wanting to believe what's happening. I shove my feet into my shoes and run out the back door, hoping to catch him before it's too late, if it isn't already.

Movement catches my eye across the yard and I stop short. Kale is sitting on the old swing under the tree, staring at the ground.

When I swear, he looks up. "What?"

"I thought you left." I walk the remaining distance, but Kale stands and gestures for me to stay where I am. The sunlight hasn't reached over the trees yet, leaving him in the shadows.

"I haven't yet, but I'm about to. So you can't be near me." His voice shakes, and then he asks. "I need you to tell me what date you saw."

I swallow and say, "January eighth."

Kale looks away and his mouth silently moves as he counts, hand fidgeting in front of him. "January eighth," he murmurs, "Okay. That gives me maybe two more travels before then."

"Or maybe more," I say suddenly, my mind going through possibilities.

Kale stops. "What?"

"I want you to try coming back earlier. And not back to that old house—I want you to come back *here*."

He's already shaking his head. "Harper, I don't think—"

"Stop." I walk up to him, keeping only a foot of distance between us. "I don't want to hear about how you've tried and how you can't control it. I think that's bullshit and I think you *can* control it. You just have to learn how."

"It's not going to change anything."

"You don't know—it could. I'm here now, and you know what that means—I don't give up. And I'm never going to give up on you."

Kale leans in for a kiss and pulls away too soon. He looks across the yard and nods. "I'll try, okay? I can't make any promises. I have to go."

He steps back and then he's gone. It's like I blinked and he wasn't ever here to begin with. Too fast to be real.

"You remind me of your Aunt Holly," Uncle Jasper says behind me.

"How's that?" I stare at the spot where Kale was standing seconds ago, wondering if I'm giving us false hope for trying. But having hope is better than having none at all. It's not over until it's over.

Uncle Jasper says, "You never give up."

39.
Kale

When I'm in the past, it's like I'm actually living in that time. I don't think much about the present because I'm not there. It doesn't stare me in the face like the past is. It's hard to explain. It's like both are real life. Equally mine but separate.

My helmet is heavy on my head and my legs are tired, grounding me to this time.

We're walking today, trying to find a new place to hold our ground. It's quiet with just the sounds of boots hitting the ground and sighs of cigarettes. No tanks or jeeps because we're too deep in the woods with little more than rough paths for roads. A squad scouts ahead for mines or any signs of the Germans. Everyone is on high alert; they could come from any direction at any time.

I still question why I was placed on the front lines. Was it dumb luck, or did the past put me in front of that officer on purpose—to make sure I made it here? Am I even doing them any good? So many questions with no answers.

Perkins walks beside me smoking a cigarette since he doesn't have to worry about Germans when he has no gun. I routinely scan the woods. Hoping we won't come across anyone today. There's not much snow on the ground, but it's cold.

I'm able to ignore how my jacket isn't warm enough when we're walking. Stiles found me a pair of gloves—I didn't ask him from where and I don't want to know—and I cut out holes for my trigger fingers.

So today isn't so bad.

Not until we come to a crossroads where the road bends out of sight. Our scouts went both directions, but their tracks double back and continue on straight. We walk on silently, and when I'm passing over the other road, a horse suddenly gallops into sight. Everyone freezes, including the German on his horse. Then he turns it around and kicks it forward.

I hear Captain Price shout, "*Jackson!*"

I have my gun up and into my shoulder before his voice is done echoing through the forest. My finger pulling the trigger right before the man is out of sight. His body jerks and then falls off the saddle. The horse startles but stays nearby, its eyes wide with the smell of blood. Price motions for a couple of us to go with him, including me and Perkins. We jog down the road, scanning the forest for more surprises.

When we come to the body, Perkins rolls him over and checks his pulse even though we already know he's dead. His eyes stare at the sky and an exit wound punctures his chest. Private Woods checks the man for any documents and only comes up with a little black journal. I don't look away fast enough and manage to see a picture of his family.

I step away and watch the woods, pretending nothing is wrong.

Someone leads the horse away

Price says between me, "Alright, let's get back."

I trail behind them and join up with the rest of the division, like nothing happened at all. I'm lying to myself, but it's better not to think about it right now. I will later, when I'm in my foxhole and alone. There, nobody can see my hands shake.

"You good?" I turn to see Perkins walking next to me again.

I nod. "Yeah."

But I'm not and he knows it, too.

I don't leave early, but somehow—and still don't know how—I'm able to come back outside of Uncle Jasper's house. I was sitting against a tree, on watch for another two hours, when the pull became so strong, I couldn't ignore it.

No . . . I didn't *want* to ignore it.

The day before, I tried to trigger it. Thinking of summer and Harper and everything about home. I got close once, I think. It's hard to tell. I was thinking about Uncle Jasper's kitchen, the way it always smells like toast or sometimes frozen pizza. Of how warm his house always is whenever I'm cold.

I felt it then. But someone shouted my name and I couldn't hold onto it.

So three days passed, and now I'm standing in the field next to Uncle Jasper's house. My skin is still cold from the winter, and I'm hungry from the rations they lowered. They've been having trouble getting supplies to us through the forest with no roads.

It's evening now, and I can hear the baseball game coming through the open window. I can't wait to see his face when I walk in the front door. My legs are a bit numb, but they warm up as I walk.

I still can't believe I did it.

For the first time in forever, I came back to a different place. A place of my choosing.

I don't bother knocking—I just open the front door and walk in. Uncle Jasper looks at me twice before his eyes go wide and he comes to give me a hug. "Harper!"

Her feet are fast coming down the stairs, and I turn to pull her into my chest. She's so warm and smells like home, and I finally realize how I came to be here. Because I *wanted* to be here, more than anything.

"You really did it," she says, pulling back to look at me. "Where did you come back?"

"Just right outside in the field." I still don't believe it. Then my stomach growls and Uncle Jasper puts a hand on my shoulder. "How do you feel about pizza?"

I take a shower upstairs to get rid of the dirt and cold, still thinking about what I did and wondering if I can do it again. This small crack in the door might be the beginning of me learning control. It's hard to have hope when I know what's to come, but at least it's something to work on.

When I come back downstairs, Miles is sitting next to Harper at the table, talking to Uncle Jasper.

Not expecting him here, I stop in the doorway. "Miles."

His face lights up when he sees me. "Kale." Miles comes around the table and throws his arms around me, but then pulls away saying, "Harper told me what happened." And that's when *I* remember. I'm supposed to die. I feel my smile fade away. Miles continues, "You know I'll do anything for you. Just tell me what."

"Right now, I could use some food."

"You're in luck; I brought the goods." He gestures to the table where an open box of pizza sits, and I take my place across from Harper. The chair is hard and familiar—making this place feel like the home I know it is. I know it's the love I have for it that made it possible for me to come back here.

And I think I can do it again.

They try to hold conversation while I eat, but Uncle Jasper glances at me every now and then, worry in his eyes and stress in his shoulders. When I'm finally done eating, they all sit silent, waiting for me.

I say, "What do you want to know?" I settle my gaze on Harper because she's biting her lip and she only does that when she wants to say something.

"I want to know how you did it. Maybe if we figure it out, you'll know how to do it again."

"I think I *can* do it again . . . but really, is there a point? Unless the report of my death is drastically wrong, I don't think I'll be coming back at all."

Harper is already shaking her head. "But you can. Whatever happens, you'll be able to leave and come back, maybe even earlier than usual. And if you come back here, maybe we can help you."

Uncle Jasper chimes in. "It's the only chance we have. You must understand that." He puts a heavy hand on my arm and I almost can't look at him. "Don't give up on us yet."

I won't break down in front them. But I feel it coming. I want to say maybe it's easier to give up. I want to say it but I don't. That's not who I am.

So I tell him, "I'm not."

"Good. So tell us what happened."

"I tried to leave after two days, but I got distracted. I felt like I was close," I shake my head, trying to remember exactly what I felt, "but I'm not sure."

"Do you remember what it felt like?" Harper asks. "What you were thinking of?"

"I was thinking about this house, actually. How it always smells like toast—"

She says, "You were thinking of details. That must be what triggers it. What about that time in the grocery store?"

Uncle Jasper looks at me, "What happened at the grocery store?"

"It was the cold from the freezer section," I tell him. "But that was more of a panic attack than anything."

"But you still had the pull to leave," Harper says. "What came to mind?"

"The snow . . . the sounds."

"Details." Harper smiles and nods. "That's what it is. You have to hone in on the details and you'll be able to do it."

"Maybe."

"What do you mean, maybe?"

"Because I can't promise anything at this point."

Miles is still silent next to me, my ever constant support when I need him. Uncle Jasper is trying not to look hopeful but it's all he has left. And Harper is more optimistic than all of us put together.

What would they think if they knew I shot someone in the back who was trying to run away? I almost tell them, just to see. It's hard to be hopeful when I have to go back to that.

I scrape my chair back and stand. I say, "I'm going home."

"I'll drive you." Miles tells me, grabbing his keys and not giving me a chance to decline.

"I'll see you guys tomorrow." Harper looks like she wants to get up and walk to me or something, but she stays seated. Just nods.

Outside, the sun is going down and the grass is becoming wet with dew. His old Camry sits behind the truck, and I take my usual seat, brushing away some old gum wrappers to the floor. It smells like him. Mint gum and the laundry detergent

275

his mom uses. The car wheezes to life, brakes squeaking as he turns around.

He looks at me and says, "Not a word."

Because I always have some about this car.

Honestly, I'm just surprised it's still running.

In no time at all, he's pulling into my driveway and parks behind Dad's truck. It feels odd being glad he's home.

"You wanna throw some ball tomorrow?" Miles asks, knowing the right words and knowing I need to do something normal.

"Nine?"

"I'll meet you there." I'm about to get out when he stops me and asks, "What is it?"

I look at him for two seconds, then say, "I shot someone trying to run away."

His mouth presses into a thin line, for once not smiling.

Miles nods.

I nod back.

That's all I needed.

That night, I can't sleep. I don't even try. Dad leaves me watching TV to go to bed around midnight. I can't really remember the last time I did nothing but stare at the television. It feels good to shut off my thoughts. To think about nothing and worry about nothing.

I must doze off in the early hours because I wake to Dad making his coffee in the morning and there's a blanket over me. The television is still on, showing an early morning news show. Dad comes into the living room, and I sit up so he takes a seat.

"Didn't know you were a fan of the *Today Show*," he says, nudging me in the shoulder.

"Is that what it's called?"

Dad's dressed for work and his shoes are already on. He would already be out the door by now, but instead he's sitting here with me. I almost wish he would call in sick but he loves working too much to do that. So I don't ask.

After a few moments of silence, he says, "I'm glad you're home. It's too quiet around here when you're gone."

When I'm gone.

And what about when I don't come back at all. What will he do then? What will happen to my body once I die—will it stay there forever or will it go back to be the proof of what happened? I'm not sure which is worse.

I have to come back. I'll make sure I do.

Screw history.

So I tell him, "I always come back, you know that."

40.
Harper

Kale goes and comes back again within the next week. He appears in the field like last time but not early, and he doesn't feel like talking at all. He mutters something about going home, his face streaked with blood and his hands dirty with brown and red. So we let him disappear into the woods without a fight.

I give him the night and then go to his house in the morning, the sky overcast with a coming storm. Kale must hear me pull up because he opens the door before I get there. His hair is that type of messy when you sleep with it wet, but Kale doesn't look like he's slept at all.

"Hey."

Thunder rumbles overhead and he looks up, like he's not quite sure what he's seeing or maybe he expected something else.

"Are you okay?"

He nods and steps aside. "You wanna come in?"

I take him up on the offer as the first drops of rain fall on my shoulders. The living room is dim with the television on, and there's a blanket and pillow on the couch.

"Have you been sleeping in here?"

"Sleeping is a relative term. I stay up late watching TV, and I'm lucky if I doze off sometime in the morning."

"Sorry," I mumble, because I don't know what else to say.

"It's not your fault."

But it is; he just doesn't want to admit it. We sit down on the couch, a good foot between us, and stare at the screen showing a muted rerun of *The Price is Right*.

"I'm sorry about yesterday," Kale says, turning around an apology of his own. "I just didn't feel like talking or seeing anyone."

I peek a glance at him. "I'm just glad you're back."

He looks down to the carpet, and I'm ready for him to shut me out like he does every other time when we try to talk about his foretold death. But instead, he smiles and looks defiant, like not even history can get in his way.

"I promised I always would be, right?" This is the side of him I've been waiting for—the Kale who doesn't give up. "I'll be back next time, too." Even though he's staying strong, his voice cracks—just enough for me to hear it. "You've shown me I can control it—I'll be able to when the time comes."

"You don't leave for another few days, right?" I say. "So let's make the best of it. Come have lunch with me and Uncle Jasper. There's no food in the house, so you know we'll go somewhere good."

At that he smiles.

The whole rest of the day goes by in a happy blur despite the weather spitting rain at us every other hour. We have lunch and then go see a movie, where Kale holds my hand in the dark so that's all I could think about. He's closed off more than usual, but I take what I can get.

I don't want to see him go again, but I don't mention it. I try not to think about it all, like I know he's trying to do. But it's there—like the clouds overhead—and not letting us forget.

Kale comes through the back door while I'm making breakfast the next day. Uncle Jasper is already in the barn. I'm about to offer him some food before I stop short. He stands barely inside the door, hands deep in his pockets, unable to look at me.

"What is it?"

The silence is deafening between us until—

"There's no point for me to wait around a couple days. I don't think I can bear it. So I'm gonna go."

"But . . ."

"Bye, Harp."

Then he's out the door before I can stop him, and I'm holding the spatula and am too shocked to move. Did that *really* just happen? He hasn't even been here for two days yet. I throw the spatula on the counter and run after him, the screen door slamming shut behind me. He's already at the tree line.

"Kale!"

He doesn't stop, and I run after him, not caring I don't have shoes on. The farther I go down the path, the more fear consumes me. I see the river around the bend, and I slow to a stop when he finally comes into view.

I let myself breathe, relieved he's still here.

"Kale?"

I walk up to him, but he spins around and puts his hand up to stop me, taking a step backward. "Harper, please don't come near me."

"Why?"

"Why do you think?" His body trembles with a shiver, telling me the answer. He's about to leave. I can't go near him, because he doesn't want to risk the chance of dragging me along.

"You don't have to leave right now. You can fight it," I say, trying to believe he'll do it. "You know you can."

Kale can't leave right now. I'm not ready for it, and don't think I ever will be. I have to believe this won't be the last time I'll see him. Thinking about it makes my throat close up.

"There's no point in waiting," he says, showing me something I'm not supposed to see—his fear. He's held it back for so long, not letting me see it, but he can't anymore. Of course he's afraid, but seeing it is something totally different. "It's either today or tomorrow, it won't change anything."

"What brought this on all of the sudden? You were fine yesterday." I take another step closer and he doesn't notice. "Kale—"

His eyes stop wandering, settling on mine. He's calm now, like he really needs me to understand. "I was trying to sleep this morning, knowing I would have to try again the next night and the next, and my thoughts wandered, knowing where I'm going and . . . I realized I'm ready to go. It doesn't make a difference. It's either now or two days from now, and I'm as ready as I'll ever be."

I step closer. "But I'm not ready for you to go."

A little color returns to his face, brightening up his eyes for only a moment before it's gone again. "But *I* am," he whispers, then his voice becomes more determined. "*You're* the one who made me ready. History isn't going to get the better of me. I won't let it."

I realize—I can't argue with him. His mind is set and he really does seem ready to take on the impossible. I knew this day would come, just not so soon. So I kiss him. Not like a good-bye, but something to be continued later. He *will* come back, because he has to.

Kale slips his fingers through mine when I pull away, my hand warm against his. I don't want to forget the color of his eyes or the shape of his jaw. I don't want to forget the way he smells.

"You have to keep your promise," I say. "You have to."

Kale tilts his head ever so slightly, not breaking my gaze. "Have I ever broken it?" He leans in, brushing his lips against my forehead.

"No." A tear escapes my eye and races down my cheek—I can't hold them in.

"Then you have to promise me you'll be here when I come back," he says. "Because I'm going to."

The breeze kicks up around our feet, bringing the smell of winter with it. I close my eyes and press into him. "I promise."

Kale steps away, his lips leaving my skin and his fingers slipping from mine. The smells of summer return, bringing warmth to the places of skin he touched.

I open my eyes and Kale is gone.

41.
Kale

The moment my lips brush against her forehead, I almost decide to stay.

I'm strong enough to resist the pull to be here when Harper opens her eyes. I want to so badly. I want summer and its warm weather. I want to be with the summer girl who's here to stay. I want a chance at a normal life.

But the past is calling me back, and if it's not now, it'll be later. I can't put it off any longer. Every day I wait is another day of torture. Knowing the truth and trying to put it off.

I can't stand it. I'm reminded of it when Harper looks at me. Hear it in her words when she talks to me.

When I step away from her, going against every instinct to hang on, I have to believe this isn't the last time I'll see her.

It's all I have.

And then I watch the world around me fade into something else.

The full trees become bare and cold. Grass turns into snow. Day turns to night. The weight of my rifle digs into my shoulder and my feet are heavy with boots.

I'm standing in the same place I left days ago.
As if no time has passed at all.
In a place where death is a constant reminder.
More now than ever.

42.
Harper

Only minutes pass before I hear Uncle Jasper behind me. I wipe the tears from my cheeks and try to remind myself Kale isn't dead. He's just gone, and he'll be back in a few days' time. Hopefully not more than two days, because that's when January 8 will be where he is. The day after tomorrow at the earliest. I can wait that long. At least, I want to believe I can.

"What's going on?" He probably heard me shout for Kale from the barn.

"He's gone." I turn around and Uncle Jasper wraps his arms around me. I bury my face into his chest, seeking something familiar.

"He'll be back."

I mumble into his shirt, "He promised he would."

Uncle Jasper pulls away and looks down at me. "And Kale has always been one to keep his promises. Come on, let's go back to the house." We start back down the path, his arm wrapped around my shoulders—he needs me as much as I need him right now.

"So, what do we do now?" I ask.

"Hope this day doesn't go by as slow as I think it will."

Around twelve o'clock, a truck comes up the driveway, towing a trailer behind it. I sit on the porch and watch Uncle Jasper back an old muscle car down the ramps—the driver using arm motions like he's trying to land an airplane, which makes me think of Grace the first day we met. It seems so long ago, and I'm lucky to have her as a friend now.

Once the car is backed into the barn, the driver pulls away with the trailer, kicking up dirt behind him. Uncle Jasper locks the barn and comes to sit next to me. The wind picks up, blowing a storm in from the west.

I wrap my arms around my legs, feeling the breeze a little cold. "You aren't going to work on it today?" I've never known Uncle Jasper not to work on a car the moment he got it.

"I won't be able to concentrate," he says, curling the bill of his baseball cap in his hands. "Not until Kale is back."

"You want to find something on TV? And I think we have another frozen pizza in the freezer," I suggest.

Uncle Jasper smiles, granting me his approval, and goes inside, the screen door squeaking shut behind him. I'm hoping some television will keep my thoughts off Kale, because I'll take anything at this point. He's only been gone for two hours, and I'm already anxious for him to come back. To know what he's going through in 1945.

I follow Uncle Jasper into the house, wondering if I'll be able to stomach food today.

It hasn't stopped raining for three hours. It pounds against the roof and the windows, a constant noise slowly making me go crazy.

Uncle Jasper slouches in his chair beside me, his baseball

cap on sideways and an empty can of soda in his hand. He stares blankly at the screen, watching golf. *Golf.*

When the commercials come on, I lift myself out of the chair and go upstairs to use the bathroom. I have an urge to crawl into bed and go to sleep, but I know even if I do, sleep won't come right now.

I splash some cold water on my face, deliberately ignoring the mirror in front of me. Before I go back downstairs, I find my hoodie and slip it on, feeling cold for the first time this summer.

Miles shows up at our door right as the sky is becoming dark, all smiles and perfect hair despite the rain, asking for Kale since he wasn't at home.

"He left early." I stand in the doorway and realize I don't want to go back inside yet. I nod to the porch and ask, "You wanna sit down?"

Miles nods, still trying to look happy despite my news. He sits next to me on the porch swing that faces the field and speaks first, "It's not easy—it's okay to admit that even if you feel you shouldn't."

That's exactly how I feel—guilty for feeling something when Kale leaves, knowing what he goes through is harder than me waiting for him to come back. "It just feels . . ." I'm not sure if I know the right word. Then I test it. "Disconcerting?"

"To put it mildly, yes," he agrees. "We were driving into the city one weekend right after I got my license and this song came on that we both liked. We sang it together a hundred times before, trading verses and me always taking the high parts. At least trying to." I smile at that and try not to laugh. "So we were singing along and then it was Kale's turn, but he wasn't singing his part. I looked over to find his seat empty."

I can say nothing except—"Shit."

Miles laughs, probably because he's never heard me swear before.

"It's expecting one thing and getting another. Something you just gotta roll with. That's why we're friends with him, right? To be here for him when he gets back. It's the side effects of being friends with Kale Jackson."

"Does it get easier?"

"You get used to it."

The rain tapers off during the night. Uncle Jasper already went up to bed, and I'm watching an infomercial about brooms. When I can't hold my eyes open any longer, I shut the television off and blindly make my way upstairs.

Without turning the lights on, I change into a pair of shorts and a tank-top. I open the windows before I climb into bed, only taking comfort in the sound of the storm tonight when nothing else comes close. While lying in bed, facing the dark windows with the sound of rain coming through them, I brush my hand over the place where Kale slept all those nights ago. The warmth of him is long gone. When Kale leaves, he leaves nothing behind except the memory of him, and it's never enough.

There is one question I've been ignoring today.

What if Kale doesn't come back? This is what Uncle Jasper must have felt when Aunt Holly died. I don't understand how life can continue on when someone so close to you goes away forever.

It's something that hurts to think about, and something I hope I don't have to deal with anytime soon.

43.
Kale

When I look up at the sky, time is irrelevant.

The clouds look the same and the sun is just as bright.

It's one thing that never changes. The only thing that brings comfort. Because wherever I might end up, the sky is always there—the sun during the day and the moon at night.

Two constant things when nothing else can be.

With my helmet hanging from my fingers, I close my eyes and soak in whatever warmth I can get on my face. Missing summer in this cold place.

"Jackson."

I look down in time to see Perkins throw me something. I catch it in my helmet and see an unopened pack of Lucky Strike cigarettes.

"Where did you find these?" I ask. I shoulder my rifle and put my helmet back on so I can have my hands free. I haven't had a smoke since last night and I'm dying for one.

"The captain gave them to me," he says.

I pull two out, hiding the rest away for later. Perkins flips his lighter open—one he found a couple days ago—and I start them at the same time, handing one to him once they've caught.

I take a long drag and silently mouth a curse word.

It's horrible and wonderful all at once.

"Why did he give them to you?" I ask, sparing him a glance. "Special medic privileges?"

Perkins tucks his helmet under his arm, running his hand through his short blond hair with the cigarette between his lips. "I wish," he says. "I never thought I would be addicted to these damn things."

I laugh once. "You didn't answer my question."

He glances over. "I told him I was trying to find you, and he just gave them to me and said, 'Here, I owe him one.'"

I can't believe Captain Price remembered the night we had a smoke together. I'm a little baffled he remembers me out of the hundreds of men in our company.

"That was a while ago," I say, still thinking about it.

At least I think it was.

Perkins shrugs, continuing to smoke. Most of the guys around us are eating lunch and enjoying the bright afternoon despite the snow on the ground. We haven't seen any Germans for two days. I still don't want to think about the last time I was here—how I came back with blood on my face and the look Uncle Jasper's gave me when he saw it.

Today, I welcome the silence.

I take another quick drag and ask, "Do you know what the date is?"

Perkins shakes his head but looks over his shoulder where a few guys sit. One of them is using an ammo box as a pot, warming some food over a fire.

"Hey, Trip!"

One of the guys looks up. "Doc?"

"What's the date today?"

"Uh—I think it's the eighth today. New Years was just last

week." He has a pretty strong Texan accent. But then he grins and asks, "Got a date, Doc?"

Perkins smiles. "What's it to you if I do?"

"I don't know, is there a sister?"

"Not one that would take a liking to you."

Trip's smile drops and the guy next to him punches him in the arm, laughing. When Perkins turns his head back, he shrugs one shoulder. "It's the eighth. Why do you want to know?"

"Just wondering." But my hands are shaking a little more and I glance at the sky again. Looking for some sort of refuge.

I finish off my cigarette and want another. I've never had two in a row before, and I don't want to start now. I've never even told Harper I smoke here. It's not like I do it at home, even though I've come close, but I wish I had told her something as simple as this.

I suddenly ask, "Do you ever think about dying?" I see him look over in my peripheral but I don't turn. I almost regret asking—though I think I would regret it more if I hadn't.

With every minute that passes, my hands shake a little more and my stomach tightens at every sound.

I'm barely holding myself together at this point.

"When did you get all morbid on me?" he asks.

"It's just a question." I shake my head, avoiding his eyes. "Never mind."

Perkins looks around, taking notice of the men around us. He nods for me to follow him and takes me further back from the camp. Picking a place where there's nobody within earshot.

"We shouldn't talk about that kind of stuff around them," he says. "It's not a subject anyone likes to bring up. What's been with you these last two days?"

"What do you mean?"

"You've been quiet—*more* quiet than usual," he points out. "I think I know you well enough by now to know something is wrong."

I take my helmet off again, feeling more normal without it on. And because I can't help myself, I pull the pack of cigarettes out, my shaky fingers making it hard. I offer another to him but he shakes his head.

"I don't know. Do you ever think you're meant for something more?" I ask. "Or that when you die, you'll die for nothing?"

With the cigarette between my lips, I wait for the flame to catch.

When it does, I stare at the ground because I can't bring myself to look anywhere else.

"All right, look," Perkins says, shifting his weight. "I'm going to tell you something, but I don't know if it'll make you feel better or worse about this. When I first became a medic, I really felt like if I only ended up saving *one* person, it would be worth it. Just one. Because to me, one life is just as important as one hundred."

"But you've saved a lot more than one person," I say. "You actually make a difference here."

"And you don't?" He motions his arm behind us, back toward the company. "Every time you take down a German, you're saving someone. Don't you get that? You look out for our asses every damn day."

I shake my head. "That's different. You're saving people, and I kill them. If it's not me, it'll be someone else. Everyone here has a gun and knows how to use it. I'm talking about like . . . changing history."

"Changing history," he repeats.

I finally flick my cigarette in the snow and turn to him, my heart pounding a little too fast. So many thoughts scream at me, reminding me and never leaving me alone. I think about the day I ruined the house and my tongue can no longer keep silent. So I explode on him. "*Yes. That's exactly what I'm talking about. Because why else am I fucking here? Why? Why?* If you know the answer to that, I would really like to know. Why do I keep coming back here if there's no point in it all?"

"Kale—"

"Because this has already happened," I gesture around with my hands, "and nothing good comes from me being here. It feels like life is putting me through one big joke." I stand there and stare at him, on the edge of breaking down. "And I don't find it all that funny."

He thinks I've lost my mind. I know he does. How can he know what the hell I'm talking about?

"Do you have something you want to tell me?" he asks.

I put my helmet back on and take a deep breath. "No. Just . . . forget I said anything."

I start to turn away, but he places a hand on my shoulder. His eyes are serious again. He needs me to know he's not joking. "If you need me to, I can see you unfit for duty. It's not something to be ashamed of."

"Isn't it, though? I didn't sign up to be sent home."

"I don't have to remind you why we're here," he says. "Every man here plays his part, but as for dying . . . there are some things you can only figure out on your own. Yeah, everyone here thinks about that every day, but it's not something you want to dwell on. Not everyone is meant for great things, but I believe everyone is a part in something bigger than us all."

I look up at that, because somehow this easygoing medic I've known for the last few weeks is making a point. It's true that I've been thinking about something bigger than me, because why else would the past pull me here time and time again?

But maybe me being here is like a pebble being thrown into a quiet pond.

Something so small can have an effect on everything.

I hear Captain Price's voice ring out behind us. "Second squad, you're on patrol! Move out."

I shoulder my rifle and look at Perkins one last time before following the others. Lieutenant Gates is with us today, and he takes point with Stiles.

"Perkins, you stay behind," I hear Captain Price say behind me. "They'll let you know if you're needed."

"I'm afraid I have to insist today, Captain. I don't like the thought of them going out on patrol without a medic nearby. And I'm not needed here at the moment. Unless you're thinking someone is going to choke on their lunch."

I stop and turn around, catching the captain's eye when I do. I don't give any indication to what I want him to say.

I'm surprised that Perkins is insisting on coming at all.

"Just be careful," Captain Price says, still looking at me. "I want my medic back in one piece. You, too, Jackson."

"I'll keep an eye on him, Cap," I tell him.

He nods, and Perkins and I move off to join the others. About twenty minutes in, the talking dies down when we come upon a new stretch of woods, not knowing if the enemy could be nearby. The trees are tall and thick, leaving no underbrush for us to push through. It makes everything quiet.

I keep my eyes sharp, looking for signs of life or flashes of metal. In the dark places where the trees shadow, it's hard to see if anything is hiding.

I've been part of a few sudden attacks before. Whether it was in a town or the woods, they all feel the same. Your body wants to freeze up like a rabbit, too afraid to run for its hole, so you have to be quicker than that. You have to be moving the moment you hear it, or else it'll be too late.

But this time when I see movement up ahead, the first thing

my mind goes to is Perkins. He stands next to me, not seeing what I'm seeing. I can't handle another one of my friends dying.

Stiles calls out before I can. Warning everyone before the woods explode with gunshots.

I dive to my left, taking Perkins down with me before he has a chance to get shot. Bullets hit the tree next to us, showering the snow with chips of wood.

My shoulder blooms with pain, as though I fell on it the wrong way.

But when I go to push myself up, I know it's something more. My vision is spotted and I can't breathe right. The adrenaline coursing through me is the only reason I'm able to push myself against the tree.

Perkins is already crouched into front of me, pressing his hands over the right side of my chest.

I look down and see blood covering his hands. *My* blood.

I wonder how it got there so fast.

It certainly can't be real.

"Fall back!" I don't know where the voice comes from. It sounds far away. Too far for me to answer. I know I need to be moving, but my body keeps me in place.

More bullets whiz past our hiding place, the tree taking a beating it doesn't deserve. The gunshots are closer now. The snow on either side of us is pelted by invisible drops of iron.

I look down at the rifle in my hand, wondering how we can get out of this. Perkins is looking for something in his satchel, swearing when he can't find it. I'm having a hard time making sense of things, and it's even harder to focus, but I grab onto what I do know.

I lift my face to the sky one last time, knowing what I have to do.

It's so blue it reminds me of home.

It reminds me of Harper.

A warm hand taps my cheek, bringing my eyes back down on my friend. There's dirt smeared on his cheekbone and his eyes are more serious than I've ever seen them. But he's alive. That's what matters.

"I'm gonna get you out of here," he says. "You're going to be all right."

I glance down at his hand, still trying to hold my blood in. I try to laugh, but everything hurts. Everything. Hurts so much I can't breathe.

There's no way I can make it back in time.

He knows it.

I know it.

"I'm not going anywhere," I tell him.

Our guys are still trying to hold them off, but the lieutenant is yelling for us to fall back. By the sound of it, we're outnumbered.

Perkins is about to stick me with morphine, but I catch his hand. "Don't, you need to save it. Don't waste it on me."

"Kale—"

"*Stop.*" He finally looks at me and I let go of his wrist, pushing the medicine back at him. "You need to go, and you are going to leave me here. The only way—" My body freezes when another wave of pain comes over me. When I'm able to breathe, my heart is pounding faster. "The only way you'll get out of here is with covering fire, and I'm not about to see another friend of mine die."

"You already saved me," he says. "Now let me save you."

"Why don't you do me a favor and make sure you stay alive first." I clench my jaw and take his hand away from my wound. My fingers are almost shaking too much, but I manage to break off one of my dog tags and press it in his bloodied palm. "Please, Dan."

"You know I outrank you, right?" he says. "I could order you to let me take you back."

"You could," I agree, trying to talk through a tight jaw. If I let it, it shakes too much. "But I'm asking you not to. As my friend. You know what you said about one life being just as important as a hundred?"

He barely nods.

"Yours is worth it." The last thing I give him is the pack of Lucky Strikes. "Tell the captain thanks for me. For more than just the smokes."

Perkins is doing everything he can to resist taking me back with him. I pull my rifle into my lap and nod for him to go. "Go the moment I start shooting. I'll keep them off your back."

When he leans in, I dip my head and bump my helmet with his. Then without saying another word, I stand, using every last drop of adrenaline I can find, pressing against the tree for support. Sweat drips from my forehead and my visions spins for a moment before I can breathe again.

I don't need to hit any targets—and probably can't in the state I'm in—but all I need to do is give Perkins enough time to get back to the line our squad has made behind some fallen trees. If he can make it there, he'll be safe.

I nod down at him once and he nods back, saying everything he needs to.

Then I swing around and start shooting.

The first three bullets hit their targets before they realize they're being shot at so close. They take cover, forgetting about the unarmed man darting out from behind the tree.

I keep shooting until I can't.

Once the clip is gone, I press myself against the tree again. Just in time. Bullets pound the wood even more.

Despite my situation, I smile, because he made it. It's then I realize—saving one person's life will be enough for me.

It might not be something heroic or something that's written into history books, but it's enough for me.

I did what I came here to do, and now it's time for me to go home.

I don't have to wait for the right time.

Or wait for my heart to tell me so.

I'm going because I want to go. Maybe the chance was within me the whole time, or maybe I'm only now able to do it.

Either way, I'm going home.

I have a promise to keep.

44.
Harper

On the second day of Kale being gone, I venture outside after dinner to breathe some fresh air, hoping it'll calm my nerves. Uncle Jasper and I haven't left the house all day, and we've barely held a decent conversation. It's like we're not living in reality right now, waiting for something to happen that shouldn't exist in the first place.

I walk deeper into the field and away from the house. The sun has set, leaving the sky red and orange with the moon already taking its place. I stand there and close my eyes, listening to the sounds of the crickets and frogs down near the creek.

"Harper."

I open my eyes, wondering how I can hear him so clearly. Then the air fills with the smell of snow and I know I can't be imagining it. When I turn around, he's standing there. Ten feet away and never looking so real.

"Kale."

He smiles, but it's wrong. Something dark is smeared on his face, and I take a couple of steps forward, having trouble believing he's really here, afraid he's going to disappear again.

"You're here." I laugh once out of relief. "You came back."

"I promised—" His eyes close, warning me something more is wrong. When he opens them again, even with the dark night, I can see he's in pain. Now that I look closer, he's unsteady on his feet and not breathing right. "Didn't I?"

Then I catch sight of something on his upper chest—a stain growing darker and darker against his white T-shirt. It's blood. I don't have to see the color to know.

Before I can help him, Kale's legs fold beneath him and he sinks to the ground.

I yell toward the house, "Uncle Jasper!"

I kneel down next to Kale, pressing my hands against his chest, where the blood is pouring from. It doesn't seem right that he's bleeding when there's no hole in his shirt.

I drag my eyes away, up to his face. "What happened?"

"Aside from getting shot?" His smile is quickly replaced when he sucks in a breath. After he relaxes against the ground, he's too still. "Our patrol was attacked and we were outnumbered. I told them to go back without me."

"But what will happen when you go back?" I ask.

"Harper?" I look up and see Uncle Jasper trying to see me through the dark. "What's wrong?"

"It's Kale!" I shout back. "He got shot!"

He runs back into the house and I look down at Kale again, not ready to lose him when I just got him back.

"Don't you get it?" he says. "I'm not going back. What you read on the Internet was what happened. I can read it to be sure, but I have no doubt. It says I was killed, because they really believed I was." Kale pulls out his dog tags—his hands also covered in his blood—and I see that one of them is missing. "It's done, Harper. I'm not going back there."

I lean in and press my lips to his cold ones. Then I tell him, "I told you you could do it, didn't I?"

The screen door slams shut and Uncle Jasper runs toward

us. "I called 911," he says, kneeling down on the other side of Kale. "What happened?"

I move my hands away and he rips open Kale's T-shirt, exposing something I can't look at. He presses a wad of cloth to it, causing Kale to wince and suck in another breath.

"He was shot," I tell him, feeling my hands shaking against my legs, still covered in blood and staining my jeans. In this light, it's like black tar spilled everywhere.

"The ambulance should be here soon," he says. "I didn't want to risk driving him myself. He might lose too much blood if I do."

Kale tenses and says through his teeth, "It fucking hurts."

"Your mouth seems to be getting looser these days, Kale." It seems an odd thing to talk about until I realize he's only trying to get Kale's mind off the pain. "After this is all over, I expect you to work on that."

I smile and look over at my uncle. "I think he picked up that habit from you."

Kale smiles but doesn't laugh. He's struggling to stay awake, I can tell.

A few minutes later, I catch sight of flashing lights coming down the main road and hear the siren. Uncle Jasper takes my hand to replace his over the wound. "Press down hard," he says and takes off toward the driveway, making sure they find us.

"How did you do it?" I finally ask, wanting him to stay awake.

"Do what?"

"You left early."

His mouth turns up at the edges. "I just thought of you and wanted to be here. I wanted to come home."

His eyes start to close and he's not moving much anymore.

"Hey, guess what," I say.

Kale looks at me through glazed eyes, barely moving now. "What?"

"I named my car." I try to laugh, but it doesn't come out right.

He smiles. "What did you name him?"

"Fiver."

"From that rabbit book you like?"

"Yeah."

"It's perfect."

The ambulance comes to a stop, and Uncle Jasper points over to us. I don't want to leave Kale's side, but Uncle Jasper pulls me away, giving the EMTs the room they need.

"Will he be all right?"

Uncle Jasper pulls me close, and we follow them back to the ambulance, Kale on a stretcher between them. "He'll be fine."

We stand and watch them load him into the back of the vehicle, my eyes glued to the rising and falling of his chest.

It's something I've always taken for granted.

We follow the ambulance to the hospital, and when they pull Kale out of the back, his eyes are closed. I vaguely recall Uncle Jasper asking if something is wrong, but they won't answer. We follow them closely through the doors of the ER, where a nurse tries to stop us from going any further.

"I'm sorry, but family only," she says.

"We are his family," Uncle Jasper says. "He only lives with his dad, and I can't get a hold of him right now."

She's shaking her head—about to protest us going back there—when a nurse behind the desk hangs up the phone and smiles at Uncle Jasper.

"Jasper, how are you?" she says. "Is everything all right?"

The nurse standing in our way answers for us. "They came in with the kid just now, but they aren't his immediate family."

A look of worry crosses her face. "Who?"

"It's Kale," Uncle Jasper answers.

The nurse behind the desk waves her hand. "Let them through, Sylvia."

"But they aren't—"

"Yes, they are," she says firmly. "Let them through."

Sylvia finally moves aside, and I see Uncle Jasper give the nurse behind the desk a smile of gratitude. We pass through the door, and I smell antiseptics and something metallic. They've taken Kale into a room to the right, and we can't get any closer other than looking through the glass. There's a half dozen people in there with him, all wearing masks and green scrubs with red-stained gloves. There's so much blood.

"I'm going to try to call Peter again." Uncle Jasper squeezes my shoulder before going to find a quiet place to talk.

When I can't watch anymore, I sit down on a hard chair outside the swinging doors and wait, something I haven't taken a liking to within the last few days. I keep telling myself he isn't going to die. He's here now—made it back and he's going to be okay. I text Miles and let him know what happened. He responds immediately, saying he's on his way.

After a time, Uncle Jasper comes back and sits down next to me. He doesn't look any better than I do. "One of the doctors asked me what happened," he says.

"What did you tell them?" I ask, turning to him.

"That it was a hunting accident. At least, that's what Kale said before they took him away, right?"

"Right."

"A police officer might come and do a report, but I'll do the talking. If anything, just nod along."

A few people come out of the room with blood stains all over their scrubs. Uncle Jasper leaves to talk with them more, and I stand to look through the window again. His heart monitor is going at a steady pace, and he's already hooked up with multiple IVs. They've completely cut away his T-shirt, leaving him only with a pair of jeans and the upper right side of his chest wrapped in white bandages.

His eyes are still closed.

All but one of the nurses leave the room, taking with them a tray of red tools. Uncle Jasper shoots me a glance before following them down the hall without saying a word.

I settle down in my chair again, watching the nurses and doctors tend to other patients, a few of them going in and out of Kale's room. I don't know how long I've been sitting there, but the next thing I know, I'm being shaken awake. When I see the young nurse who has woken me, I almost panic, thinking something happened to Kale.

"Everything's all right," she assures me, "they just moved him down the hall now that he's stable."

"So he's going to be okay?"

"He's going to be fine. It's room 110."

She points down the hall and I shuffle away, my legs not working properly yet. I pass by rooms already filled with patients, some awake and talking to their families and some alone, sleeping the night away. I'm almost to his room when Uncle Jasper appears behind me, glancing over his shoulder.

"Where did you go?" I ask. "You've been gone forever."

"I actually wasn't gone that long."

"I fell asleep."

"That's because you haven't slept in two days."

I don't argue with that and ask again, "Where did you go?"

He nods his head a little, motioning me to sit down next to him. He waits for a doctor to pass before taking something from his pocket. A misshapen bullet sits in the palm of his hand.

"Is that . . ." It's the bullet Kale was shot with.

Uncle Jasper puts it away, glancing down the hallway again. "He's lucky he wasn't shot with something bigger. I'm guessing it's from a sidearm. Maybe an officer's gun, if I could guess."

"How can you tell?"

"Because he would be dead otherwise."

A couple of nurses walk by, and Uncle Jasper's eyes follow them like he's going to be caught doing something.

I narrow my eyes. "How did you get that?"

"We can't let them examine it," he says. "How could I explain a bullet from World War II being lodged in his shoulder?"

I nod slowly. "That would be a tough one."

He settles deeper into his chair and looks over. "Did he say anything about what happened?"

I tell him everything I can remember. About Kale being shot and his squad thinking he was already dead before he left. As far as they knew, he died in those woods on January 8.

"So they marked him as killed in action because, to them, that's exactly what happened. But instead, he came back home." Uncle Jasper takes off his hat and lays it on his knee, sighing.

"I'm glad you turned out to be right," I tell him.

"About what?"

"About history being wrong." I lean my head on his shoulder, finally able to rid the worry built up within me. "I don't think I'll ever be able to look him up on the Internet again."

"Hopefully you won't have to. Before he started going back to World War II, he was rarely in any kind of danger. To tell you the truth, it doesn't make sense if the past pulled him back only to be shot. Did he say anything about what happened before?"

"No, nothing." I lift my head to look at him. "But I do remember something about the article online, because it wasn't about him at all. Kale was only mentioned in it."

"What was it about, do you remember?"

"It was about this guy who was a medic in World War II." I shake my head, unable to recall what it said. "I should read it again and ask Kale about it. It'll probably clear up everything."

"I would be curious to know," he says. "Whatever it was, I hope it was worth him going through all that."

A little while later, Miles shows up, followed by Kale's dad, his hair in disarray and his shoes tied in hasty knots. I watch silently from my chair—too tired to listen or even move—as the nurses try to tell him Kale is going to be okay, but Uncle Jasper is the only one who's able to calm him down.

Miles sits next to me, for once not smiling or trying to make a joke.

Peter says a few words to Uncle Jasper before following the nurse into the room. I would give a lot to see him right now, but I would give even more to have him healed and back home where he belongs.

After a little while, the nurse tells us we have to leave—family members only, even when there's only one right now, and I can't fight to stay, even when I want to. Miles says he's going to stay a while longer and the staff don't fight him about it. I follow Uncle Jasper through the maze of halls and then outside to the truck.

At some point on the way home, without even knowing it, I fall asleep. Not even waking when Uncle Jasper carries me up to my room.

The blood stains on my hands when I wake in the morning are the only proof I need to know that what happened with Kale wasn't a dream.

45.
Kale

After three days of being in the hospital, I'm on my way home.

My shoulder is sore but healed, something the doctors were more than curious to know about. They had a hard time letting me go home, but after having no excuses for me to stay under observation, they didn't have much choice.

I blamed my fast healing on one of the nurse's "loving touch," and while they were laughing at that, Dad and I made our escape.

Those three days went by excruciatingly slow. I still had a hard time sleeping—whether it was sleeping in a hospital bed, or something else, I don't know. The first thing I did when I woke up after they took the bullet from my shoulder was make Dad promise he wouldn't call Mom.

The fewer people who know about this, the better.

I don't want her to think I'm not fit to live with Dad—not like she took any notice before—but it's something I don't want to risk. Libby would never be able to come back home if Mom found out. That's why I made him promise not to ever tell her about anything.

Some things are better left unknown.

Even something as big as this.

As for Uncle Jasper and Harper, I haven't seen them since the ambulance drove me away from the house. It's my fault, really, because I told them not to visit.

They already saw me at my worst, and I didn't want them to see me until I was myself again. And I know it's hard for Uncle Jasper to be in the hospital—especially the same one Aunt Holly died in. I wanted that whole hospital thing to be over as soon as possible.

And now it finally is.

"How are you feeling?" Dad asks. "Are you all right? We can go back if you need to."

"I'm fine, really."

He keeps glancing over. "Are you sure?"

"Dad, really. I told you I heal a little faster than normal, so why don't you believe me? Plus, even if you don't believe *me*, you can at least believe the doctors."

Dad nods and turns his attention back to the road.

"I just . . ." He hasn't said much over the last few days. Maybe now he's finally able to say what's been on his mind. He probably thinks I haven't noticed, but I have. "I was really worried about you, Kale." He looks over. "I've always had this fear of you never coming back. And when I got the call about you being shot, I thought that was it. That I would be never get the chance to be the dad you deserved to have."

It's not something I expected him to admit.

"I'm sorry," I say, wanting to say something more, because he has every right to feel that way. I'm the one who leaves people to worry about me while I'm gone.

"You don't have to be sorry for anything," he says. "It's not like you had a choice."

"Maybe if I tried harder . . . if I was stronger." I don't know.

The truck slows down, and he pulls over to the side of the road. He slowly takes his hands from the wheel and looks over.

"Kale, whatever made you believe you aren't strong—or if someone said something to make you think differently—it's not true. Don't think that. We all go through trials in life, but yours are just harder than everyone else's, and quite a lot different. I don't think there's anyone in the world who could have been through what you have and came out stronger in the end. Do you hear me?"

I nod, not trusting my voice enough to say anything. I feel anything but strong. But I survived, so that's better than nothing.

"You're strong because you kept coming back," he says. "It's more than I deserved."

I think back on all the times I came home after days of being gone, not wanting to go home because I didn't want to face the mess I had made there. It never felt like enough—like I was a burden more than anything.

"I'm sorry," I say again.

"For what?"

"For not being the son you wanted." I taste salted tears on my lips. "For not being *normal*." I wish I could take back everything I've put him through. That I was strong enough to change the past instead of having this curse I can do nothing with. "I'm sorry," I whisper again, because it doesn't seem like enough to say it once.

Dad leans over the seat, wrapping his arms around me to bring me into his chest.

"You're more than I ever could have hoped for," he says, holding me tight. "I'm proud of you, Kale."

And before I know it, I'm hugging him back.

After we get home and Dad leaves for work, I go upstairs to take a shower. I stand under the hot water, relishing it because I feel anything but cold.

I'm home now, and I'm not leaving anytime soon.

It's time I exercise the control Harper swears I have.

When the hot water runs out, I get changed into a clean pair of jeans and a T-shirt. I walk out the door, leaving my sweatshirt behind. I glance under the tree where my car is usually parked, forcing my legs to keep walking toward the woods.

That car always felt like it was a part of me. I know it's just a piece of metal with a name, but it was the first thing I ever called my own. I worked on it for hours. Cut my hand open on the broken exhaust. Lost sleep over trying to figure out what was wrong with the starter.

I stop thinking about it.

I should know better than anyone—the past can't change.

Even before I reach the back door, it opens and Harper comes out. Her Chuck Taylors once again untied and her eyes brighter than I've seen them in a long time. She stops on the bottom step, looking down at me.

"Hey," she says. "You're back."

"Why do you keep saying that like I won't be?" I step up to join her, struggling not to touch her.

Then I think: Why?

All my life I've held myself back.

I don't need to now.

I trail my fingers up her arm to her shoulder, all the way to her jaw, slipping my hand through her hair. I kiss her, not sure how I'll ever be able to stop. Harper slides her fingers through the belt loops of my jeans, pulling me closer.

It's enough to make my heart go crazy.

The screen door opens, and for the first time, we don't

break apart right away. I smile against her mouth and open my eyes, turning to see Uncle Jasper standing there.

"Uncle Jasper," I say.

"Kale."

He looks between me and Harper. "Come inside, I have something to show you."

"Is it a gun?" I ask. "Am I going to get shot again?"

"Not today, smartass."

"There's that language again," I say, smiling.

Uncle Jasper looks like he wants to say something else, but he stops, looking down at Harper's thumb still hooked in my jeans. He suddenly shakes his head and goes back inside.

"Too soon for the gun jokes?" I ask her.

"Maybe a little. Give it another month or two."

Harper sneaks me another kiss and I follow her into the kitchen. We sit down in our respective chairs, Uncle Jasper looking at me differently than he usually does.

"I'm glad you were able to recover so quickly," he says. "How does it feel?"

"A little stiff, but nothing too horrible." He keeps fingering a piece of paper on the table, and I can't stand waiting for him to tell me whatever he's holding back. "What?"

"We weren't sure if you wanted to see this," he says, "but I wanted to at least give you the option."

I glance at the paper between his hands. "What is it?"

Harper answers for him. "It's the article I found online. The one that told us you were going to die."

"I don't know if I—"

Uncle Jasper leans forward, cutting me off. "That's not what we wanted to show you. This man wrote a short piece about his time in the war, and he mentions you. We thought you might want to see it."

"Who wrote it?"

"A medic," he says, and I instantly know who he's talking about. I can see him like I'll suddenly go back there—blue eyes, blond hair. The only friend I was able to save. "Do you want to see it?"

I don't know if I want to see it. Uncle Jasper slides it over, face down. I finger the corner and catch his eye. "Why did you look it up again?" I ask him.

"Because I needed to know if it was all worth it."

I glance down at the paper, already knowing the answer to that. "It was," I say. "I don't need to read it to know that."

I slide it back to him.

"So it's true then?" he asks.

I nod. "It's true."

Uncle Jasper folds the paper and gets up to put it away in the drawer where he keeps old newspapers, mostly those that have crosswords he couldn't finish. "If you ever want to read it, it'll be here. But there's something you should know about it."

"What?"

He sits down and finally smiles. "It was only written two years ago."

I sit up straighter and ask, "He's still alive?" This is something I hadn't expected. Most World War II veterans have passed away by now.

Uncle Jasper nods. "He got married and had four kids, and he now has six grandchildren. If you hadn't saved his life, Kale, that whole family never would have existed. So I think you're right—it was worth it."

The last memory I have of Perkins was him looking at me before I told him to run. There was blood and dirt streaked on his face—his eyes the only things in color in that whole world. It was the moment I knew he would live.

That was what I had gone there to do. Save him.

Ripples in a pond.

That's all the past is.

It's almost unbelievable that one person could have such an effect on it. It makes me wonder about the small things in life, and how much they have to do with the bigger picture. How many times have I traveled to the past to do small but important things? I'll probably never know.

We're not all meant for great things, but we all play a role somehow, no matter how big or small.

It's my first night home from the hospital, and I can't sleep. I should be able to because sleeping in the hospital is terrible. People always coming in your room in the middle of night, wanting to take blood pressure or make you take pills.

I should be able to sleep, but the nightmares still come— something that might not ever go away. I know war can give you scars on the outside. I never thought about the scars left on the inside once it was over.

Ones that may never heal.

In the morning, not long after the sun peeks through my curtains, there's a knock on my door. I push myself up and Dad comes in, pausing before sitting down on the bed.

"Do you always wear your jeans to bed?" he asks, eyeing me like maybe I'm not feeling well or something.

I shrug. "Sometimes."

It's not like I can sleep anyway.

He keeps glancing at the single dog tag around my neck, his mind elsewhere. Talking with Dad can still be an awkward occurrence, something I'm sure will become easier with time.

"What's going on?" I ask.

He comes back to the present, giving me an unexpected

smile. "I have something for you. I've been wanting to tell you for a while now, but I needed to make sure I could get it first."

"You got me something?"

His smile falters a fraction. "I needed to do something, and this is the only way I know how."

"Dad, you didn't need to do anything," I say, really meaning it. "You being here and believing me is more than enough."

"I know," he says. "But this is something I needed to do, and I don't want to hear you complaining or telling me I didn't have to. I did it because I'm your dad. Doesn't that give me the right to give you things?"

I finally return his smile. "What is it?"

"It's downstairs." He stands up and tosses me a shirt off the floor. "Come on."

I pull my shirt quick and follow him down. I'm a little caught off guard when he leads me outside. I squint against the morning sun and glance around.

Then I can do nothing but stare.

"Dad . . ."

I hear him pull keys from his pocket, and he presses them into my hand. I look down and see that they're *my* keys. Mine.

"I told you I would try fixing things, didn't I?"

"Yeah, but—" I don't know what else to say. My car is parked in my spot like it never left. Except it's not the same. It's so much better than I could have done myself. I could never afford to do any body work, and now my car has suddenly transformed into what I've always dreamed it could be. "This is . . ."

My words become forgotten.

I have my car back.

Dad puts his arm around my shoulders. "You don't deserve any less," he says. "Uncle Jasper was kind enough to help me with it, and I don't want my son driving in a car that looks like a piece of shit."

I laugh because that's the same thing the guy said when he took it from me.

"But how did you pay for it?"

"I've had things laying around I didn't need anymore."

It doesn't take me long to think of it. And when I do, I suddenly don't want this anymore. It's too much. For what I put him through, he shouldn't have done it.

"Your baseball cards," I say. "Dad you shouldn't have—"

"They were collecting dust in my closet." He flies his hand aside like it doesn't matter. "I knew I would need money one day, and that day just came a little sooner than expected."

I look down, where my keys lay so familiar in my hands.

I can only say, "Thanks, Dad."

He pulls me in tighter, and we stand there together and look at the day like it's something brand new.

I'm glad I made that promise to Harper all those years ago.

And it's one I intend to keep, even if I have to prove history wrong all over again.

46.
Harper

I stand in front of the mirror, trying to convince myself the dress fits right and my hair isn't too boring. I haven't worn a dress in months, and I kinda missed it. That's really weird for me to admit, but sometimes dressing up is fun.

Grace drove me to the mall and showed me the only stores worth going into, and she helped me pick out something that worked. The whole time I wished Mom could've been there, too.

In the end, though, I'm glad the way things worked out, even when my thoughts betray me. If I went to live with Mom, I wouldn't be here right now. I wouldn't be going to school in the fall with Libby—who finally convinced her Mom to let her come back after agreeing she'd go to college somewhere near her.

And I wouldn't be with Kale.

I've known him for a long time, and yet I've never been so nervous about seeing him before. It's like something old and new, all at once.

"Harper, he's here!" Uncle Jasper yells upstairs.

I take one more look at the white and blue summer dress, thinking maybe I should have picked something different. It's too late now. I grab my purse off the bed and go downstairs. Uncle Jasper waits by the door, smiling when he sees me.

"Nice choice of shoes," he says, meeting me at the bottom step.

"That's all you have to say?" I ask, glancing down at my Chucks.

"Be home before midnight?" Before I can slap him in the chest, he says, "You look beautiful. I wish Holly was here to see you."

I glance over his shoulder where her chair still sits by the window. "Me, too."

Uncle Jasper kisses me on the forehead, the same way Dad used to when I was little. "I know she would be proud of you, just as I am." Then he nods toward the door. "He's waiting outside."

I stand on my tiptoes and hug him. "Thank you," I whisper into his ear.

After a moment, Uncle Jasper clears his throat and pulls away. "You should go," he says.

I plant a kiss on his cheek, smiling because he's trying not to cry. I leave, not wanting to torture him any longer. Kale is waiting for me in the driveway and succeeds in making my heart skip a beat and start over too fast.

Never in my life have I seen Kale wear anything except jeans and some sort of casual shirt, something I'll surely never complain about because he looks good in anything. And when he asked me out on our long-belated first date, I knew somewhere in the back of my mind he would dress a little better than normal.

But I didn't except him to look so *good*.

His black slacks look new and fitted, and he's wearing a white dress shirt, the sleeves rolled up to his elbows. And to pull everything together, a black tie hangs slightly loose at the neck.

And what surprises me most of all—his hair is styled. Not messy or in his face, but arranged in a way I never imagined he could pull off.

I have to remember how to walk. Kale watches me the whole time—his hands in his pockets. When I'm close enough to see the specks of blue in his eyes, I say, "You look . . . amazing."

He smiles and glances down at himself. "I've been known how to dress well, if need be."

"Known by *who*?" I ask. I catch sight of the car behind him, not at all sure about what I'm seeing. "Is this *your* car?"

His eyes never leave me. "It is." The old Mustang looks brand new, its black paint shining and without a scratch. "I needed something decent to pick up the girl I love."

I force my gaze off his car, feeling so aware of what I'm going to say. "The boy I love should know these things don't matter."

Kale's smile turns into something else—a side of him I've only seen a handful of times. Every one of those times being the moments before he's kissed me. It's a side of him I've grown to love.

"Do you remember when we first met?" he asks. "When you were covered in mud and said we had something in common because we both had weird names?"

"It was on the back porch."

Kale nods slowly. "There hasn't been a day since then when I haven't thought about you. Not even when you were gone all these years." He steps closer, his eyes never leaving mine. "I can't think straight when you're around, because you're all I'm ever thinking about. And I don't think I would be here if it wasn't for you. You're my anchor in a timeless world, Harper.

I felt it the moment I met you, and I feel it even more with you looking so . . . unbelievingly beautiful."

I let a smile creep onto my lips, never wanting to kiss him so much. "You want to know what I feel when I look at you?"

He leans in closer. "So much."

"Something I've never felt around anyone else."

"Is that a promise?"

I stop inches from his lips and whisper, "It's the truth."

Kale might not be a superhero or someone who will change the world, but he's the only one to ever make my heart pound like it does.

And I wouldn't have it any other way.

47.
Kale

The sun is low, and yet sweat beads down my temples and neck.

My arms hang heavy. Tired. But the pain I feel every time I throw another ball, through my shoulders and down my back, is better than feeling nothing.

I'm alive out here.

Something I'm feeling more and more every day.

I still wake in the night, my voice hoarse and my skin damp, but now Dad is there when I need him the most. When I'm haunted by something I'll never go back to. But also something I can never forget.

I haven't time-traveled for two weeks. Before that, it was a week. But never back to WWII. Always somewhere else, sometimes with a purpose of helping someone and sometimes not. Soon, I might even be able to control where I go.

It's getting better.

This is where I want to be, now and forever.

Under the sun, breathing in the air of summer. Standing in the field I used to know so well. When I dig the toe of my shoe into the dirt, the wind carries the dust away. Over the tall grass and farther until I can't see it at all.

I bend down and take another ball from the bucket. I turn it over in my hands, my fingers tracing the stitches.

I take a deep breath and bring it to my chest, my leg coming up in a motion I could do in my sleep. My arm comes back and then the ball flies. It hits the net.

Thump. Thump. Over and over.

The bucket of balls is slowly dwindling to none. It's the first week all summer Miles couldn't make it. Grace's name came up, and I didn't ask more than that.

From over the long, seeding grass, the sound of the screen door slams shut, its hinges screaming for oil.

I don't turn to see whose footsteps are coming my way. Now that everyone in the house is gone—until Libby gets back—it can only be one person. Even still, I'm a little surprised.

It's been a long time since he's been out here.

Now that I know he's behind me, I'm conscious about my throw.

I miss the mark. About a foot high.

"Do it again. Relax your shoulders," he says.

I can picture him behind me—arms crossed over his chest, brow firm with judgment. I used to see that face at every game I played. Dad being competitive enough for both of us.

Taking a deep breath, I turn the ball over in my hand again, readying myself. I throw, not taking my eyes off the mark.

After it hits dead center, joining the others on the dusty ground, I turn to see him smiling.

"It's good," he says. "Have you been practicing?"

I nod. "I haven't stopped. I meet Miles down at the school once in a while."

"Well, they don't know what they're missing out on."

I only nod and turn away, getting ready to throw again, still feeling like I had a whole chunk of my life torn away.

But even though I'm on a different path now, it doesn't mean it's a bad one. If anything, it's the opposite.

"Maybe I can still go to tryouts in the spring," I say.

He smiles at that, giving me a hope I haven't had in so long. I throw my last ball.

"I miss coming out here," Dad says behind me.

So I take a chance on something I wouldn't have a couple months ago. "Do you want to play?" I ask, turning around. "Tossing the ball around helps my shoulders loosen up." I shrug like I don't care, but really, I'm afraid he'll say no.

But he smiles and gives me the only answer I hoped for.

"I would love to."

So while the sun slowly sets, we play catch and lose balls in the tall grass when we try to fake each other out.

But then later, after our shoulders are sore and our backs wet with sweat, Dad goes into the barn and starts up the tractor.

I sit on the back steps and watch him mow the grass until its short. Like it was all those years ago. Back when nothing was complicated.

I've wanted to be normal my entire life.

And it wasn't until I embraced who I was that I realized I never would be.

I might be a time-traveler and a dropout. Someone who never thought they would go to college or have a job.

But I would rather be no one else.

I'm a boy who keeps his promises.

Even when history tells me otherwise.

Acknowledgments

Not many people read the acknowledgments, but I think it's the most important part. Because without these people, this book never would have been made.

First and foremost, I have to thank God for giving me this gift to write and create stories to share with countless others. I might not be good at math or school in general, but I can write books and I wouldn't have it any other way.

To my amazing agent, Rachel Brooks. Thank you for being by my side through everything, especially that stuff we never thought we'd have to deal with. Without you picking my book from the slush pile, I wouldn't be here. In addition, thank you for Brenda Drake for hosting Pitch Madness, and Summer Heacock for choosing Cold Summer for #TeamFizzy—those were the first steps to putting me on this path.

Big thanks to my editor, Nicole Frail, for shaping this book into what it is now, and to the whole Sky Pony team for what you do behind the scenes to make this book possible. Special thanks to Sammy Yuen for creating such a beautiful cover.

To my early readers, Wendy Higgins, Diane Stiffler, Kari Martin, Christie Martin, Leigh Ann Burcham, Theresa Latourelle, Heather Gaines, Natasha Razi, and Caroline T. Richmond: Thank you for reading terrible first drafts and still finding the good in them.

To my newer critique partners, who might not have helped

me with this particular book, but helped shape my writing into what it is now: Scott Reintgen, Kevin van Whye, Dave Connis, and Tricia Levenseller. Thank you for putting up with my emails and texts and everything that comes with being a new author. I'm beyond lucky to have all of you.

Many thanks to old and new friends, you each had a part in this journey: Sandy Perrin, Carrie Smith, Hannah Hunt, Meagan Rivers, Alan Ramirez, Meghan Sullivan, Michelle Larsen, Sarah Glenn Marsh, Dan Perkins, and Kristen Simmons.

To Corri: Thank you for saying, "You should try writing." You were my first reader and first person to tell me to not give up.

Thank you to my whole family, and especially my parents: Mom, you've always been nothing but supportive and my biggest fan. Dad, thank you for all the books you read to me when I was young, and giving me books when I was older. I'm sorry I got published instead of going to college.

Special shout-out to the other 17er debut authors. Thank you for listening and letting an introvert find it easy to make new friends. You all rock.

To the Insomniacs: Thank you for being the most awesome people and talking about inappropriate things at inappropriate hours.

To my husband, Joe: Thank you for putting up with my many hours of writing and letting me go unemployed for two months so I could write this book. As Chris Traeger would say: You are literally . . . the best husband ever.

Last but definitely not least: Thank you to my readers, without you there really would be no books.